BROKEN HEART WOOD

By Eleanor Jones

***

Heart break, survival, new beginnings and an ancient

mystery

Prepare to be enthralled

***

Broken Heart Wood

Broken Heart Wood

First published in Great Britain, December 2012

*Re-published (revised version) November 2024
(Copyright Eleanor Jones December 2012)*

Illustrator Pollyanna Valente 2024

***

*This book is a work of fiction.
Names, characters, places and incidents are either a product of the author's imagination or are used fictitiously.
.Any resemblance to actual people, living or dead, events or localities is entirely coincidental.*

Broken Heart Wood

Dear reader

Thank you for picking up this story. It will, I hope, appeal to all those who enjoy an emotional drama, believe in true love and also love horses, dogs and the countryside, as do I.

I do hope you like it and I would love to hear your comments. Please feel free to contact me by email. holmescalesequestrian@gmail.com

All Best Wishes   Eleanor Jones

BROKEN HEART WOOD

By

Eleanor Jones

CHAPTER ONE

Images flashed relentlessly through Grace's mind. The stallion's gleaming silver coat, splattered with bright crimson, his dark eyes slowly fading as he heaved his final sigh. Tom's handsome face, crumpled with horror and pain.

A silent scream bubbled inside her and she fought back the memories, tightening her hands around the wheel… Molly was the only one who mattered now and she needed to focus on that.

All around was grey, dark and oppressive, the rain a torrent that ran down the windscreen of Grace's small car. The rhythmical swish of the windscreen wipers beat a pattern into her brain as she glanced in the mirror, relieved to see that Molly still slept contentedly in her car seat, free from the confusion that filled her life right now.   For how could a three year old possibly understand why her safe little world had suddenly turned on its head?

When Grace's thoughts slid inevitably to Tom a sharp shaft of pain tore her in two. Through everything, the accident and Sliver's death, there had still been trust between them, or at least she had thought so. Now though even that was broken... so what else could she have done but leave. She had to try and find herself some space to breathe before she could deal clearly with her own confusion.

Narrowing her eyes she peered through the mist that slowly drifted down from the huge mass of the fell. It moved mysteriously, blanking out the world, leaving her feeling very alone in what felt like a harsh and hostile place. Its severity suited her right now though she realised and she had loved it here once, in a vague childhood memory; perhaps she could come to love it again.

Broken Heart Wood

Friday afternoon and the motorway was busy. Pinpricks of light through the murky mist buzzed along in spaced out rows, tyres swishing through surface water, blank faces closeted in their own small space, heading who knows where. Grace glanced back again at Molly, quietly sleeping still, trusting her. A car overtook them throwing spray across her windscreen and for a moment she fought with the wheel, her knuckles white as the buffeting wind took the vehicle in its grip.

A stony faced man in the driver's seat of the passing vehicle glanced at her and then glanced away as if she was invisible. Loneliness was a solid lump inside her. If something happened to them now then who would know. How long would it be before someone informed Tom… and would he even care? Oh yes, the answer was immediate, he might not care about her but he would do anything for Molly.

Struggling to concentrate she moved across into the slow lane, turning up the radio to keep her thoughts at bay. A voice blasted out into the silence. "Welcome to Lakeland Radio, this is your local DJ Chris…" She flicked it off again, preferring the silence and afraid of disturbing Molly's sleep.

It had seemed strange though to hear that broad Northern accent again after all these years… her mother's accent. Nostalgia swept over her; perhaps she *could* find some peace here then after all, at least for a little while.

Way, way above her the huge mass of the Pennine fells loomed against the skyline, awesome in their magnificence, making everything else seem small. They had stood here since time immemorial she realised and would stand here still, bleak and wild and yet so beautiful, even perhaps when all the people in the world had gone. Her problems seemed puny in comparison.

The motorway swept round in a curve, centrifugal force dragged her small car sideways. Grace closed her hands more tightly than ever on the wheel, focussing on her driving. The road magically levelled off again and suddenly the sun burst through from behind the grey clouds, casting a golden light upon the harsh slopes ahead, softening their austerity and resting upon... a shape, a perfect shape. Ten thousand shades of shivering green set against the blues and greys of the fell in the form of a perfect heart.

She took her foot off the throttle, entranced; it seemed like a sign. The bang hit like a sledge hammer, exploding inside her head as her car span round in the road. Behind her Molly screamed and survival kicked in. She couldn't let her child die here... like this.

Cars sped by as she fought with the wheel, flashing in and out of her vision, red and silver and white. Blank faces, eyes opened wide with horror as they narrowly missed her spinning vehicle, relieved that it wasn't them. Molly's screams went on and on, mercilessly portraying their plight; for Grace though it seemed as if the world stood still whilst she observed the proceedings from afar. Just she and Molly facing death together on the soulless motorway; so was this it then, would she never see him again? Her lips formed his name, clinging desperately to what she had lost. "…Tom!"

As quickly as it all began, everything suddenly became still. The car creaked gently as if in protest whilst above them the mighty fells still loomed, motionless, overseeing the scene with the wisdom of time. Faceless drivers still flashed by, uncaring of their plight… except for one.

An urgent tapping on the window brought Grace back to now. She looked up in a daze as Molly's screams began again.

"Mummy… Mummy!"

As Grace leaned through into the back seat, unbuckling the straps with fumbling fingers, Molly's small arms reached out for the only comfort they knew. "It's okay sweetheart… Mummy's here."

Broken Heart Wood

And then at last she was holding her so tightly, breathing in her sweet smell, embracing the warmth, the life of her. "Hey Molly… It's okay you're safe now."

The car door opened slowly, groaning its objection, to reveal anxious bright blue eyes in a world worn face beneath a fringe of silvery white.

"Are you all right dear?"

A sob took Grace's breath when she saw the kindness in the old lady's face. Was she alright? "I… I think so," she began, determined not to cry. "I mean… Yes, thank you."

The woman smiled a gentle, caring smile. "Well you'll never be so lucky again you know, how you missed all those cars I'll never know. I saw it all from further back, and then you even finished up on the hard shoulder… Look…" The concern was back in her blue eyes, genuine and real. "Why don't you just leave your car here? It doesn't look too badly damaged but you must be in shock. There's a slip road just a bit further on and my house isn't very far way. Let me take you there and I'll ring my son to pick up your car."

Grace's eyes caught hers and held. A lifeline, she had been thrown a lifeline.

"Oh but I couldn't…" she began half-heartedly.

"…Nonsense!"

Already the old lady was helping her from the car, leading her off towards an unlikely looking four by four with giant wheels and a shiny chrome bumper.

"You need a four wheel drive for our winters," she explained with a smile. "My name is Annie by the way, Annie Allbright."

Grace looked at her, momentarily speechless. "I am Grace," she eventually managed.

"And this is...?" Annie smiled gently at Molly who gazed back through a blur of tears.

Grace pressed her cheek against the silky softness of the little girl's hair, relief flooding over her in a warm comforting wave. "This is Molly," she said.

"Well hello Molly, you are going to be all right now. I have a lovely book to show you at my house. It has pictures of horses... do you like horses?"

"Hawses," repeated Molly solemnly, thrusting her thumb firmly into her mouth.

Annie drove confidently, her large silver vehicle nosing its way determinedly along the tiny lanes that ran through the valley bottom way below the looming fells. Vague, formless memories of her childhood, invoked by the familiarity of her surroundings brought a wave of nostalgia.

"Have you been to Cumbria before?"

Annie's question was delivered in passing, a comment designed to break the silence. Grace's answer surprised her.

"I was born here."

"What…you mean *here*… in Greythwaite?"

"Well… near here. My mother was brought up on a farm called Fellclose; we left there when I was five though."

"The cumbersome vehicle suddenly slowed right down as Annie turned to look across at Grace. "You're Sarah's daughter," she exclaimed in a high, excited tone, and then a shadow fell across her face. "…How is your mother?"

"She died when I was six."

Silence fell for a moment, a heavy brooding silence. A shaft of pain flashed across Annie's face and she let out a sigh. "So that's why she stopped writing so suddenly and I thought…"

"You knew her…?"

"Oh yes."

She glanced across at Grace again, nodding her white head slowly. "Your mother and I were best friends right from childhood. I'm so sorry to hear that…"

"It was a long time ago," cut in Grace. "But I just needed to get away and this seemed like the obvious place to come."

"Well you're very welcome," said Annie, standing on the brakes to negotiate a narrow entrance. "And this..." She raised one hand from the wheel, proudly drawing Grace's attention to the long, grey stone cottage ahead of them, "... is Hillside. It used to be a farm but I rented off the land and buildings when my Edward died. I take in guests now."

A sense of release flooded over Grace. For a moment she felt as if she was home as something about the house sprang a chord deep in her memory.

"Have I been here before?" It came out more sharply that she intended and she tried to smile. "I mean... It seems familiar somehow."

"When you were just a little girl you used to come round here with your mother..."

Suddenly Annie's face crumpled. "Oh I wish I'd known that she was dead. And all these years I've thought..."

Molly wriggled in her arms and Grace held her tightly, breathing in the warmth, the life of her.

"Thought what?"

Broken Heart Wood

Suddenly it seemed so important for her to know more about her mother's life, here, at Greythwaite.

Annie turned the key and the engine died, spluttering into silence.

"Oh it's nothing now, just a silly misunderstanding really. I thought that she didn't want to hear from me again when she never answered my letters; that she'd moved on and forgotten about her life here. Eventually I just stopped writing…"

"But why didn't my dad reply?"

It didn't seem to make any sense to Grace.

Annie shook her head, opening the car door.

"Your father and I never saw eye to eye about a lot of things."

Realising that the subject was closed Grace slid from the passenger seat. Molly began to wail, a loud annoying high pitched cry and she reached back into the vehicle for her bag.

"She wants a bottle," she explained awkwardly. "She's too old really I know but it gives her comfort."

"And that is exactly what she needs after everything," Annie agreed. "Come on, let's get her inside."

Vague memories flooded in again when they entered the low ceilinged hallway, familiar and disturbing. It felt to Grace that she had been here in a dream... or in another life. She felt so close to her mother that it hurt deep inside and all her insecurities rushed in, threatening to overturn her false mantle of adulthood and turn her back into a clinging, needy child again.

Annie caught her eyes and smiled.

"Come on," she said kindly, reaching out her hand. "Give me the bottle and I'll go and warm it up for you."

Thankfully the kitchen held no ghosts for Grace. It was sunny and bright and unexpectedly modern. She settled gratefully down onto a chair, cradling Molly against her shoulder.

"Shush now sweetheart," she murmured. "Everything is okay."

The microwave pinged and Annie handed her the bottle. Molly took it with eager fingers, drawing hungrily on the teat.

"Now," she said decisively. "I think a nice cup of tea is what we both need... I've spoken to Ben and he's going to get Andy -that's my grandson- to bring the car back here. He'll take a look at it first himself though, to make sure that it's driveable."

"I really do appreciate it," mumbled Grace. "I'll pay him of course."

Broken Heart Wood

Annie shook her head. "You will do no such thing. I would have helped you anyway but now that I know you're Sarah's daughter... well..."

She blinked hard, lost for a moment in nostalgia.

Grace's face crumpled. "I'm so sorry my father didn't reply..."

Annie shook her head with a determined smile. "It's all a very long time ago now, water under the bridge so to speak. Perhaps your mother even sent you here eh, who knows what determines our lives."

"It was the heart," announced Grace, suddenly remembering. "I saw it against the fell as the rain cleared. A perfect heart... I lost concentration and..."

"Ah yes..." Annie's voice held a kind of awe. "It's easy to forget just how it affects people the first time they see it, especially at this time of year with all the fresh greens of spring... there again." She smiled at the memory. "You should see it in the autumn."

"It must be amazing to see the colours change with the seasons," sighed Grace, suddenly wishing that she could. "It was just such a surprise though, to see a perfect heart against the stark grey slopes of the fell, like a sign almost. How does it come to be there?"

"Now that," replied Annie, pouring the tea. "Is something we would all like to know."

Broken Heart Wood

She handed Grace a white china mug bespattered with red poppies. "There are all kinds of stories of course but no one has ever really found out the truth of it. Perhaps they never will."

Grace took a sip of the steaming liquid and placed her mug carefully down onto the table. Suddenly it seemed very important to her to know more about the heart shaped wood, as if somehow it could help to heal the pain that tore at her own heart.

"But surely someone must at least know who planted it."

Annie shrugged. "Not really. Some say that it was a young woman whose fiancée crashed his plane there in the first war, and there are those who believe that it was planted to celebrate a wedding. There's a huge house up on the hill, overlooking the valley; it's been made into apartments now but a Lord Dinsdale once owned it. In fact he owned everything around here so perhaps it was for his son or daughter… who knows."

"Are you rambling on about that daft wood again gran."

When another voice cut in on their conversation Grace looked round to see a dark haired youth lounging against the doorjamb with all the casual swagger of the young.

Broken Heart Wood

Annie's blue eyes lit up. "Andy, meet Grace, she's the daughter of a very dear friend of mine... and this is her daughter, Molly."

Hearing her name Molly stirred, handing her mother the now empty bottle.

"Hewo," she said, with her most appealing smile.

Annie's grandson grinned, entranced. "Hello," he responded. "Would you like to come and see the rabbits?"

To Grace's amazement Molly scrambled down from her knee and held out her hand trustingly.

"Wabbits," she repeated solemnly.

He laughed, wrapping his broad palm around hers before glancing back at Grace. "Is it okay?"

"They're just outside on the lawn," reassured Annie. "They're wild really but they know that no one bothers them here so they get quite tame... and don't worry about Andy, he's good with children."

Andy jerked his chin forward, rolling his dark eyes. "I've had to be, with two little brothers," he explained.

"Wabbits," repeated Molly determinedly, tugging on his hand.

Grace smiled, feeling calmer than she had in days. "Go one then but don't be too long."

Broken Heart Wood

Andy hesitated at the door before stepping out into the breaking sunshine. "Your car is outside by the way," he said. "Dad told me to let you know that it's just a dent and he can knock it out if you want. He's calling round later on his way home from the garage."

When Andy and an excited Molly had disappeared into the garden, Grace glanced awkwardly across at Annie. "Please thank your son for me but you've already done so much for us…"

Annie sighed, placing her hand on Grace's arm, knotted veins and fingers worn by time. Her mother's hands would have been like that now Grace realised with a sudden rush of emotion.

"Your mother and I were very close when we were young," Annie said, remembering. "Things happened that drove her away from here, bad things I suppose, but we still kept in touch. She was the sister I never had. When she stopped replying to my letters I was devastated. I thought that she'd moved on without me, that our friendship had meant so little. Now that I know the truth though I want to make amends and by helping you it makes me feel as if I am finally able to help her too. I can see that you're distressed and I'm not going to pry but, well you are more than welcome to stay here… if you having nothing else planned I mean."

"Here!"

Grace gawped at her, absorbing her kind offer with a sudden sense of relief. She had been so desperate to get away that she'd given no real thought to where she was going… let alone staying.

"Look," Annie leaned towards her. "You really would be doing me a favour you know. This is a guesthouse after all and I have no one staying at the moment. I'd enjoy the company."

Grace exhaled, all the emotion of the last few days threatening to overcome her. She had kept herself strong for Molly's sake but with this one act of kindness it seemed that all her strength was draining away.

"So that's agreed," smiled Annie. "Come on, I'll show you to your room while Andy's looking after the little one. You can get your bags later."

Grace stood in the sunny brightness of the bedroom that Annie proudly showed her into. Memories flooded over her in a wash of colours; the bright pink fabric of her mother's dress clutched between her sticky fingers, soft against her skin; a glorious splash of blue from beyond the window, and all the grey: The grey desolation of her mother's tears. She turned to look at

Annie, overwhelmed by the memories she'd stifled for so long, needing to know. "Why was she crying?"

Annie shrugged, clasping her hands together as she turned away. "It's a long story, I'll tell you about it another time; you just get some rest," and with that she was gone, leaving Grace alone to face the turbulence that bubbled inside her. Closing her eyes she pushed the vague memories back into their hiding place, storing them away until later. Now was about Tom, about his treachery, about trying to get her life back on track.

She stepped across to the window, watching Molly running around in circles on the smooth green lawn. And beyond the garden, way, way up towards the vast blue sky, she could see the wood, a perfectly shaped green heart set against the harsh beauty of the fell. What secrets did it hide?

A rush of emotion made her shudder; perhaps here she *could* find some kind of peace… if there was such a thing to be had anymore.

Broken Heart Wood

Broken Heart Wood

Broken Heart Wood

Broken Heart Wood

Broken Heart Wood

Broken Heart Wood

CHAPTER TWO

Everywhere smelled fresh after the rain, clean and earthy. The pavement glistened, turning its grey façade into something more magical; even the birds twittered in unison from the hedgerows sharing their jubilation with the world.

"…Morning Tom… lovely day."

Clare Healey's greeting fell on deaf ears as Tom Roberts walked determinedly by.

She called out again. "Whatever's eating you this morning, Tom, late for work is it? Not that it matters when you're the boss though I suppose."

He looked round vaguely, running his hand through his thick blonde hair.

"Sorry Clare… didn't see you there."

She took a step towards him, a determined smile on her round plain face. "Are you all right?"

Tom nodded curtly. "Yes, I'm fine…"

As he marched on down the road she watched him go, a troubled frown crumpling her forehead. It was so unlike Tom to be down in the dumps, why, even when Grace was bad for so long he'd always managed a smile. And where *was* Grace come to that, she hadn't seen her for almost a week?

"Tom!"

He hesitated, looking back, shading his strong clean-cut features from the bright spring sunshine.

"...Is Grace okay."

"Yes... of course, she's fine."

His words were a dismissal. She turned away reluctantly to retrieve her mail from the box at the end of the pathway. She would ask Nell, the elderly woman who did some part time secretarial work for his firm, Quicksilver, she decided.

Tom glanced back at his good natured but inquisitive neighbour; Clare had been a real help to him and Grace when they first moved into Ivy Cottage. They'd soon come to realise though that *their* business would be everyone's business if they let her too far into their lives. He was already screwed up enough right now about Grace leaving without the entire village offering tea and sympathy; anyway, he didn't deserve any sympathy.

Noting her disappointment at his lack of information, Tom turned away and headed off along the lane. There was only one thing that was stopping him from losing it altogether and that was work. If... no, *when*, Grace came back then at least they would still have a business.

But what if she didn't come back, what if he never saw her again? Agony coursed through his veins as he fought off a rush of fear. Of *course* she'd come back. She was his girl there was no doubting that; they were both his girls. An image of Molly filled his mind's eye and for just a moment he closed his lids, holding his face between his hands. Oh how could he have been so stupid... so selfish. If only Grace had stayed around long enough for him to make her understand... there again how could he ever expect her to understand? Even he didn't understand why he'd done such a terrible thing so why should Grace even listen to his lame excuses?

It was only a couple of hundred yards from Ivy Cottage to the old stable yard where they parked the vans. Tom walked hurriedly towards it, not wanting anyone else to start asking awkward questions.

All around him everywhere seemed to be bursting with new life. Hedgerows shimmering in the sudden breeze with a thousand shades of vibrant green, birds singing their sweet spring songs and swooping up into the clear blue sky. It was a morning for living and he felt as if he was dead inside.

Withdrawing a key from his pocket he fumbled with the padlock on the yard gate, a wave of emotion bringing a tremble to his fingers as he saw the key ring that Grace gave him just last Christmas. There they all were in a tiny picture, so close, so together. So how had come to this?

A heavy pain swelled inside him, sticking at the base of his throat. His heart began to beat in a fast painful rhythm and he clung to the wooden gate for a moment, trying to get a grip on his emotions by concentrating his attention on the day ahead.

Their three silver Ford vans were parked in a row on the cobbled yard, front bumpers drawn right up against the doors of the stables that had once housed their dreams. For a moment he allowed himself to remember how it had been back then, bustling with life, horse's heads peering out over their half doors, the clatter of buckets from the feed room right at the very end of the yard. It was an office now.

Waiting for the piercing pain those memories always invoked, he hesitated for a moment, for once though it didn't seem to hit so hard. Having to give up on his dreams may have been tough but it was nothing compared to a future without his two girls.

'QUICKSILVER,' the name of their delivery company, was written in black italic writing right across the side of each van. That had been one of Grace's brainwaves; she was always good at things like that.

He took a breath, sucking air into his lungs, remembering the moment when she'd turned to him with her bright idea, her lovely face shining with delight.

'Quicksilver, that's what we should call it. It will be an honour to him… a tribute to what he was to us.'

He'd loved the idea; a real tribute to a very special horse. So why was it then that just when everything seemed to be going so right it had suddenly seemed to go so wrong? Was that what life was all about then he wondered, disappointments and regrets, or did bad things just happen to him?

'And there you go again,' he murmured, giving himself a mental kick in the head, "feeling sorry for yourself."

His mind flicked back relentlessly to Grace. Her luminous grey eyes alight with laughter, always positive, always there for him… 'You make your own luck,' she used to tell him and he *had* made his own luck, hadn't he; his own bad luck.

Unlocking the door into the tiny office he sank down onto a chair, for once allowing his memories a free rein. His eyes rested on the picture above his desk, of the noble grey stallion, Quicksilver, for who the company was named. Everything would have been so different if he was still alive.

If he had been insured then there might have been a slim chance of carrying on, once they'd got their lives back on track again that is. At the time though it had felt as if there *was* no way forward, no way left to live out the dream. After the accident his dream hadn't seemed to matter anymore anyway, nothing had seemed to matter. And then he'd made his other stupid, weak mistake, the mistake he was paying for now. He'd been a fool, a selfish fool who'd thought only about his own disappointments, because, if he was honest, it had all started with *his* dream. Had he ever actually stopped to ask Grace what she really wanted, or had he just presumed that they shared the same goals? He discarded that thought at once. Grace had been just as keen as he was, he knew that. In fact she was the one who'd believed in Silver right from the start when he was a

Broken Heart Wood

scrawny, leggy youngster that no one else appreciated… if only…

Memories rushed in too painful to bear. He clicked them off at once, shutting them out of his mind. If only was a waste of time; what was gone was gone and the only important thing in his life right now was to get back what mattered to him most, Grace and little Molly, the loves of his life. Somehow he had to find them, had to make Grace understand why he'd let her down so badly. He desperately needed to get his family back… for without his two girls then what was there left to live for?

The clock on the wall ticked loudly in the silence. Six thirty am, too soon to set off yet and Mick wouldn't be in for another half hour at least. He flicked the switch on the kettle, craving a strong hot coffee to fill the void inside him. Food wouldn't seem to go down somehow and those three double whiskies he'd downed last night had been a really bad idea. Perhaps he should let his other driver, Geoff Dobson, do the first run for he didn't feel as if he was fit to be behind the wheel.

The coffee scalded his throat as he gulped it down. Where could she be though, where would a broken hearted young mother with a two year go to get away?

He had rung everyone they knew, trying not to let them know that something was wrong, making small talk whilst his whole world was crumbling around him. What else could he do?

The name caught his eye again, 'Quicksilver,' across the top of the leaflets on the desk. If the talented grey stallion hadn't died on the road that day then he would still have been chasing his dream with Grace beside him.

It hadn't been easy, trying to make a living in the tough world of show jumping, but she'd always been there in those early years, pushing him on, keeping the yard going while he was away at shows, doing the entries, mucking out, grooming, and riding exercise... until that ordinary day when tragedy struck and changed their lives forever.

There was no way they could carry on after that. Their only really talented horse was gone, none of the youngsters they'd bought had lived up to their promise and eventually there had been no choice but to cut their losses and sell up. The money they had left bought their first van, an elderly Ford transit with which they'd eked out a living, trying to build up a reputation for express deliveries of very special items. Now they had three almost new vans, all with their logo emblazoned across the side, *QUICKSILVER,* in memory of the horse that might have been great if things had gone differently.

Grace's words flashed once again into his mind. 'You make your own luck in this life,' she used to tell him. Well then maybe it was about time that he made *his* luck change he decided, for there was no way he was going to give up without a fight. Reaching for the phone book he rifled through the pages yet again for the numbers of her old friends, someone had to know where she'd gone. His eyes fell on a familiar name. Maddison, Mary Maddison. He shut the book with a thud, the bile of self-loathing rising inside him. Oh God how could he have let that that happen? Perhaps he didn't deserve to get her back.

Images of Molly flashed into his mind. Her wide, trusting smile, the way she called out to him, reaching up her chubby arms. The way she nestled down in the bed between them when she woke in the night… and Grace's soft sweet smile.

Lowering his head down onto his arms he fought against a wave of pain, battling with the rush of emotion that threatened to take him over.

"You OK mate"

He struggled to regain some composure under Mick Harris's concerned scrutiny, standing up abruptly and turning to the list on the wall, clearing his throat to try and disguise the break in his voice. His reply seemed to come from someone else, a distant echo in his ears.

"Yes... thanks. I'd like you to take the first job for me today. Geoff will go to York."

Mick studied his boss's broad back, raising his eyebrows. Tom always seemed so focussed, so under control, he'd never even seen him lose his temper. Whatever was eating at Tom Roberts now though was definitely not a place where he would ever want to be; the poor guy looked like death. "Whatever you say boss," he responded reaching for his keys.

As the silver van disappeared out into the lane the phone began to ring, a relentless jarring tone that vibrated around inside Tom's head. He stood abruptly, walking outside into the sunshine, suddenly unable to find the strength to pretend anymore.

He could never undo the wrong he had done but he could make amends. He just had to find them... somehow.

CHAPTER THREE

Grace rolled over, feeling Molly's small form against her, warm and soft. She cuddled her close, automatically reaching out beyond her to find... an empty space.

"Tom?"

She opened her eyes, blinking away the clogging dust of sleep, disorientated and confused. Awareness filtered in bringing a wave of panic, closely followed by a heavy emptiness.

"Tom..."

His name tore at her heartstrings, Tom, her Tom. But he wasn't her Tom anymore was he? The answer came back at once for deep down inside he would always be her Tom, for all the things they had been through together, entwisting their lives, would be etched in her memory forever. He had just moved into another place that's all, a place where she couldn't go.

Beside her the sleeping child stirred. Grace stroked the silky fair hair back from her face, pressing her lips against the warmth of her skin, taking comfort from her

Broken Heart Wood

neediness. Molly was the most important person in her life right now.

Sleep was a long time coming. Memories plagued her. Quicksilver, that noble and beautiful stallion, his silver coat crimson with blood; the expression of despair on Tom's face when he saw his lifetime's dream slipping away … The pain of his treachery…

Turning her mind sharply back to now she stared determinedly from the window, out into the vast navy sky where a million tiny stars twinkled above the sleeping heart shaped wood. Who had planted those trees she wondered, and was their inspiration rooted in joy, or heartache? Somehow it felt so important for her to know.

So many things seemed to have gone wrong in her life, from that vague, miserable day when her parents took her away from this place, to her poor dear mother's death and then… She closed her eyes against the images that swirled around inside her head. She'd thought that she had reached her lowest ebb, that the very worst had happened, but then… there was this. Just how much more could life throw at her?

"Mummy…"

Small fingers, clutched around her own, a tiny heart, beating next to hers…No, she must never ever think like that. 'You make your own luck', how many times had she said that to Tom? Now she had to prove it to herself.

Unbelievably, when she opened her eyes again it was almost nine o clock. Her hand scrambled for Molly, finding only a cold and empty place where her small body had lain.

She leaped from the bed, dashing downstairs in her cream silk nightdress, cheeks flushed with sleep, dark hair a tousled cloud around her face.

"Molly!"

Annie was standing by the solid fuel cooker, a spatula in her raised hand.

"Ah," she exclaimed with a smile, "just in time for breakfast."

Grace took in the scene before her, suddenly acutely aware of her state of undress. She ran a hand awkwardly over her head.

"Molly… whatever are you doing, you should have woken mummy!"

Annie nodded, motioning her towards the table. "She's having some breakfast, aren't you poppet?"

Broken Heart Wood

Molly looked up, her mouth stuffed with cereal, milk dripping down her chin as she stared at her mother with Tom's twinkling eyes.

"Bwekfast," she announced solemnly.

"You go and get dressed and I'll make you some too," insisted Annie. "Go on... Molly will be fine with me."

Grace hesitated. "But..."

"But nothing," Annie waved her spatula. "It is an order."

"Not that I mind you wandering around in next to nothing," remarked a deep voice from behind her.

She looked round in horror to see Annie's son, Ben, whom she had met fleetingly the night before. Then he had appeared shy and slightly awkward but now his kind, plain face was alight with a broad grin.

"Get away with you," cried Annie, shooing him off.

Grace fled her bedroom, the pink flush on her face deepening to crimson.

The warm rush of water over her naked skin felt so good, as if she was cleansing away some of the heartache. Here, where the pace of life was slow, so very far away from her other life, maybe she could try and make some sense of the mess *her* life had become.

Broken Heart Wood

Annie's reedy voice floated up the stairs. "Breakfast is ready…"

For the first time in days she actually felt hungry, Grace realised, hurriedly rubbing herself dry. Last night she had merely picked at the wonderful meal Annie had prepared, watching guiltily as she removed her almost untouched plate and scraped it into the bin. Her apology had been met with good grace but she could tell by the way the elderly lady kept looking at her that she was very eager to know just what she was running away from.

She pulled on jeans and a sweater, running her fingers through her damp curls. Maybe it was only fair to tell Annie the truth, she decided. She had been so kind to her and it wasn't fair to keep her guessing. Not today though, she needed to get everything straight inside her own head first. It was just so hard to suddenly be one on your own when you had been one half of two for what seemed like a lifetime.

For a moment she paused to stare from the window, unable to get over the stark beauty right on her doorstep. Her eyes drifted across the bleak sweep of the fell side and rested yet again on the vivid greens of the heart. It drew her like a magnet. One day, she decided, she would walk up there and see it close up.

"Are you coming dear...?"

Annie's voice brought her sharply from her reverie and she raced downstairs to find Molly still sitting at the kitchen table, but now she was drawing on a huge piece of paper, a large red wax crayon clasped in her chubby fingers.

"Sorry," she apologised. "I don't know what's come over me; I haven't slept so well in days. I hope Molly hasn't been a nuisance."

Annie placed a plate of scrambled eggs and toast in front of her. "Now how could such a lovely little girl ever be a nuisance?" she smiled.

Grace laughed. "Oh believe you me she does have her off days."

She ate in silence, suddenly desperately hungry. What would Tom be doing now she wondered, driving somewhere, or maybe...? No, she wouldn't let herself go down that road, wouldn't let herself even think about him being with someone else. The food in her mouth suddenly seemed to turn into cotton wool.

"What day is it?"

Annie looked across at her, surprised by her question. "Why, it's Sunday of course. I'm off to church soon but you stay here and rest. We'll talk when I come back shall we?"

Grace's heart began to beat in a rapid rhythm that left her breathless. Did she want to talk? Did she want to bare her soul to this kind eyed elderly stranger? But there again, she wasn't really a stranger at all; she was her mother's dearest friend.

"Will you tell me about my mother?" she asked, blurting it out. It felt like a pact, an exchange of information, but she wasn't sure that she was ready to talk about her problems just yet.

Annie nodded. "Of course, I'd love to."

Whilst Annie was gone, Grace bathed and dressed a reluctant Molly, wondering if perhaps she should have gone to church too. Vague memories filtered in, of a narrow pathway leading up to a grey stone church on the hill, her hand held tightly in her mother's. Excitement prickled inside her; suddenly she wanted so much to know more about the mother she had almost forgotten. Here, in the place where Sarah Hall was brought up, the place where she had met and married her father, Donald Bryant, Grace felt a whole new bond with her sweet, softly spoken mother -but what to tell Annie in return?

Broken Heart Wood

Oh what was she doing here, so far away from Mossdale, the sleepy little village she had thought of as home? For a moment her mind slipped back to happier times, with Tom. To their delight at moving into the cottage, working side-by-side on the stable yard, scrubbing and mending and painting; hard graft but so satisfying when it was to help fulfil their dreams. Tom had always thought that the dream was his but she cared about it just as much as he did, revelling in the work and the close companionship of the horses in her care. His success was her success, his hopes her own, until they were cruelly ended on a sunny summer's morning by one crazy, thoughtless, reckless driver.

She closed her eyes against the memories, the shriek of tyres, the sharp crack of shattering glass, and all the screaming.

She thought that they'd dealt with it, that they'd moved on with their lives and learned to live with the tragedy, but perhaps it had just been too big a tragedy for Tom to deal with after all.

So was that why it had happened then? Was it some kind of retaliation to the pain she had caused them both? Perhaps she should have stayed there and fought her corner, confronted him and listened to his lies –for any excuse he gave would have had to be a lie. How could

Broken Heart Wood

she have stayed though when everything she'd believed in had crumbled. They had crumbled; her and Tom.

Something contracted inside her, like a hand squeezing her guts. She shook her head, determined not to break down, grabbing hold of Molly and swinging her up onto her hip, clinging to her neediness.

So what *was* she going to say to Annie? 'I have run away because the man I love… the man I love…' There, she couldn't even say it to herself.

Was she a coward then… is this what cowards did, just run away when the chips were down? No… because she wasn't running away was she. She was running back, back home to find herself again.

"Dad…dee."

Molly looked up at her with Tom's unusual, beautiful eyes, their colour changing with every shift of light, just like his.

Her bottom lip puckered. "Daddy," she repeated quietly."

Grace's heart twisted. "We'll see him soon sweetheart." Suddenly Annie's kitchen seemed stifling and she headed for the door.

As she climbed the steep slope with Molly getting heavier by the minute, Grace felt her heart lightening.

She stopped beside a stunted tree to catch her breath, setting the little girl down onto the coarse grass of the fell and crouching besides her.

There was Annie's cottage, way below them, and the church. She could see a small stream of people pouring from the entrance, stopping to talk in the spring sunshine, all content in their own little worlds; but where was her world now? She couldn't stay here forever, couldn't impose on Annie like this for long and Tom would be wondering where they'd gone... wouldn't he?

When her heart jolted she shut out the pain harp, concentrating her attention on Molly, who was starting to wail.

"Look sweetheart," said, pointing across to where a baby rabbit hopped slowly towards them, oblivious to their presence.

Molly's tears dried like magic. "Wabbit," she cried gleefully, clapping her hands. The tiny creature lifted its head, bright eyes staring in their direction, and then it was off, racing for the safety of its burrow.

"Wabbit," screamed Molly.

Grace lifted the little girl back onto her hip again. "Shush now, the rabbit has gone home for his tea. We'll go back soon and see Annie's rabbits."

Broken Heart Wood

Way up ahead she could see the trees of the heart shaped wood, rustling in the breeze. For a moment she hesitated, longing to go just a bit closer. There was something about the wood that drew her, a kind of link, as if she had been there before. Somehow, crazily perhaps, ever since the moment when she'd first seen it from the motorway she had felt that it held the key to her peace of mind and she was determined to go there at least once before she went home.

Home... An image flashed into her mind, of the two up two down crumbling cottage where she and Tom had lived and loved and cried together. But where was her home now?

Molly's restless grumbling brought Grace's attention back to now. "There, there," she soothed, cradling her close. "Come on, let's go and get you a bottle and then you can have a nice sleep."

"Bockle," repeated Molly, wrapping her chubby arms around her mother's neck.

Grace breathed in the essence of her, overcome by a sudden rush of guilt, for Molly had done nothing wrong yet she and Tom had turned her life into total confusion. And it wasn't just Tom's doing, if she was honest, for if only she had gone another way that day, or set off five minutes sooner, then he would never have been in that situation. An image of his familiar face flashed into her mind, his wide smile, the humour in his hazel eyes, the love… Oh how she missed the comfort of him.

Annie was back in the kitchen when Grace burst in through the door. She had already removed her 'church' hat and was about to start peeling vegetables at the sink. Taking one look at the sleepy, whimpering child, draped across Grace's shoulders she immediately reached for a bottle and placed it into the microwave.

"I know what you want," she smiled, pressing the button and Molly reached out her arms.

Grace sank down onto a chair. "Thank you," she said. "We walked up the fell…"

Annie nodded. "To Heartwood I suppose?"

"Not quite… but I am going to go there before I leave."

The microwave pinged and Annie reached up and removed the bottle, testing it on the back of her hand before handing it to Molly, who grabbed it eagerly, sucking happily on the teat.

"You're not thinking of leaving *too s*oon though are you?" she asked with dismay. "I won't get any summer visitors for a few weeks yet so there's plenty of room here."

Broken Heart Wood

To Grace it felt like a haven. "Are you sure?" she sked uncertainly.

Annie's lined face lit up. "It would be my pleasure."

"I'll pay you of though of course…I can't let you keep me for nothing."

Annie shook her white head gently. "It's not necessary, really, but if it makes you feel better about it… Stay as long as you need to, and you really must go to Heart Wood. Your mother and I used to spend hours there when we were children."

Molly's eyes drooped shut and Grace placed the bottle down onto the table. She felt at home here, safe and comfortable, perhaps she really could stay for a while, or at least until she had her head straight again, if that was ever possible.

"Thank you," she said. "…And you'll tell me more about my mother?"

"Anything you want to know," agreed Annie. "It will be nice to remember her."

It wasn't until much later that evening, when Molly was asleep in bed, before Grace touched upon the subject of her mother again. Annie was sitting in her favourite chair next to the large stone fireplace. Her head was slowly drooping forwards and when the magazine she was reading slipped from between her limp fingers, falling to the floor with a rustling sound, she looked up with a start.

"Sarah!" she cried. "... No... of course not. You must think I'm a silly old fool. You just looked so like her for a minute."

"Do I?" Grace leaned forward earnestly. "Do I really look like my mother?"

Annie smiled gently. "You are every bit as beautiful," she sighed. "Oh I wish I'd been able to see her again after she left."

"But why... why didn't you stay in touch with her and why didn't my father tell you that she'd died?"

For a moment the old lady remained silent, a faraway look in her eyes. "People's lives often don't go the way they expect," she said sadly. "We all do things we shouldn't, get carried away by the moment I suppose you'd call it, and your mother was no exception. She gave up everything for your father on a whim, everything she loved... And look where it got her."

Grace tried to cast her mind back to the time before her mother's death. Her parents had always seemed happy, hadn't they? It was all such a long time ago though and she had been so young. She closed her eyes briefly, vaguely recalling raised voices in the dead of night. She used to pull the covers over her head when she heard her father shouting and then next morning everything would be all right again.

"What was it, Annie?" she asked. "What was it that made her cry on the day we left?"

Annie nodded her head, a sigh on her lips. "She compromised on love… Never do that Grace, always follow your heart wherever it leads."

"But how…?"

"…How what?"

She looked round with a start to see Ben in the doorway, his large frame blocking out the light. "I hope you're not listening to my mother's daft stories," he said, smiling.

Is that what it was, wondered Grace, just a daft story, or had her mother really compromised on love?

"I'll sort out your car tomorrow if you like," he offered. "The dent will easily knock out and I have the right paint for it in stock."

"But I can't expect you to…"

"Of course you can," butted in Annie. "It's what he does best, fix cars. Strange job for a farmer's son I know…"

Mother and son exchanged an affectionate glance. "No money in farming anymore," a broad grin lit up his whole face. "Anyway, I like my weekends off too much. Oh, and by the way mother, Carol said to tell you that you don't need to look after the boys tomorrow because she's off work."

"How many boys do you have?" smiled Grace. "And... well, thanks for offering to fix my car."

He nodded. "No problem... and it's three with Andy, you've met him of course."

"Andy, Will and Tim," filled in Annie proudly. "Will is eight and he's just like his mum. Tim is just six and he's a cross between the two of them, he looks like Andy and Ben but he has Carol's red hair."

"She calls it strawberry blonde." The affection in Ben's tone pulled at Grace's heartstrings. They had once been a family like the Allbrights, she and Tom and Molly, a complete unit. It was smashed now, disbanded, as if it had never been.

"Thanks again... for the car," she mumbled, already moving towards the stairs. "I think I can hear Molly." The flood of tears that welled behind her heavy lids began to burst before she'd even reached her room. Shutting the bedroom door firmly behind her she flung herself onto the bed, sobbing for everything she'd lost.

When Annie passed by a few minutes later she heard the muffled sounds and stopped outside the door, raising

Broken Heart Wood

her hand to knock. Thinking better of it, with a heartfelt sigh she lowered it again. Perhaps the poor girl needed her solitude, needed to cry away her pain. Oh how like her mother she was, poor Sarah had cried like that on the day she left after… after making the daftest decision of her life. How different things would have been if she had stayed here with Sam, they would have been real sisters then. So what was best, to do the right thing or to follow your heart? Sarah had done what she considered to be 'the right thing' and look where that had got her.

When her tears eventually dried, Grace dragged herself up and washed her face in the sink. What must Annie and Ben have thought about her disappearing so suddenly? She must tell Annie what was wrong; she owed her that at least. Tomorrow, she decided, she'd tell her tomorrow.

Decision taken, Grace took a deep breath and walked determinedly across to the window, staring out at the fells. Life went on no matter what and those majestic hills must have overseen so much heartbreak over the years… like her mother's, for instance. But why *was* she crying that day she asked herself… whatever could have made her so unhappy?

Broken Heart Wood

The sun was slowly sinking over the horizon, a glorious orange glow against the looming dark shapes of the Pennines, turning the endless sky into red and gold and glorious flame. Grace thought about Tom, alone in their small cottage... or was he alone? Was he missing her? Was he worried about her? Should she at least phone to tell him that they were okay? She fumbled in her pocket, closing her hand around her mobile phone. She'd switched it off the moment she left home, so that he couldn't ring her, now the thought of hearing his voice brought both longing and dread. She'd do it later, she decided, before she went to bed. First she had to go and see Annie.

The old lady was still sitting in her chair beside the empty hearth. She looked up with a smile when Grace entered the small cosy room; the late evening sun cast a rosy glow upon her white head.

"Do you feel better now dear?"

"Yes... thank you. And I'm sorry for..."

"No need for sorrys."

She stood stiffly, waiting for her old joints to ease. "Would you like a drink of hot chocolate or maybe a cup of tea?"

"You stay there," Grace insisted. "I'll make it."

"Why don't we make it together," Annie suggested. "Then perhaps we can talk."

They sat together next to the stove, fingers wrapped comfortably around their mugs of hot sweet chocolate. What to say wondered Grace, where to begin?

"I've left my husband," she eventually announced, emotion rising like a tide inside her.

Annie nodded. "I thought as much... another woman?"

"It is so much more than that though," Grace cried, suddenly realising the truth of it. "Something terrible happened, an accident... it changed our whole lives and..."

"Look." Annie reached across and touched her arm, a simple caring gesture that meant everything to Grace. "You don't have to tell me about it now if you're not ready, but you do need to come to terms with it yourself and think it through properly. Why don't you write it all down, right from the beginning, then maybe you'll be able to see things more clearly? ...And you don't have to let me read it unless you really want to."

Grace covered Annie's gnarled fingers with her own.

"Thank you," she said quietly. "I think I'll do that, and you will be the *first* to read it I promise."

"And you'll stay until it's done?"

Suddenly Grace felt as if she had a purpose again.

"Yes," she agreed. "I'll stay."

CHAPTER FOUR

Grace stared at her phone. If she didn't contact Tom soon then he would probably have her listed as a missing person. Her fingers trembled as she pressed the on button and watched the screen come to life. Its familiar tune blasted out into the silence. What if he tried to ring her now before she had time to send her message though? For a moment she hesitated, longing to hear his voice and yet very aware that she wouldn't be able to bear it, knowing what she now knew. Her whole life had been a lie and she needed to face up to it.

She typed hurriedly, *'We are both ok will ring soon,'* pressing send and then switching the phone off with shaking fingers. It was done. At least now Tom would know that they were safe.

Settling herself down next to Molly on the comfortable double bed beneath the window, she tried not to think about how he might be reacting to her message, tried not to think what he might be doing now. Maybe her going away was what he'd wanted all the time; maybe it was his opportunity to… No, that wasn't fair; their life together had to mean more to him than that. They'd always been like two pieces of a puzzle, each lost without the support of the other... until now.

The barely contained well of emotion flooded back, blocking her throat and filling up her chest: She turned her face into the soft, smooth cotton fabric of her pillow, breathing in the faint familiar scent of spring flowers, refusing to give in to her emotions. She had to stay strong, for Molly. She would do what Annie suggested, she decided; write everything down from the beginning. Maybe then she'd be able to make some sense of it all and move on.

Decision taken, Grace cuddled up next to Molly's small body beneath the flowered bedspread, watching the silver moon cast its pale beam upon her daughter's beautiful little face. Perfect skin unmarked yet by life; oh how she wished it would stay that way forever. The little girl whimpered in her sleep and she gently stroked her cheek; of course it wouldn't and she didn't really want it to, for without pain how can we truly appreciate pleasure and without some sadness there can be no real joy.

Closing her eyes she snuggled down determinedly. She would start her story tomorrow she decided... but where to begin? She was still mulling it over in her mind as sleep came to claim her.

Ben was already in the kitchen, chatting to his mother, when Grace appeared next morning with Molly perched on her hip.

He flashed them a warm smile of welcome. "I'll have to take you to meet Carol," he told her, in a voice as huge as himself. "You two will get on like a house on fire I'm sure and she'd love to have a little girl around for a change; it's all boys at our place."

Grace settled Molly down into a chair and looked up to meet his shining dark eyes. "Thank you," she said, meaning it. "I appreciate how welcome you've all made me… as well as fixing my car of course."

"Ah yes." He nodded. "…Your car. It should be ready by tomorrow morning, I'll bring it round."

"And now," interrupted Annie. "Why don't you both sit down and I'll make you some breakfast?"

"Not for me thanks." Ben removed his cap and slid it back onto his slightly balding head, tweaking the peak. "I'm late for work as it is. "I'll call in tonight mother, and maybe bring Carol and the kids."

"Well then why don't you all come to dinner?" Annie suggested.

Broken Heart Wood

He nodded eagerly. "Thanks mum. Ring Carol then and ask her, she did have a school thing on but I think it might have been cancelled.... See you later."

The door shut behind him with a heavy bang and Annie shook her white head in feigned despair. "He always did do everything loudly, even as a small boy he used to shout all the time."

"Well he is a big guy I suppose," added Grace, upon which Annie burst into a fit of laughter.

"Oh yes..." she gasped. "And just wait until you meet Carol; she is *soo* tiny. I couldn't believe it when he first brought her home."

Grace couldn't help but join in with her infectious outburst. "Oh Annie," she cried. "You sound more like a teenager than..."

"...Than an old woman you mean..." finished Annie.

Grace felt a rush of warmth colour her face at that but Annie just laughed some more. "That, Grace," she said, hand on heart. "Is because although you may see me as wrinkled old has been, inside here still beats the heart of a seventeen year old."

Grace's bottom jaw dropped. It was something that she'd never really thought about before.

Annie just laughed, twirling around in a circle with a flourish of her hand. "Well if I'm honest I feel more like twenty seven than seventeen… but I definitely don't feel seventy."

"And you don't look anywhere near seventy," cried Grace.

Annie shook a finger at her. "Just remember, Grace, you are only as old as you feel. Now, have you started to write yet?"

"Today," Grace promised. "When Molly has her nap."

At the sound of her name Molly waddled towards them but to Grace's surprise she stared at them both in her solemn little way and then held out her arms to Annie.

"Wabbits," she announced determinedly.

Annie smiled with delight, reaching down to pick her up. "There you are then," she said. "She wants to stay with me, so why don't you have your breakfast and then make a start this morning; you could do with some quality time on your own. Have a walk up to Heart Wood if you like, it's a lovely day; you could just sit on a tree stump, get out your pad and pen and start writing."

Grace panicked at the thought. The idea was good but how would she know where to start?

"At the beginning," Annie remarked, reading her mind. "Just think of something from what you consider to be the beginning and let your mind go."

Grace felt vaguely excited about the idea and yet the thought of leaving Molly, even for a short while, brought out an empty space inside her. Her... *their* little girl had seemed like her only reason for living these last few days.

"But are you sure?"

Annie shrugged at Grace's reservations. "I'll enjoy it," she insisted. "All we have in our family is boys; it will be nice to have a bit of female company for a change, won't it Molly?

The little girl looked up, her hazel eyes sparkling. "Wabbits," she repeated, wriggling up and down.

"See," said Annie. "All she cares about is rabbits anyway... oh, and you'll find a writing pad in the top drawer of my desk, the one in the office next door to the kitchen. Help yourself."

Grace felt suddenly weak and shaky and yet there was something else, a seed of positivity germinating somewhere deep inside.

"Thank you," she said quietly. "I won't be long."

"Be as long as you like," Annie insisted.

Broken Heart Wood

By the time she had walked half way up the steep slope to the wall that surrounded Heart Wood, Grace's legs ached and her breath came in heaving gasps. It felt good she decided, physical effort, something practical to push aside the heavy weight that had been draining her for days.

She gazed back down into the valley, vague recollections bringing a sense of déjà vu. Way below was the village, a higgledy piggeldy collection of grey stone houses that seemed to have been built with no positive plan and further along, at the very base of the fell was… For a moment she hesitated, the square white house with its cluster of shabby outbuildings stood out from the rest. It felt so familiar. Could it really be Fellclose, the farm where she had lived until she was five years old? Memories rushed in; her hand, tight in her mother's grip as they carried her grandfather's coffin down the narrow aisle of the old stone church. The heavy, musty smell, weighed down by such a sense of melancholy that she'd started to scream. And then someone else had picked her up and taken her out into the sunshine.

So many vague memories of forgotten emotions, an awareness of another life, but why hadn't she thought about it up until now, why hadn't she wanted to come back here sooner?

It all seemed so long ago though... *was* so long ago. She left here when she was just five years old so that would make it... For a moment she hesitated, working it out inside her head. Twenty-eight years. It was twenty-eight years since she and her parents walked away from here and never looked back.

A vague memory of her mother's face flashed into her mind, the sadness in her eyes, and suddenly she knew... Sarah Roberts *had* looked back; every single day of the rest of her life she'd looked back...

Grace shook her head, trying to clear it of the long forgotten and unwanted emotions that were rushing in. She moved on up the hill, walking doggedly and embracing the pain in her limbs, to where the soft greens of Heart Wood beckoned. She stopped at the old grey stone wall, touching it reverently, moving along its crumbling defence. There was no gate, she suddenly realised, so this place was obviously not put here for pleasure as visitors were unwelcome. So why was it here then then?

Placing her pad and pen on the topping stones, she scrambled awkwardly over the wall, falling heavily on the other side. The serenity of it took her breath away. Rabbits hopped slowly, curious but unafraid of their unexpected visitor; a red squirrel stopped on the branch above her head, peering down at her with bright shining eyes. And a blackbird sang a sad sweet song that so perfectly reflected her emotion.

She pushed her way through the tangle of undergrowth where no pathway marked a trail. Silver birch grew tall above her head, their pale glistening bark catching the sun that filtered through the branches. Clumps of holly, dark and shiny, blocked her way. The strong trunk of a horse chestnut tree finally gave respite and she leaned against it. How long ago had it been planted here and by whom, she wondered, or had it simply germinated from a seed, dropped perhaps by a passing bird? Ahead of her she saw a patch of light, in an open space near the centre of the small wood. She hurried towards it, oblivious to the thorns that caught her skin; perhaps here she could start to write.

The sun beamed down, warm and comforting, bringing a mellow air of serenity. Grace sank down onto one of the long, smooth, moss covered rocks that had formed the small clearing by denying the trees and bushes a place to grow. Wild plants still fought there for survival though. Flowers and grasses and creeping

Broken Heart Wood

weeds squeezed through the cracks between the rocks, bringing a magical beauty to the place. Had the wood been planned around them deliberately, for someone to come and sit in total privacy, just as she was doing now? Or was all this beauty here purely by chance?

Turning her face to the sun, for just a moment she allowed herself to think about Tom. She closed her eyes tightly against the memories. Where was he now? Driving perhaps, doggedly staring ahead and thinking… what? Was he hurting too with the same raw ache that was dragging her down… did she want him to hurt? She shook her head to clear it, picking up her pad and raising the pen. Right, where to start…? 'Think of a beginning' Annie had told her 'and then just let your mind go.'

'It all began when…'

When what…? When did it all begin? Was it after the accident when everything changed? Surely though it all began much sooner than that, when she first saw Tom that day at the Fair for instance, or maybe even here, at Greythwaite, when she was just five years old.

Fifteen minutes later there was still just the one same line, surrounded now by doodled circles and sweeping shapes. She stared at the paper, raised her pen, and then ripped the sheet from the pad, stuffing it into her pocket. Tomorrow, she would try again tomorrow.

Broken Heart Wood

Slowly she stood up, easing her cramped limbs; would it be any different tomorrow though… or on any new tomorrow? She remembered reading somewhere that tomorrow holds yesterday's dreams, her yesterday's dreams were gone though so what now? The future stretched before her, bleak and empty.

Suddenly she longed for the feel of Molly's chubby arms about her neck, her happy smile, her innocence. What if she was crying for her mummy, what if she was hurt? What if Annie had tried calling her and she had no signal? Hurriedly she pushed her way through the undergrowth, searching for the chinks of light that would reveal the edge of the small wood and open fell side beyond.

She came upon it suddenly, beyond the crumbling remnants of the old stone wall. The huge space of open sky, the far horizon, the tiny houses way down in the valley. Nostalgia flooded over her, nostalgia for all that had once been. This place was her home, no matter what, and it always would be.

When Grace burst into the kitchen filled with dread, her fears proved falsely grounded. Molly was standing on a chair next to Annie, helping to mix something in a large bowl. She looked round at her mother, raising her hands, small chubby fingers covered with cake mix. Her hazel eyes were wide with delight. "My making a cake, she announced proudly, licking the sticky substance from her fingers.

Annie smiled a welcome, nodding towards a cooling tray. "We have already made some biscuits; have one if you like."

Grace deliberately chose a misshapen biscuit and took a bite. "Delicious," she exclaimed.

My baking wiv Ann…ee," Molly said, her little face glowing with pride.

"And did you see the rabbits?"

"Wabbits," shrieked Molly, scrambling down from the chair."

"Sorry Annie," groaned Grace. "I seem to have lost you your helper."

Annie smiled. "Well then why don't you take her out to see the rabbits again while I finish up here," she suggested. "I'm sure I can manage on my own."

"A whole lot more quickly than with Molly's help I'd imagine," laughed Grace.

As soon as Molly ran across the smooth green lawn the rabbits disappeared as if by magic.

"Don't frighten them," cried Grace, grabbing hold of her daughter. "Look… Sit down here with mummy, nice and still; I'm sure they'll soon come back."

For a moment they sat in a rare silence, watching and waiting as Grace crouched down with Molly perched on her knee. It reminded her sharply of another, similar moment, when her mother had held onto her hand as she walked away from Fellclose farm for the very last time. Tears pressed the backs of her eyelids. Perhaps *that* was the beginning then she realised; the moment when her whole world first turned upside down.

The idea germinated in Grace's mind as she helped prepare a meal for Ben, Carol and the boys, whilst Molly sat happily on the floor, playing with some old toys that Annie had given her.

"Someone may as well get some pleasure out of them," she'd announced, determinedly dragging the box through from the garage. "My three grandchildren would rather play with computer games nowadays."

When Molly dived in with glee, spreading the colourful pile of toys across the kitchen floor, Grace smiled with genuine delight. When had she started to smile again she wondered?

"Perhaps I should take Molly upstairs for a bit," suggested Grace, tidying up the mess half an hour later. "After all it is your family meal and I don't want to intrude."

"You'll do no such thing," insisted Annie. "Anyway," Her face crinkled into a smile. "Carol is only coming to see you so the least you can do is stay around."

"To see me?" echoed Grace.

The old lady looked up from where she was putting the finishing touches to her pie crust, her blue eyes bright and vital against the faded parchment of her skin. "Yes, didn't you know, you are the talk of the village?"

"But why would anyone want to talk about me?"

"Think about it. A mysterious, beautiful young woman arrives from nowhere with a small child in tow. A woman who was born here, in the village, all those years ago, and whose mother was brought up here too, only to run away one day, never to return. Obviously everyone from around here will be talking about you."

Grace carefully dried the last of six crystal glasses, placing it carefully down with the rest. "Well, I suppose, If you put it like that," she said, glancing sideways at Annie... "Why *did* my mother run away though, Annie, and why was she crying?"

Broken Heart Wood

A heavy silence fell as Annie digested Grace's question. She let out a sigh, closing her eyes for a moment as if better to remember. "Oh it's all so long ago now, water under the bridge so to speak, but to be honest…" She hesitated, as if unsure of whether or not to go on, afraid of releasing the sleeping demons.

Grace leaned earnestly forward. "Please Annie. I would really love to know."

"Your father found out that she was in love with someone else." A sense of relief flooded over Annie as she blurted it out. "…He was her first love you see and she'd never got over him; when your father gave her an ultimatum she did the right thing by you both and moved away with him –much good that it did her."

"But who was it?" Grace's mind went wild. "Who did she love?"

"Well I don't suppose it matters now because he's gone too…"

Still Annie hesitated, and then she walked quickly across to take a picture from the side, handing it to Grace. A dark eyed, ordinary looking man looked out at her with the kind of smile that made you want to smile right back.

"My younger brother, Sam," breathed Annie, her voice so low that Grace could hardly hear it. "They were inseparable from childhood, best friends rather than lovers then but I think they both believed that eventually they would be together, Sarah wouldn't settle though, would never commit. I had been married to Edward for over two years but she was still free and single -she was younger than me of course but still.... She was always looking for something more you see, when all she really wanted was right under her nose."

Annie heaved a sigh, her mind lingering in the past whilst Grace waited patiently; her imagination buzzed with unexpected images of the mother she lost so long ago.

"Your father came along with his fancy talk you see," went on Annie. "He swept her off her feet... then you arrived and..."

"And my dad found out that it was Sam she really loved," cut in Grace. "So he took her away from here."

"That's about the top and bottom of it," agreed Annie. "Your father was away a lot on business you see and Sam often called in on her, to keep her company and to do little jobs in the house, so he said. Sarah came to realise then just how much she loved him, how much she had lost, but it was too late.

She almost changed her mind about leaving, right at the last minute. Sam asked her to stay you see. He said that true love meant more than just a wedding ring."

"And my mother said no…"

"Annie nodded. "Sarah said that it wasn't fair on you or Donald; she had made a promise and she had to keep it."

"And now, when I look back, I can see that they were never really happy," Grace admitted. "After she died he soon met someone else, someone he really loved. They went to live in Spain with their two young children when I was sixteen…"

A heavy pain lodged itself inside her chest as she remembered the day she started her first job at the stables. Her father took her there with all her belongings and that was when he delivered his blow.

"Terri and I are moving to Spain love… We've wanted to go there for a while but we thought we'd wait until you were settled. Now that you have a job you like and somewhere to live, well…"

She had wanted him to hold her, to give her a little of the love she had lacked since the day her mother died so very long ago. Holding had never been his thing though, apart from when it was with sharp tongued, olive skinned Terri of course. She got plenty of hugs… and so did little Isabella, the apple of his eye.

Grace stood quite still, absorbing Annie's information. Everything seemed so much clearer to her now. "Do you think she did the right thing?" she asked.

Annie shrugged. "It wasn't so easy to follow your heart in those days… Do you see your father then, now that you have Molly?"

"No," Grace admitted sadly. "He's still in Spain with Terri's family. He rings sometimes and sends presents at Christmas; to be fair to him he does always ask me to go and visit but…"

"But you've just kind of drifted apart," finished Annie.

Grace nodded. "It didn't seem to matter when I was with Tom. Perhaps I'm as bad as he is, too busy with my own life to think of anything else…"

Suddenly she looked right at Annie. "You think my mother should have stayed don't you?"

Annie shrugged "Life is never perfect and we all make mistakes but… yes, I think your mother should have followed her heart and stayed here with Sam."

A heavy sadness settled over Grace. "Perhaps she would still be alive if she had."

Annie shook her head. "That we will never know; all we can do is to try our best to take the right decisions in life and if we take the wrong road, well… we just have to make the best of it."

The melancholy mood was suddenly broken by high-pitched laughter from outside the window. "Oh my Lord," cried Annie. "They're here already and I haven't even set the table yet.

The Allbright family tumbled into the kitchen, a mass of colour and brightness and life, talking, laughing, and joking. Carol –it had to be Carol, decided Grace– walked quickly across towards her, holding out her hand. She took it, surprised by its strength and vitality, but there again everything about Carol Allbright spoke of strength and vitality, despite the fact that she hardly reached up to her husband's chest. Her bright red hair fell in tumbling curls around her shoulders, having obviously escaped from the clip on the top of her head, and her round face beamed with delight at meeting Grace. In fact everything about her was round, from her ample hips to her huge, perky breasts, and yet somehow it all seemed to work.

The smallest boy, who had hair as red as his mother, started to wail; Carol released Grace's hand to grab hold of her middle son, a bright faced boy who looked exactly like her, apart from having dark hair like his dad.

"Will," she cried. "Leave Tim alone…"

"They are always at each other," she remarked to Grace apologetically. "Tim is too soft and Will winds him up all the time, now where is this little girl of yours?"

Molly, it seemed, had taken the Allbright onslaught in her stride. She stood beside Andy, her tiny hand tucked into his, watching the two younger boys with delight. Timmy, smiling now, sank down beside her.

"Hello," he said. "Shall I build you a tower?" and without waiting for her response he fell onto his knees and began piling one brightly coloured block on top of the other… until his brother noticed that is. With an impish smile the tall gangly eight year old touched the top of the looming stack, crowing with glee as it tumbled to the ground.

Tears welled in Molly's hazel eyes and Andy reached down to pick her up, swinging her round and around.

"Right boys," he announced. "That is enough; now tidy up this mess and say sorry to gran."

It surprised Grace that it was Andy who disciplined his brothers, whilst his father appeared oblivious to the melee.

Broken Heart Wood

"Never gets rattled my Ben," remarked Annie. "His dad was just the same, letting the world flow over his head. Andy now, well he takes more after his mum."

"What, you mean a tiny round fireball," suggested Ben with his usual lazy grin.

"I'll fireball you," cried Carol, applying the same treatment to her huge husband as she had just delivered to her middle son.

Ben simply laughed, hiding hopelessly behind his diminutive mother.

"Whatever would you do with them?" asked Annie with a smile; suddenly Grace realised, that for the first time in what seemed like forever, she was laughing fit to burst.

After that the evening settled down. Once seated at the table the Allbrights turned their attention eagerly towards the delicious meal that Annie had prepared, applying all their energy into eating as much and as quickly as they could. After which the children announced that they were off out into the garden to play. Grace was a little cautious about allowing Molly to go with them but when Andy promised to take good care of her, she reluctantly agreed. Aware of her concern, Carol squeezed her arm with a gentleness that revealed a very different side to her flamboyant character. "Andy's great with kids, she'll be fine," she promised. "Now, why don't we take our coffees into the lounge and have a nice chat."

Later that night, with Molly sleeping quietly beside her, Grace thought about the Allbrights. They had certainly helped to take her mind from her problems; no one could spend time with them without becoming drawn into their slightly eccentric world. She had found herself laughing again and again at the boy's antics, not to mention Carol's observations on life in general. Their 'little chat' had left her squirming, for the vivacious redhead had no reservations about asking Grace the kind of direct questions she had been dreading. Despite her managing to evade any direct answers, Carol, it seemed was very quick to come to her own conclusions.

"You can't give up your whole world for one daft mistake," she insisted, putting two and two together. "Give the poor guy another chance."

***

Later that night, restlessly tossing and turning in her bed, Grace couldn't help wondering if Carol was right.

Should she have given Tom another chance, or at least the opportunity to explain, before she left… there again what explanation could there be? Surely Mary couldn't have made it up and anyway it had all made sense, answering a lot of the questions that had been plaguing her since the tragedy that broke her and ended Quicksilver's life.

Their closeness had somehow been lost after that. They had found a way to move on with their lives but it had felt as if there was a distance between them, going through the motions without the passion and joy of before.

Grace rolled onto her side, bringing her knees up to her chest, remembering how Tom had always used to say that they were like two pieces of a puzzle that fit perfectly together. But when one of the pieces was broken, she realised, perhaps they just didn't fit anymore.

CHAPTER FIVE

"So..." Annie looked up from the morning paper, scrutinising Grace from over glasses. "Have you written anything yet?"

Grace squirmed, taking a gulp of her coffee and almost scalding her throat. "I'll start today," she promised.

"Well why don't you make a start now, whilst Molly has her nap," suggested Annie. "Perhaps you could walk back up to Heart Wood."

"But it's not fair of me to expect you to baby sit again," Grace objected. "You've done quite enough for me already."

"Look," Annie removed her glasses and put down the paper. "It is as much for me as you. I told you. I like the company and I love having Molly about the place. She's a breath of fresh air"

"I think your whole family are a breath of fresh air."

Annie laughed at Grace's response. "A breath of *hot* air don't you mean?"

Ten minutes later, armed once again with her pad and pen, Grace found herself heading up the fell towards Heart Wood. She felt a niggle of guilt at leaving Molly again but Annie had been so insistent.

She glanced at her watch. Eleven o clock, what would Tom be doing now? On a sudden impulse she pressed the button on her phone. *'One new message,'* when had that come in? She'd had the phone switched off all the time, apart from when she sent the text. Tentatively she clicked *'listen to message'* her whole body turning to jelly as Tom's voice flooded into her ear.

"Grace, where are you? God I'm so sorry, please, please let's talk about it and…"

His voice cut off mid-sentence and she stood stock still, her whole body shaking. Oh why had she switched the damned thing on? Over the last couple of days she'd become distanced from the emotion that bubbled inside her, now though it rushed back with new ferocity; the shaft of pain just as sharp as in that endless moment when Mary Maddison, her one time friend, had calmly destroyed her whole life with a few short sentences.

Shaking her head she pushed the phone back into her pocket and set off again, embracing the physical pain in her leg muscles and the ache in her lungs that took her thoughts away from the uncertainty that churned inside her.

Heart Wood was just as tranquil as she remembered from the day before and Grace felt a kind of calm steal over her as she sat down once again on the now familiar, moss covered rock. There was something about the whole place that brought her a kind of peace, distancing her from the world beyond its crumbling perimeter. Oh how she longed to know who had planted it and if they too had once sat in this very spot. Picking up her pad she raised the pen.

'My whole world first turned upside down when I was five years old… It realigned itself one Summer's evening over twelve years later… on the night I met Tom.'

So was that the beginning then? She thought long and hard about her life after Greythwaite. Her mother had been so ill and then suddenly it was just she and her dad. He had tried his best of course, at least at first, once he'd met Terri though he seemed to have less and less time for her. To be fair Terri had tried to include Grace but she'd just been so busy with her own things, first her career –whatever that was –and then her babies, which followed each other in quick succession.

Grace remembered the ugly jealousy she'd felt whenever her father fussed and cooed over tiny, perfect, Isabella and Maria. Right from the first the little girls had been beauties, with their mother's exotic foreign looks and inborn elegance. They had seemed to her like a perfect unit, the four of them, whilst she stood on the outside looking in.

Horses had been her saving grace. Every day in the holidays and every weekend, she spent all her time at the local stables and when she left school at seventeen, horses had been her obvious career choice.

Little Oaks livery stables, near Beverly, had accepted her as a working pupil. She remembered how she'd felt on the day her father drove her there, apprehension and excitement jostling for first place in her emotions. And then he had delivered his blow and her turbulent emotions were suddenly channelled into a paralysing panic. They were moving to Terri's native Spain and she was to be left there all alone…

"You can come and see us every holiday," he had promised. "I'll send you the fare…"

To be truthful her father would have sent her the fare had she asked for it. He sent her sporadic letters too; it was she who rarely replied. And then she met Tom and she hadn't needed anyone else, for he became her whole world.

Picking up her pen again she began to write, for now she knew exactly where her story should begin.

***

"I loved my life at the stables, early mornings and hard work that left me sleeping by nine o clock each night, but also the close companionship with some of the most gentle and noble creatures in the world. When Julia, one of my workmates, asked me to go to the summer festival in the local market town of Allonby, at first I said no. What did I want with stalls and shows and fairground rides?

'It's just for kids and families,' I told her.

She looked at me in exasperation -long blonde hair, long brown legs and a figure to die for. "Oh Grace, you are just so boring, it's not for kids after dark.'

Her pretty face lit up. "There's a band playing and the fairground goes wild at night. I hooked up with a travelling guy last year... he was something else.'

Broken Heart Wood

She wrapped her arms about herself, as if remembering the feel of him, and I jumped to my feet giggling.

"You, Julia, are a total tart."

"I know," she responded. "And it's sooo great. Oh please say you'll come with me Grace. I can't exactly go on my own. I'll pay for the taxi."

It took all afternoon for her to persuade me but by five pm I was already deciding what to wear. By six thirty I had changed my mind again but there was no such word as no in Julia's vocabulary. She knocked once on the door of my caravan before yanking it open and barging inside.

"Come on," she insisted. "I've got a taxi outside and you haven't even put your make up on yet."

With a heartfelt sigh I brushed on some blusher and picked up a lipstick. "I had decided not to go..." I began.

"You, Grace Bryant, need a life," she announced. "And I am about to make sure that you get one."

Colours and lights and a buzz of sound lit up the usually quiet meadow, down by the river in the sleepy market town of Allonby. As we jumped out of the taxi a fierce and unexpected excitement brought a tingle to my nerve endings. When one of the latest hit songs boomed out into the velvety darkness of the night I felt totally alive.

"Come on," cried Julia, throwing a twenty pound note at the taxi driver and grabbing hold of my arm.

I had been to fairs and festivals before of course, but only as a child. Now I realised what Julia meant, for after dark the whole scene took on a whole new life of its own: Music, colour, sound and the electric buzz of rampant hormones from the crowds of teenagers that moved to the heavy beat of the rock band, or just stood around the Waltzer watching the rotating cars flash by.

Julia managed to get us into a space, leaning back against the wooden balustrade, shoulder to shoulder with the heaving crowd of youngsters. She hissed something in my ear but her words were whipped away by the melee of sound as the cars rolled to a stop. The thumping beat of the music pounded through my whole body.

"Come on," she cried, grabbing my arm and dragging me towards an empty car.

"No!"

I held back but she yanked at my sleeve.

"In you get girls."

When a sparkly eyed, dark skinned boy flashed us a grin, holding the car still, I felt Julia melt beside me. Her eyes grew huge and her full lips softly parted.

"Tart," I hissed but she just threw back her head and laughed, a high-pitched vivacious sound, whilst all the time she held his electric gaze. The buzz between them put them both into a private place that left me floundering in the cold.

I felt awkward and sick as we spun faster and faster, longing for the dubious comfort of my caravan and the company of Forrester, my favourite horse. When our car finally rolled to a stop three other teenagers piled in. The dark skinned boy reached out to take Julia's hand, holding it for an endless moment as the Waltzer rolled into action again, before applying his flashing gaze upon another welcoming, nubile female.

"Isn't he gorgeous!" she groaned as we settled back against the side rail once again.

"He's trying it on with every girl who looks at him," I told her.

"But did you see the way he looked at me," she cried. "That was totally different; we had a connection."

She quivered, half closing her eyes and I glanced around in desperation to see if there was anyone else here from Little Oaks. If Julia ended up going off with her exotic Romeo then where did that leave me?

I don't know quite when I first noticed the blonde haired boy on the other side of the whirling cars. His eyes connected with mine across the distance before self-consciously slipping away again. Did I know him? When I sneaked a look back and caught his gaze again I felt a strange quiver deep inside me, a kind of longing that left me feeling weak. What was happening to me; I was as bad as Julia. I stared determinedly at the whirling cars, refusing to let myself be drawn into her dangerous world and then there he was again, and again, and again... Somehow it felt as if there was just the two of us in the whole place, as if our eyes had a special connection that cut right through the throbbing atmosphere.

Ten thirty and the fairground took on a dangerous feel. A gang of lads wearing skimpy tee shirts that showed off their tattoos appeared, lounging against the wooden boards, jostling and laughing and eyeing any girl who looked in their direction. Julia was far too connected to Romeo to notice but I felt uneasy. I tweaked her arm urgently. "Come on, let's go,"

Broken Heart Wood

"He goes off at eleven," she murmured, totally oblivious to me. "I'm meeting him at the burger stand."

My heart skipped a beat. "...But what about me?"

Her eyes were still locked on him as she replied. "Oh there are loads of taxis, you'll soon get one."

I made a stand. "Well I'm going now then and you'll have to come with me to find one?"

"Look," Julia turned to look at me and I felt like a fractious five year old. "I think you are quite old enough to get yourself a taxi, Grace, and if you can't find one then just come straight back here. I won't be going anywhere for another half an hour."

She giggled deep in her throat. "After that though... who knows."

I made my way out into the car park, head down and hands trembling. I'd never been good at this sort of thing. When the group of lads from the Waltzer materialised from nowhere, shouting after me as I made for a row of taxis, I tried to ignore them. "Not going already are you darling, why don't you come along with us?"

They surrounded me, laughing, jostling. Panic constricted my throat, taking my breath. "Come on," they insisted. "We'll show you a good time."

Broken Heart Wood

I tried to push past them, holding back tears, and then I felt a firm hand on my arm. A clear calm voice rang in my ears. "Back off lads, she's my sister."

When I glanced up to meet the intense gaze of the blonde haired boy from across the Waltzer, my whole body turned into a quivering mush. "Here," he said, pushing me into a waiting cab as the group of youths slouched off. The door slammed and relief flooded over me as I collapsed onto the seat.

"Where are you going love...?" The cab driver peered round, elderly, solid, reliable.

"Erm...Little Oaks Stables please," I mumbled, trying to still the quiver in my voice. A vacuum seemed to settle inside me as I realised that I would probably never see him again -the boy who'd helped me- and I hadn't even had the chance to say thank you.

The day I did eventually get that chance was just as fresh in my mind now as it was all those years ago.

Almost a month had passed since my night at the fair but the boy with the hazel eyes still flooded my mind. I liked to think about him when I settled down to sleep in my lonely caravan. I could never quite remember his face but his eyes were emblazoned on my brain, bringing a delicious shiver right down into my very core.

Broken Heart Wood

Julia, my crazy companion that night, no longer worked at Little Oaks, for on the morning after the fair she didn't turned up for work. She did eventually appear towards lunchtime, bleary eyed and full of excuses, but the boss, Trevor Adams, never one to bite his tongue, hit the roof and ordered her straight off the premises. I was mortified but Julia just rolled her eyes at me from behind his broad back and laughed.

"I was getting sick of it here anyway," she told him, picking up her bag.

To my surprise then, he had looked right at me. "Right Grace," he said. Right what? I wondered cautiously.

Trevor was a brilliant horseman. No one could produce youngsters like he did. Firm but fair was his motto, for both horses and for people, and he expected everyone around him to put in the same kind of effort that he did. I suppose some people might say he was ruthless. He lived for his horses though, just long as they performed for him, and he had a way with them no doubt about that.

Clients sent youngsters from miles away to be schooled at Little Oaks. If they weren't up to the job their owners wanted them to do though, Trevor would tell them straight. He didn't waste time on no hopers. We lost a lot of liveries too, with his high handed manner.

As Julia disappeared down the lane that day I shivered as he looked at me. Huge barrel chest, short, slightly bandy legs and a wide chin tilted determinedly forwards, did nothing to improve my confidence.

"You..." he announced, "will now have to take over Julia's job, looking after the competition horses and youngsters in for schooling."

It was a daunting thought as my responsibilities had, up until now, been just with the liveries. I suppose it was, in a way, a promotion, but I loved working with the hairy cobs and ponies that made up the yard's livery section. In most cases the owners were middle-aged ladies who had longed to own a horse for most of their lives but only found the time and funds when their children were older. They totally adored their super safe mounts and had no aspirations to do anything other than amble around the country lanes. I totally understood how they felt for I worked with horses purely for the love of them, not the glory. I couldn't ever see myself being a competition rider, although I did love schooling. The thought of taking responsibility for Trevor's highly strung and extremely talented team of horses worried me slightly, but I must admit I was longing to ride them.

"There's a new girl starting tomorrow," Trevor told me. "She can take over the liveries. And I have a lad coming in to see me after lunch. I'm employing him mainly as a rider but he can help you with some of the stable work too. Give me a shout when he turns up will you."

He turned to march off then, stamping down the yard as if he had all the worries of the world on his shoulders, just as a figure appeared, riding a bicycle. The youth hesitated at the yard gate, peering up at the sign as if to make sure that he was in the right place, before pulling off his helmet and leaning his bike against the wall.

"Morning he called," striding towards me.

For a moment I just stared at him, hit by the familiarity of his long easy stride and mop of dark blonde hair. Then he looked at me with those fathomless eyes I remembered so well and something warm rushed through my whole body. "Hello," he said. "So, we meet again, I hoped that we would but I didn't expect it to be here. I'm Tom Roberts by the way... to see Trevor."

He reached out his hand and as his firm fingers closed around mine the warm sensation inside took away *my breath. In that moment I never wanted him to let me go, and he hadn't... until..."*

***

Grace put down her pad and pen, crouching forward and covering her face with her hands as the memories surged in.

"Oh Tom," she groaned as the first wracking sobs engulfed her. Where had he gone, that gallant young man from Little Oaks? What had happened to the awesome love they had shared for so long?

CHAPTER SIX

A screaming sound filled Tom's whole head; cutting into his reverie and bringing him sharply back to now. He stood on the brakes... "Damn... Damn... Damn..."

This was the last thing he needed. The package was already late and if it didn't get there by midday then no doubt he'd lose another customer. He had to get his mind back on track before his whole business went down the pan; trouble was his business didn't feel as if it mattered anymore. He was just going through the motions, holding it all together until Grace came back... *if* Grace came back. No, he wasn't going to think like that. Grace and Molly *had* to come back, for if they didn't then there was nothing worth living for.

His silver van slithered to a halt, slewing sideways, narrowly missing the back bumper of the car up ahead. He jerked on the handbrake before jumping out to see what was going on. The screaming sound appeared to have come from the wheels of an elderly red Ford pickup.

Broken Heart Wood

"It just ran out in front of me," cried its diminutive driver, her voice quivering with tears.

Tom glanced at the middle-aged woman's horrified face and slid to his knees beside a white bundle on the ground. Blood covered the little dog's pale fluffy coat and a shaft of agony sliced right through him as another image flashed into his mind's eye... a flow of crimson against gleaming silver and the stern, set face of a man, holding a gun. No. He shook his head to clear it... This was now.

Suddenly it seemed so important to him that they saved the little white dog, it was hardly more than a pup. Gently he eased his fingers beneath its limp body, lifting its pretty head. At least it was breathing he noted with relief, glancing round urgently at the small crowd of observers. "Where is the nearest vet's surgery?"

A large, kind faced woman detached herself from the crowd, stepping forwards. "Nether Street, just round the corner on the left as you leave the town. Here..."

She rushed to open the door of his van, watching with concern as he gently placed the half conscious dog down onto the passenger seat.

"I'm so... so... sorry," groaned the tiny woman who had caused the accident.

Broken Heart Wood

Tom shrugged, pulling a wry face. "It's done now; let's just hope the vet can save it."

It wasn't until he was sitting in the waiting room half an hour later that Tom suddenly remembered the urgent package in the back of his van. It was supposed to be delivered to an address in Skipton by twelve noon. He glanced at his watch, eleven thirty; too late now. Or was it?

He leaned over the counter, calling out to the tall slim blonde who was rifling through a filing cabinet.

"Can you tell me how the little white dog is getting on?" he asked urgently.

She smiled half-heartedly. "I'll go and check."

Five minutes later, during which Tom kept glancing nervously at his watch, she reappeared. "It's still in surgery. If you want to come back in an hour or so I'll be able to tell you more…"

Tom was out of the door before she finished her sentence. He had lost too many clients lately to risk upsetting another and Ronald Fenwick was one of their best customers.

He drove determinedly, rushing through the town centre as the town hall clock clicked round to twelve noon, glancing down at the directions that were scrawled on a piece of crumpled paper. There it was, Brownlow and Sons.

A dark suited, worried looking man hovered in the doorway, awaiting the delivery. Tom handed over the small square box with a sigh of relief.

"Samples," explained the man, scribbling his name on the acceptance sheet. "I've an important client waiting for these."

Tom shrugged and nodded, thinking how strange it was, the way the world went round. He had come to realise of late though what was really important and it definitely had nothing to do with delivering packages.

As he drove back towards the vets his mind kept going over and over the same painful memories. Where had it all gone so wrong? Why had they given up so easily? Why had he been such a bastard? An image of Grace's smiling face clicked into his mind, and Molly, so small, so perfect. Oh God what was he going to do. He had to find them, had to make it right.

Pulling over into the side of the road he pulled his phone from his pocket and scrolled down to Grace. The dial tone relentlessly rang in his ears and then clicked off. *'...This person is unavailable, please try later...'* How many times had he heard that empty voice today already?

Broken Heart Wood

But what if they were hurt, what if they needed him? He closed his eyes for a moment against the grey misery inside his head, opening them again to see it reflected all around him.

Rain ran in tiny rivers down his windscreen and people scurried by, heads down and jackets firmly fastened. Even the weather was against him. Wearily he nosed his van out into the road again and headed back along the busy street. Knowing his luck the little dog would probably have died.

When the receptionist showed him through into the back of the surgery, to his surprise a tiny white bundle of fur with button bright eyes, was sitting up in its cage smiling at him.

A tall, slim girl wearing a white coat appeared from a side door, smiling brightly. "Hi," she announced, "I'm Beth, a veterinary nurse, and I'm pleased to tell you that your little dog has made a remarkable recovery."

"Opening the cage door she carefully withdrew the little dog, cradling it in her arms as it wriggled up to smother her in kisses. "You'll never be so lucky again," she said, smiling across at Tom. "Fortunately the wounds were more superficial than they first appeared to be. "We've stitched him up and given him something for the pain and to fight off any infection. All he needs now is a bit of love and attention so just keep a close eye on him and bring him back next week to have the stiches out."

Tom was surprised by the surge of relief that hit him. It had seemed so important that the little dog was going to be okay, kind of like a sign. Reaching out his hands he carefully extracted the squirming creature from the girl's arms. "Thank you so much... I guess that's what we should call him then... Lucky. I'll come and settle the bill now. Oh...and."

For a moment he hesitated. It would be so easy to just claim the dog as his and take it home with him. But it wasn't his was it and some child might even now be crying for its loss.

"I don't know whose dog it is to be honest; I just found it in the street. If I leave my name and number perhaps you could inform anyone who is looking..."

The girl, Beth, nodded. "Of course, but don't hold your hopes out. We have a lot of abandoned dogs around here. It may be a stray. I can contact Animal concern to come and get it if you like..."

"No...! I... I'll look after it. My little girl will love it."

A rush of excitement overtook him as he imagined Molly's face when she saw the cute little dog.

Broken Heart Wood

As soon as he was back in the van with Lucky sitting up on the passenger seat beside him, Tom clicked down to Grace's number again… and again… and again; every time he was greeted by that same message, delivered in a clipped, impersonal tone.

"Damn, Damn, Damn," he cried out loud. The little dog squirmed, wriggling his whole body and wagging his tail.

"Sorry boy," Tom reached across to rub his head. "…Nothing for you to worry about."

The dog stared at him, its gaze bright and interested, piercing his loneliness. Suddenly Tom realised that he was smiling for the first time in days

By the time he got back to the yard the dark clouds overhead were rolling back to reveal an ocean of blue. He glanced up at the sky remembering something his grandmother used to tell him. *'If you can see enough blue to make a sailor's jacket then it's going to be a nice day.'* Her words echoed around inside his head, words from another place and another life, when he was someone else. They were all gone now, his gran, his mother, his father…. And Grace… was she gone forever too? No… Grace and Molly were coming back if he had to move heaven and earth to find them.

Pushing aside his melancholy, he snapped his thoughts back to now. The other two Quicksilver vans were already parked up he noted, side-by side with their noses against the wall. Clambered from his vehicle he eased his stiff legs, blinking in the sunshine as Geoff Dobson, the more experienced of his two drivers, appeared from the door of the small office.

"Glad I caught you, boss," he announced, in a loud forced tone. "I've left you a letter but I'd really rather do this in person."

Guessing what was to come, Tom nodded. "Go on then,"

Geoff looked at the ground, twisting his toe in the dirt as if to stamp out an imaginary cigarette butt. "I know this isn't the best time for you," he began awkwardly.

Tom glanced around the yard. Clematis in full bloom trailed all across the back wall. The late afternoon sun cast a golden glow on the gleaming paintwork of the silver vans and the vague aroma of honeysuckle hung heavy in the air. How could everything look so bloody glorious on the outside when his whole world was tumbling down around him?

"Geoff, if you want to go then just tell me." His voice sounded as if it belonged to someone else, a stranger who inhabited his body.

"It's not that I *want* to go." Geoff looked up at him, faded blue eyes peering out from his drawn, lined face. Why hadn't he noticed just how old and tired the man looked, Tom asked himself uneasily?

"Thing is…" Geoff's shoulders drooped. "Nelly wants me to retire you see. We've a bit put by and she wants to move nearer to our daughter in Scarborough."

With a stab of guilt Tom placed a firm hand on his shoulder. "Sorry mate, I've been a bit preoccupied lately. Of course I'll be sad to see you go but family comes first."

Geoff's whole face brightened. "I'll work my notice of course."

When the old man had gone Tom sank wearily down onto the bench by the wall, the one that Grace had placed there a lifetime ago. He closed his eyes, hearing her voice. *'We can come and sit outside to have our lunch, or at coffee time; it's a real sun trap this corner,'* God how he wished that she was sitting here right now.

It was only as he stood up to leave, twenty minutes later, that Tom remembered the little dog. It stood on its back legs as he approached the van, working its tiny front paws up and down the window glass.

"Sorry Lucky," he apologised, opening the door. The pup looked up at him through button bright eyes, head tilted to one side and pink tongue curling out from the side of its mouth. With one huge leap it deposited itself into his arms, licking his face ecstatically. Tom's mood lightened. "Come on then," he said, smiling for the second time in as many days. "Let's go home."

As Tom walked along the lane towards Ivy cottage, the tiny, two bed roomed cottage where he and Grace had lived since they moved in together all those years ago, he found himself remembering the day when they first came to look round.

He had held her hand tightly in his as the tall, stern faced estate agent, ushered them in through the front door. Grace had giggled when he showed them into the bedroom, reaching for his hand and curling her fingers around his. God, how young they had been, how sure of their love. It could have been a pig sty for all they cared. And when the stable yard down the road came up for rent it had seemed as if the whole world was smiling down on them. Heeding the signs they'd taken the plunge, left Little Oaks and started up on their own. An unbeatable combination they had believed themselves to be, especially with Quicksilver to take him to glory. And then they'd grown up... had to grow up whether they liked it or not. But why had he given up on horses altogether, he wondered, why hadn't he just gone back to riding for someone else?

It had taken so long for Grace to recover from the accident though. She had needed so much care and what with little Molly to look after too... it had been too good an opportunity to miss, finding another business to go into so quickly, right out of the blue like that. When he'd bumped into an old school mate, George Appleby, quite by chance, and found out that he was moving abroad and needed someone to take over his delivery business as soon as possible, the price he was asking seemed just too good to miss.

Perhaps it hadn't been such a good opportunity after all though, for if he hadn't met George that day then things would have been very different. Maybe even, when everything had gradually settled back into some kind of normality, he and Grace might have found a way to carry on with the horses.

Broken Heart Wood

Memories overpowered him, memories he usually kept well at bay. The warm aromas of horses and hay and leather, the feel of the stallion's awesome power as he exploded into the air over a fence... and those long winter's evenings, cuddled up together with Grace in front of the log fire in their tiny lounge, discussing their plans and dreams for the future. They had been so... together then, so focussed.

A heavy lump lodged itself inside his chest as he thought about Molly, clambering up onto his knee... holding out her chubby arms; 'daddy's girl' Grace used to call her.

He gulped, holding back the flood of emotion that threatened to drown him.

"She's not back yet then?"

Clare Healey was the last person he wanted to see at that very moment. She peered at him accusingly, her usually friendly eyes tempered now with steel.

Tom held the little white dog tightly in his arms, fighting for self-control, hearing Grace's voice in his ears.

'Bite your lip and hold your temper Tom Roberts....'

"She's visiting a friend," he heard himself say in a cold unfriendly tone.

"Well if there is anything I can do..."

Clare's voice trailed off and he marched past her, proud of his self-control. You see, Grace, he said to himself. I haven't forgotten.

The front door banged shut behind him and he deposited Lucky on the ground, his mind still exploding with the past. It was Grace who had taught him to curb his quick hot anger, to channel his energy into positive thinking, and they'd been so successful for a while… a real team. Was that why he did what he did when she wasn't there to guide him he wondered? Was he just a waste of space without her by his side? Well now he had the chance to prove that he had the strength to get it all back again. This time he wouldn't stray, wouldn't stop until he had Grace and Molly back here with him again…. And just maybe… an idea began to form in his mind, the seed of an impossible dream. Or was it?

"Come on Lucky, let's go and find you some food."

Tom was settled in front of the TV with a ready meal on his knee when the phone rang in the hallway, a harsh trilling sound in the silence of the evening. He clambered from his chair, depositing his tray on the ground the ground. Perhaps it was Grace.

"I believe that you have our dog…"

His heart fell with a heavy thud, right down into his boots.

"Yes I..."

He coughed, clearing the spittle that was lodged in his throat, trying to get the words out.

"Small and white, answers to Sandy..."

"Sandy," he echoed in disbelief.

"Don't even ask," giggled the woman. "I'll come and get him right now."

Tom gave her the address in a clipped tone and replaced the receiver with a bang, glancing down at Lucky. The little white dog wriggled its whole body in delight, whining and scrabbling at his leg. Tom reached down to scoop it into his arms, feeling the heavy pressure of tears behind his eyelids. Is nothing going to go right for me ever again, he wondered, loathing his wave of self-pity whilst unable to hold it back.

When the doorbell rang half an hour later he opened the front door with a firm hand. Lucky wasn't his and it was selfish of him to want to keep the little dog when he already had a home.

A tall lanky woman stood on the doorstep. She held some kind of dog carrier in one hand and a lead in the other. Tom disliked her at once.

"I've come to collect Sandy."

Broken Heart Wood

Lucky stood behind Tom, rubbing up against the backs of his legs.

"Come on," she called, reaching out for him.

The little white dog sniffed at her hand and backed away, flattening his ears against his head.

Tom bristled. "Are you sure this is your dog?"

"Sandy," called the woman more urgently now. "Sandy…"

He reached down to pick Lucky up, cradling his squirming body protectively in his arms as she leaned forward, peering at the dog through pink rimmed spectacles.

"Well do you know," she admitted. "I don't think it is. It looks a bit like Sandy but she was maybe…?"

"It's a *he*," Tom told her, a broad smile slowly spreading across his face.

"Oh," the woman stuttered, taken aback. "Then I suppose it can't be Sandy."

As Tom watched her walk away, back down the pathway towards her small green car, his heart was singing. "Perhaps my luck is on the turn then boy," he said, hugging the little dog close. "Maybe there's hope for us yet." Somehow he had to find Grace and Molly, had to tell her… but tell her what?

Reaching for the phone book he ran his finger down the names and numbers that were written in her flamboyant hand writing. Someone had to know where she'd gone, but who...? Suddenly it dawned on him. Perhaps she'd gone to her father in Spain; his number must be down here somewhere. Already, in his mind, he was buying a ticket, walking into her father's house unannounced and taking her into his arms. No matter how much she protested he would just hold her and beg her forgiveness. His fingers trembled as he dialled the number.

Grace's father was out it seemed but Terri, his wife, sounded pleased to hear from her son in law. They had met once, briefly, just after he and Grace were married. Then he had thought her hard and brittle, like a piece of glass, now though she was all coos and smiles. 'No, they hadn't heard from Grace in months," she told him. "...And you must please ask her to ring her father. He really misses her."

'As if,' thought Tom, whilst promising to pass on the message. He said his goodbyes with a heavy heart as another avenue closed.

Broken Heart Wood

As the days rolled by with still no word from Grace, the emptiness in Tom's life began to feel like a huge vacuum that was slowly sucking him in. As soon as Geoff Dobson left he sold his van and ran just two; there was no heart in him anymore to go looking for another driver… And then came the day that brought back hope.

Mick marched into the office one bright Wednesday afternoon, jangling his keys on the end of his finger, a self-satisfied smile on his face.

"What have you got to be so happy about?" snapped Tom, hating himself even as he spoke. Mick just laughed, he'd become well used to his boss's ill humour of late.

"I think you might cheer up a bit when you hear what I have to say," he announced, tossing the keys up into the air and catching them again before throwing them onto the desk.

Despite himself Tom felt a prickle of interest.

"I've seen her."

Ton's heart stopped, flipped over and started beating again, with huge erratic thumping jolts that left him breathless. Mick grinned, dark eyes sparkling with delight.

"Today… Grace I mean. I saw Grace in Meredale…"

CHAPTER SEVEN

Annie motioned towards Grace's writing pad. "Have you started your story then?" she asked.

"Yes..." Grace nodded self-consciously. "It feels a bit weird though, putting it all down on paper."

"And you finally found the beginning?"

"It found its self," she admitted. "Once I got started... and I'm sorry I've been so long. Is Molly okay?"

Annie smiled. "She's always okay. Anyway, she's been asleep for well over an hour so I've hardly seen her. She just climbed up onto the sofa, popped her thumb into her mouth and went out like a light."

"There's no stopping her when she gets like that," Grace smiled, heading through into the cosy sitting room. "I'll just go and check on her."

"And I'll put the kettle on," Annie called after her.

Molly lay on Annie's floral print sofa, her thumb still tucked firmly into her mouth and her knees curled up to her chest. Grace's heart lurched. It was such an unusual position for the little girl to sleep in, almost foetal;

normally her arms and legs were splayed out wide. Was it a sign she wondered, did it mean that she felt insecure; were the problems between her and Tom affecting their daughter more than she'd realised?

Guilt washed over her. "I'll make it right sweetheart," she promised, gently stroking back a lock of silky hair from the smooth translucence of her cheek. But when, when would she make it right… and how?

Molly stirred in her sleep. "Mummy." she murmured, rubbing her eyes.

Grace reached down to pick her up, burying her face in the soft sweetness of her hair. Who was she kidding, she couldn't stay here forever. It wasn't fair on Molly. Soon she would have to go back and face her problems and then she would talk to Tom.

"Wabbits," cried Molly, squirming in her mother's arms.

"We'll go and see them in a minute sweetheart, come on, let's go and get a drink first."

"My want bockle."

"Bottle please," Grace reminded her with a sigh. She had been trying to gradually wean her off the bottle but now was not the best time; the little girl needed all the comfort and security she could get at the moment. "Come on then," she said, in a forcedly cheerful voice. "Let's go and see Annie and I'll get you a bottle."

***

"You'll have to speak to him you know."

At first Grace ignored Annie, sipping her tea and closing her ears to the old lady's advice.

"You need to talk things through with him, make sense of it in your own head."

"I know." Grace concentrated her eyes upon Molly, who was playing on the floor, trying hopelessly to make a castle with brightly coloured blocks."

"I'm going to do as you suggested," she said. "You know, write it all down and then decide what to do." Her face suddenly crumpled as she looked up at Annie. "It is still all right for me to stay here isn't it? Please say if you need the room."

Annie reached across and placed a hand on her shoulder. "You know it's all right. I just worry about you, you know, your future and everything. I mean… well… what about your friends; do they know where you are? And work maybe."

Grace shook her head. "My best friend… my best friend moved away and I don't really have anyone close, not anymore. It has always been just me and Tom really. We both work in our own business, Quicksilver, and I've never been one for socialising much."

"And there lies your problem," sighed Annie.

Grace narrowed her eyes. "What do you mean?"

"Well when you are so close to someone and so sure of your love, when the person you love lets you down it must feel as if the bottom has dropped out of your entire universe."

"How did you know?" The familiar well of tears rushed in, pressing against Grace's eyelids.

Annie shrugged, smiling gently. "I suppose it's just life. You don't get to my age without having a bit of heartache you know."

"And I'm being so selfish…"

"No… You're just hurting at the moment that's all, your whole life has turned upside down and you can't make any sense of it. Stay a while longer, until you've finished your story at least, and then perhaps you will be able to meet up with him and talk it through."

She stood then, picking up the cups and heading towards the sink, hesitating for a second to look back at Grace. "You will let him know that you are both all right though? He must be worried sick."

"I already did," Grace admitted. "I sent him a text... but I think you'll find that it's just Molly he'll be worried about."

Annie sighed. "Oh love, are you sure about that? And what is wrong with good old-fashioned conversation anyway, never mind all this texting."

"Annie?"

The old lady looked round from where she was rinsing the mugs under the tap."

"I really do appreciate all you are doing for me you know?" Grace said. "If I hadn't come across you that day on the motorway then I don't know what I would have done."

Annie smiled. "...And you don't know what you are doing for me. It's like having your mother back home again, my chance to make amends."

"...Amends for what?"

"Amends for not trying harder to make her stay I suppose. Doing the *right* thing was more important though in those days. Oh lass, we all make mistakes; follow your heart, that's the secret. And don't expect perfection in life for there's no such thing... Oh, and by the way, Carol has invited us to tea tomorrow if that's all right and Andy is coming round after work today, he'll look after Molly for a bit if you like. Perhaps you could get on with your story."

With a sudden rush of emotion Grace gave her a quick hug. "And being with you is like having my mum back again too," she told her.

"That," said Annie. "Is the nicest thing you could ever say to me."

***

Tea at the Allbright's proved to just as interesting an occasion as the last time they met, when they all came to Hillside Cottage. Carol delivered a wonderful meal of roast beef and all the trimmings, still managing to smile as she dashed around the kitchen, whilst Ben relaxed in his favourite chair discussing his day's work with his mother. Her offer of help refused, Grace watched Molly playing with Will and Tim, both of whom were fighting for her attention, until Andy came in that is. He picked the little girl up and swung her round and around making her squeal with delight.

"Wabbits," she shrieked.

"You and your rabbits," he laughed. "There are no rabbits here; we'll see them at Gran's tomorrow."

"I have a book with some rabbits in," Tim eagerly suggested.

"Oh good... well then go and get it," said Andy. "If the little lady wants rabbits then rabbits she shall have."

"I always wanted them to have a sister."

At the sound of Carol's voice Grace looked round to see her watching the children play; a wistful expression clouded her features.

"Well there's plenty of time for you yet I'm sure," she told her.

"I really am so grateful to have three such brilliant kids," went on Carol. "But I must admit that it would have been nice to have had a girl too."

Suddenly she smiled. "...Don't tell the boys I said that though."

"Your secret's safe with me," Grace promised.

Carol sighed. "I had some trouble when Tim was born you see, so there'll be no more babies for us now I'm afraid."

Grace fell silent, her heart dropping as she realised that Molly was unlikely to be having *any* sisters or brothers now.

"You need to talk to him you know," Carol said, sensing her mood. "I don't mean to pry and I have no

Broken Heart Wood

idea what your problems are, but just remember, life is never perfect and if it was then it would become very boring –human nature I'm afraid. Forgive and forget that's my motto. Take happiness where you can, Grace, and don't let jealousy and small mindedness stand in your way."

"I'm writing it all down," blurted out Grace. "Right from the start, so that I can remember all the good times and maybe make some sense of it."

"And I'm guessing that was Annie's idea."

Grace nodded. "Perhaps I'll let you read it when I'm finished."

The small, exuberant, red haired woman grinned, giving Grace a nudge, her brief moment of dejection suddenly forgotten. "Depends on what you put in there. Maybe it will be x rated eh…?"

Grace's mind flashed back to Tom, his tender love making, the way his fingers stroked her skin, shivering at the memory. "No… I…" she began.

"Mine certainly would be," giggled Carol. "He's more man than you think, my Ben. I could tell you some tales…"

Noting the way Grace squirmed she laughed out loud. "Don't worry, I'm not going to. Now come on everyone," she yelled, changing the subject. "Tea's ready. Boys, into the dining room *now* please."

They all thronged dutifully through the hallway with Grace following slowly behind. Never had she met anyone like Carol, anyone who wore their heart on their sleeve as she did. *Her* heart was tucked neatly away deep down inside where only Tom could reach it… and Molly too of course. But the love she had for her child, that fierce protective passion that knew no boundaries, was a very different kind of emotion.

"Come along my dear," urged Annie, taking her arm. "Don't go all maudlin on us. Forget your troubles for a while; it's easy in this household."

***

It was easy to slip into the slightly frantic and very merry world of the Allbrights realised Grace, as days turned into weeks. Tom and Ivy Cottage and the sleepy little village of Mossdale seemed a million miles away, in another life. Writing down her story and re-living the past became her main focus. The urge to finish it was a driving force. What would happen after that she didn't know, but allowing all the emotions and memories of the last fifteen years to emerge, felt like a healing process.

Broken Heart Wood

Every spare minute she had was spent scribbling on her pad. Late at night, when Molly was sleeping, and, best of all, whenever she could get away to Heart Wood where her mind flowed most freely. Somewhere, in the distant future, she knew that she had to find out more about the wood, had to get to the truth of who planted it and why. Sometimes she almost felt a kind of presence there, as if someone was watching over her. For now though, all she needed was its tranquillity, the soothing presence of the timeless trees that whispered in the breeze above her head.

Picking up her pen, eager to re-live the past again, her mind slipped back to embrace those long gone happy times, when the future stretched out before her, full of dreams and promises... the day when she met Tom again.

***

'An embarrassing rush of heat flooded my face as his hand closed around mine, warm and firm and vibrant, I dared to glance up, my gaze connecting with those familiar, glorious eyes. His presence electrified me, making me feel weak and stupid but oh so alive.

"I really can't believe that it's you," he said. "I mean... I can't believe that we've met again so soon."

"I guess I need to thank you," I began. My voice came out as a quivering high-pitched squeak that seemed to belong to someone else.

"I'd have done the same for anyone in that situation," he admitted.

My joy deflated like a pricked balloon. So it wasn't just for me then, it wasn't because...

"...Anyway," he went on, smiling. "I suppose I should really thank those lads, for giving me the chance to talk to you."

He had wanted to talk to me... he had wanted... what; and what did I want from him? I stared at the ground, stupidly speechless.

"Mr Adams said that you'd show me the ropes," he said, changing the subject. "You know, tell me what needs doing around here."

Glad of the opportunity to get my spinning head back on track, I nodded, already heading off across the yard.

"So," I announced, more confidently now as he fell in beside me. "I'm guessing that you must be the new rider."

Broken Heart Wood

His smile lit up his whole face. "Well, not just a rider, I have to do yard work as well, but riding is my main thing."

When he glanced across at me I could see the passion in his eyes. "I want to be a show jumper," he announced. "One of the best, you know, travelling abroad to shows and everything... Trouble is..."

"What?" I asked. "If you want it so much then where's the problem?"

Our feet were in step as we crossed the yard; after that we always seemed to be in step, but was I striding out to keep up with him or was he shortening his strides to match mine. And when did our steps get so out of sync?

"Money I suppose," he admitted. "It's an expensive sport."

"But there's sponsorship," I told him. "And you can ride for other people. There is always a way if you want something badly enough you know."

***

Grace put down her pen, her stomach churning at the memory. Had she *really* said those words, *'there is always a way if you want something badly enough.'*

Broken Heart Wood

Where was that thought now then, when she needed it so much; where was that open hearted, naïve young girl?

Closing her pad she glanced down at her watch, stumbling awkwardly to her feet on wooden legs. It was almost teatime and she needed to get back; it wasn't fair to put on Annie all the time.

Way below her she could see Fellclose, the sprawling whitewashed farmhouse that brought back so many memories. Dare she go there? Dare she take her memories that far? Suddenly she shuddered, turning away, wondering why she loved this place so much when all it seemed to speak of was heartache?

Behind her, Heart Wood rustled, singing in the breeze. A bird flew up from the safety of its branches, embracing the wild free beauty of the endless sky, rising up on fragile wings towards the drifting clouds. There was so much to know here, so much to find out, but for now... for now.

Seized by a surge of strength she pulled her phone from her pocket, clicked the 'on' button and scrolled down the screen. *Tom*... when his name jumped out at her she took a deep breath and wrote a quick text. *'Will be in touch soon, we are both ok.'* Was that it, she thought, was that all she could find to say to the boy with the glorious eyes, her soul mate? But he wasn't her soul mate anymore was he she remembered, pressing send with a heavy heart.

The warmth of Annie's kitchen and Molly's chubby arms called out to her; she would worry about what happened next when she had finished her story she decided. And until then she would just live day-to-day, going through the motions… surviving.

CHAPTER EIGHT

Grace narrowed her eyes, struggling to see beneath the yellow light of her small bedside lamp, whilst beside her Molly slept peacefully, in the innocent all-consuming slumber of the very young.

Her fingers worked quickly across the page, her mind firmly fixed in the past, re-living those long gone times when she and Tom were different people. Or were they; were they really different or had the world just changed around them?

Her eyelids drooped as the fingers on the wall clock clicked on to two am but she jerked herself awake again. She desperately needed sleep but there was just so much to say, so many memories jostling for first place. The hopes, the promises, the passion... all so needlessly lost...

***

'Tom and I may not have quite got it together then, but I remember that I couldn't even look at him without my heart rate rising. We worked together every day,

Broken Heart Wood

skirting around each other in a hidden dance, our eyes revealing the feelings that were never voiced. As strangers it would be have been easy, but as work mates there was always that fear; if it didn't work out what then, where would it leave us?

And so we held on to our tentative friendship, glancing at each other with a longing that neither of us admitted to...or at least not to each other, at night he filled my dreams. It was only a matter of time though until our emotions over took our common sense. I remember that moment so well.

Tom had been at Little Oaks for just a few weeks but he had already made his mark. He thought nothing of riding eight or nine horses a day and I never tired of watching him work his magic. Dilly, a nervous three year old, had been totally unrideable until he took her over. His dream of being a top show jumper seemed inevitable, the talent was inborn. All he needed were the chances... or an influx of cash. The chances seemed to come thick and fast, the cash was not so forthcoming.

It was after his first competitive show jumping success, when he arrived back on the yard with a kind of elation in his eyes that we first gave in to our feelings for each other.

He leaped down from the lorry with a whoop of joy, reaching out his hand to me. I took it and he twirled me round.

"Oh Grace," he cried. "You should have seen the way Touchstone performed. I was ahead by seconds in the jump off..."

And then I was in his arms, wrapped up in the scent of him; horses, sweat, leather and something else, a kind of musky masculinity that sent a delicious shiver right down to my toes. When his warm, soft lips, passed fleetingly over mine, I knew that I was lost.

"He did well today the boy," remarked Trevor with a grin.

Tom turned towards him, his arm still thrown around my shoulders. "He's going to the top that one."

Trevor laughed. "To the top of the price charts you mean."

Tom's whole body tightened and I felt his dismay, the beginnings of the frustration that carved out our future.

After that first sweet kiss, delivered in the heat of the moment and driven by the elation of Tom's success, we became almost a couple, spending time together and yet still not ready to discuss the way we felt. Perhaps we just didn't need to. Our dreams were the same and our

Broken Heart Wood

goals...? My goals were tending for the horses in my care, being involved with their training, charting their success... and loving Tom Roberts forever. His were... What were his goals? Success I suppose, the glory of winning, and yet there was so much more than that.

We both loved to work the horses in the school, stopping now and again to discuss their progress, helping each other. I rarely saw him compete as someone always had to stay home, but in the long summers evenings we would sit together on the bench beneath the oak tree in the corner of the yard, going over every single detail of the day. Each small mistake, each cleared pole, re-lived by Tom just for me, until I felt as if I really had been there.

The first time that I actually got to watch him jump at a show though would stand out in my memory forever. I felt so proud of his obvious talent and a deep determination grew inside me that day, to help him succeed no matter what.

Jen, the young girl who came to work on the on the yard the same day as Tom, rang in to say that her car wouldn't start and she was going to be late. She was usually the lucky one who got to go off with them in the horsebox, leaving me in charge of the yard. Today they were due to leave at eight, the horses were loaded and ready to go and when she hadn't arrived by ten past, Trevor started the engine.

"You'll have to come with us Grace," he said. "Everything's fed. Jen will just have to manage things here. Leave her a note of what's to do and I'll give her a ring."

Ten minutes later I was snuggled up next to Tom in the front of the horsebox with butterflies fluttering inside me. I reached for his hand and he curled his fingers around mine, glancing round to catch my eye. His shone with excitement and I could almost smell the adrenalin that was coursing through his veins. This was what he loved, the whole thing. The apprehension, the excitement, the promise of the day ahead; he competed to win not just to take part and there lay our difference.

Don't get me wrong, I wanted the horses to win just as much as he did, but for me it was not such a need. To see them work and do their best, to see them improve, that was my joy. For Tom success was everything.

The day passed by in a haze, unloading the horses and loading them up again, redoing boots and bandages, tacking, un-tacking, and walking horses endlessly round. And of course there were the highlights. Watching Tom cruise around the courses with masterful ease brought an ache into my heart, especially when Touchstone touched a pole at the last fence. It fell with a clatter and the crowd groaned.

I expected to see disappointment on Tom's handsome face as he galloped out of the ring, there though he surprised me. He may have an inborn desire to compete and win but he handled losing far better than I would have ever imagined.

He rode towards me and vaulted off the big, dark grey gelding, his feet landing more heavily on the ground than usual.

"Never mind, Tom," I said, with a sympathetic smile, "You can't win all the time, and if you did then it wouldn't mean as much anyway."

He handed me the reins before going to mount his second horse, an angular bay named Tramp. "I suppose so," he admitted, his mood visibly lightening. Then he flashed me a grin. "And to be honest it was my fault anyway. I just pushed him too hard to that last oxer."

The day ended with two second rosettes. "It's not so bad," declared Trevor, negotiating the narrow entrance onto the busy main road. The horsebox settled into a rumbling rhythm and we all sat back. "At least we've been in the ribbons every time out. Now, next week *there's The Northern horse show at Wetherby and then..." His voice droned on as my eyelids drooped and before I knew it we were back at the yard with a couple of hours of work ahead of us.*

And so the days wore on. Electrified by the constant close proximity of each other where each glance and touch of the hands brought a rush of excitement culminating in gentle, secret kisses, we were content. Of course we both knew deep down that our relationship couldn't stay like that. Our lives though were so full, so busy, that I suppose we were too afraid to move on, for totally committing to each other would change everything

The inevitable took us totally by surprise... or was it just me who was surprised?

Of the last batch of horses that had arrived from Ireland, only one proved to be difficult. The rest were soon moved on, schooled diligently by Tom until their jumping was up to scratch and then sold on at a fat profit for Trevor. Tom got so frustrated when the really good ones went, he would plead with Trevor to keep at least just one or two and let them realise their potential. He was a dealer though, through and through. They were all there to sell and that was it. I secretly dreaded the day when he would tell us that Touchstone was sold but I never mentioned it to Tom.

One difficult horse, Hobo, a coloured four year old with an explosive temperament and feet like dinner plates, was not kept on longer than most for his talent however; in fact it was rather the opposite. It took Tom almost three months just to back him and then he had to be turned away for a while for there was no way that anyone would buy him until he'd had some more schooling.

It was autumn before we brought him back in to work again. Trevor, worrying about money as usual, insisted that Tom got the attractively coloured youngster going well enough to be sold as quickly as possible.

"You've spent enough time on him already," he grumbled. "The damned thing's just eating away at my profits…"

When the highly-strung gelding was finally ready to hack out I went along too, riding Marmalade, the quietest horse in the yard, to help to keep Hobo calm.

"If we meet any traffic then you go first," Tom told me. "And wave your arm to slow it down."

Everything went fine until we reached the wood on the outskirts of the village. The day was as warm as it

Broken Heart Wood

can get in autumn. Dappled sunshine filtered through the trees, making patterns on the ground and the trees above us were in full, glorious colour, red and gold and flame, their leaves floating gently down around us like golden rain. I thought it seemed magical but Tom laughed when I told him.

"Come on," he cried, a broad grin plastered across his face. "Never mind the dead leaves. Let's have a canter."

He set off ahead of me and I followed eagerly, revelling in the thud of hooves on the woodland path and the surprising power of my plucky little mare. Ahead of us Hobo's brown and white-patched rump bunched beneath him as his stride lengthened and Tom glanced back at me again, waving his arm to urge me on.

I don't know what spooked him first; Tom's arm above him or the black and tan crossbred dog that suddenly appeared from the bushes with a rabbit in its mouth, but suddenly Hobo gave a mighty leap, twisting sideways. Before Tom quite regained his balance the big gelding was off at full gallop, his huge feet thundering along the track. I thought that Tom was just acting crazy at first, until I saw him hauling desperately on the reins. My stomach lurched.

"Whoa boy!" I yelled helplessly.

Broken Heart Wood

My gentle mare waited for my instructions and we followed at a slower pace, afraid of spooking Hobo further by getting too close. Surely Tom would manage to slow him down in a minute.

I saw the branch before he did, hanging awkwardly down across the overgrown track. Tom looked up, too late, and then he was falling, bouncing along the ground whilst his horse veered into the trees and pulled up in a small clearing, nibbling happily at a clump of long grass as though nothing was wrong.

My heart was pounding in my ears as I leaped to the ground, flinging my reins over a branch before running to where Tom lay, totally motionless, a bed of moss and dry bracken cushioning his crumpled body. I sank down beside him, cradling his head on my knee and stroking his forehead, tears dripping down my cheeks. Gulping, I tried to control them, but they ran on in a river that splashed down onto his pale, silent face.

"Tom," I cried, hugging him close. "Tom!"

And suddenly he was looking up at me with those glorious eyes, eyes that seemed to change their colour with every shift of the light. Now they were as dark as night, dark with...?

Something deep inside me quivered. I tried to look away, afraid of their intensity, but my gaze seemed to be glued to his; it felt as if we two were one entity, alone in our own secret place. I shivered, dragging my eyes away from his and glancing around the small clearing to make sure that the horses were ok.

The little dog was still there, watching us with interest, the rabbit at his feet. He looked straight at me and wagged his tail, then picked up his prize and disappeared once again into the undergrowth, totally unaware of the damage he had caused. The big coloured gelding, Hobo, grazed calmly, happy now that he had his own way, whilst my placid little mare just waited patiently with half closed eyes. Mine slid unbidden, back to Tom. The blood pounded through my veins like liquid fire when I saw the passion in his face.

I wanted to ask of he was all right but my tongue felt like cotton wool inside my mouth. His head on my knees was warm and heavy. My eyes helplessly held his...

"Oh Grace," he murmured, reaching up to touch my face. When he curled his long fingers around the back of my neck, drawing me down until my lips found his... I knew that I was lost... forever.

Whilst our horses grazed unconcernedly in that quiet peaceful woodland, far away from the prying eyes that seemed always to surround us, we reached a place I had never even imagined could exist. His fingers burned my flesh as they trailed across my skin, making my whole body quiver with such and intense longing that nothing else seemed to matter... nothing but Tom Roberts and the sensations he aroused in me. And when at last he loved me, sweetly, gently and yet with such passion that it brought a pulsating pleasure to my very core, I realised that I was weeping, trembling in his arms with an uncontrollable joy that made me finally realise... I loved Tom Roberts with all of my heart and body and soul... but did he love me back...? I hoped so, oh how I hoped so.

Our lives slipped, unbelievably, back onto an even track after that amazing awakening. We felt no shame, no embarrassment and no regret for it was as if we were meant to be together. We never spoke of love for there was no need, our love was as natural as breathing and our commitment needed no words.

Trevor had strict rules about my caravan –no male guests, lights off at mid-night, and other crazy things that we tended to ignore. Sometimes Tom would sneak in late in the evening and we would spend a whole delicious night together, and occasionally we found moments like our first awakening again, at one with nature making love beneath her vast canopy.

Broken Heart Wood

Days drifted into weeks and months, horses came and went and then, right out of the blue the inevitable happened. Trevor called Tom into his office and informed him quite bluntly that Touchstone was sold to a wealthy American. It shattered Tom's world.

He had never forgotten his dream. To reach the top had always been his goal, jumping against the best, travelling the world over, achieving glory. Touchstone had been his chance to make that dream real and now that chance was gone.

He pleaded with Trevor but the burly dealer was immovable. "Look lad," he tried to explain, placing a broad hand on Tom's shoulder whilst I looked on with the heavy weight of tears behind my eyes. "I'm in this job to make a living. He'd have gone months ago if it wasn't for you and I just can't refuse Ross Walker's offer. It'll keep the rest of the horses for a year. Tell you what... As payment for all the work you've done on the horse I'll let you have a youngster from the next batch for free, something for you to keep."

"What...?" I could see Tom's mood lightening already. "You mean for me... to own?"

"For you to own," agreed Trevor, nodding his head.

Broken Heart Wood

The loss of Touchstone weighed heavily but the thought of actually owning his own horse lightened Tom's black mood. In fact, once Touchstone was finally loaded and gone out of his life for good, he could talk of nothing else. His very elderly parents had never been able to afford to buy him a horse and neither of us made enough money to even dream of it. This was his chance, his opportunity, and he seized it with both hands.

It was another three months before Trevor went to Ireland on a buying trip again and both Tom and I watched with bated breath as Little Oak's silver horsebox rolled back into the yard. Its wheels crunched across the gravel and then shuddering into silence as the engine died. The driver's door opened with a groan and Trevor's burly figure appeared, a broad self-satisfied grin spreading across his face as he landed on the ground with a heavy thud.

"You're back then," called Tom, walking across the yard towards the horsebox with long easy strides; his blonde hair lifted in the breeze I remember, revealing the dark locks beneath its sun bleached surface. "...You must have had a good trip if your expression is anything to go by."

"Take a look at these beauties," urged Trevor, unfastening the ramp.

As it swung to the ground with a begrudging groan a cloud of steam poured out, drifting off across the yard and spiralling up into the sky. The scent and sounds of nervous horses filled my head, clinking on their lead ropes, snorting at the strange new world beyond their small enclosure. I always felt so sorry for these new arrivals that clambered trustingly up into the wagon in Ireland, not knowing that they would probably never see that lush green land again.

Trevor slid the first bolt, looking sideways at Tom. "Don't worry, I haven't forgotten my promise. Yours is at the back."

A spooky black mare leaped down the ramp in two huge bounds, snorting at the chickens that were taking a dust bath on the edge of the yard. I took her lead rope, standing her up for the two men to look over.

"Nice limbs," remarked Tom, running his hand down her fore legs and feeling the ridges of hard clean tendons.

"Put her away then lass," ordered Trevor. "Let's have the next one out. Now this one really is a beauty..."

Broken Heart Wood

And so the horses were paraded one by one, Tom and Trevor discussing their conformation whilst all I could see were their terrified eyes. My job would be to settle them in and gain their confidence, Tom's was to train them on whilst Trevor found their best market... except for one of course, the one that Tom had earned with all his hard work.

It came out last, stepping gingerly down the ramp, a gawky, silver grey colt with huge dark eyes and a kind of presence.

"It looks a bit rough at the moment of course." Trevor sounded awkward, as if he was embarrassed by his choice. I thought that the colt was glorious.

"It has some growing up to do that's all," remarked Tom. I caught his eyes and saw that he felt the same as me.

Trevor frowned. "I'll throw in his keep too if you like, only if you do a good job with the others as well of course."

"Don't I always?" Tom said, smiling broadly.

"Yes, you do, that's why I'm giving you this chap. I just hope that I don't live to regret it."

Tom winked at me. "Oh you'll definitely do that," he announced.

And so began the rest of our lives, lives that were bound around our dream, Tom's and mine. The future stretched out before us like a pathway of promise; safe in the knowledge that no one could take Quicksilver... And oh how wrong we were...

***

Grace opened her eyes suddenly, her whole body aching. The pen was sticking into her cheek, the light from the bedside lamp still glowed and her body was twisted uncomfortably. Molly whimpered and she cuddled her close, crooning a lullaby, longing to get up and stretch but afraid of disturbing the little girl.

She closed her eyes, her mind still full of Tom. The scent of him, the passion in his eyes… Where had it all gone? And it *had* gone. Suddenly she realised for the very first time just how much he'd changed after… after his dreams died. She'd been so busy just trying to get her own life back on track that she hadn't noticed the change in him. Not until tonight, when she had re-lived those early days, remembered their hopes and their dreams… their passion. Scrambling for the pad she took her pen to scribble out the section in the wood when they had first made love. She couldn't let Annie read that.

Her eyes flickered over the page one last time before she erased it, the familiar ache a heavy lump in her heart. Writing about those early, happy days, when their love was new, brought back so many memories -memories that only heightened the pain she was feeling now. They were so confident then, so sure of each other. How could he have thrown all that away? How could she have let him? Or was it her who had thrown it away on that grey day when Quicksilver, the horse who carried their dreams, breathed his last breath on the cold hard road.

A little cry from behind her took her attention and she looked round to see Molly's sleepy face.

"Mumee," she called, holding out her chubby arms. "My want Bockle."

The low light from their bedroom glowed out onto the landing but the hallway down below was in darkness. Grace lifted the little girl onto her hip, creeping down the stairs so as not to wake Annie, feeling carefully for each step. The house was in total silence, dark and brooding, the warmth from the kitchen stove bringing a homely comfort as she pushed open the door. She flicked on the switch, blinking as light burst into the room.

"Does she want a bottle?"

Annie's voice made her jump. "Oh... yes," she responded, looking round with alarm to see the old lady sitting in her favourite chair beside the stove. "Are you okay?"

She started to stand up. "I couldn't sleep... here I'll get the bottle."

"No," Grace insisted, settling Molly down on Annie's knee. The little girl pushed her thumb into her mouth, snuggling close.

"She is very like you were at that age," murmured Annie, touching her lips to Molly's forehead.

Grace filled a bottle and placed it into the microwave. It pinged, buzzing into life and she sighed. "To be honest she's more like Tom," she admitted. "Sometimes looking into her eyes is just like looking into his."

"You miss him, I know."

It was more an observation than a question but Grace wanted to answer, needed to explain.

"We were together so long... and we went through... through so much... There was a terrible accident you see and..."

"It's okay," Annie reached up to wrap comforting fingers around Grace's arm. "You don't need to explain it to me but you *do* need to talk to Tom, maybe arrange to meet up with him and try to talk things through. There is always a way if you both still love each other; forgiveness is the key to lots of problems you know."

"I am going to talk to him… when I've finished my story, but I don't know if I'll ever be able to forgive him." For a moment Grace's face contorted as she fought off her demons. "I used to believe in him you see, believe in us… He betrayed me though, gave up on us; I don't think I can get past that."

Annie took the bottle and settled Molly back in her arms. The little girl grabbed it; eyes half closed now as she eagerly accepted its simple comfort.

"None of us are perfect," she sighed. "We all make mistakes. Look at your mother for instance. Deep down I think she had loved Sam for all of her life, she was so afraid of missing out on something better though that she would never admit it, even to herself, until it was too late. She loved attention you see and she was so beautiful that she got plenty of that. I think most of the local lads were at least half in love with her. Your father was different though, he made a fuss of her, wined her and dined her, flattered her witless and the next thing she knew… There were no abortions in those days you see, no second chances. You made your mistakes and you paid for them. Your grandfather had them married in a flash..."

Grace closed her eyes fleetingly, remembering the muffled rows before her mother became ill. "But surely if she really loved Sam then..." she said.

"Oh it wasn't as easy as that," sighed Annie. "You father loved you. He had rights too and your grandfather would never have forgiven her if she and Sam had lived together, here in the village."

"And she never saw Sam again?"

"She never saw any of us again."

"I am so sorry." Grace covered her face with her hands. "Why do we make such a mess of our lives?"

"We are human that's all, we are weak sometimes, and selfish. We all make mistakes."

Half an hour later, snuggled down beneath her duvet next to Molly again, watching the silver moon rise through her bedroom window, Grace pondered on Annie's wise words. Had the person who planted Heart Wood made mistakes she wondered, maybe heartache had been the inspiration behind the carefully planted heart shaped wood. It could have been to a lost love perhaps, or maybe it was a tribute to a true love shared?

Broken Heart Wood

Well someone must know and she was determined to find out the truth of it. For now though she had to sort things out in her own mind, re-live her life right back to now… and then see Tom. The longing that flooded over her just at the thought of him was too much to bear. Her options were impossible… for how could she ever forgive him when trust was gone?

CHAPTER NINE

For Grace it felt as if re-living the past and writing down her story, took over her whole life. On the surface she chatted to Annie, helped with the chores and cared for Molly, whilst all the time her mind was simmering with long gone memories of so many precious moments. One by one she remembered each and every one, with a painful joy that left her floundering in no man's land, trying to come to terms with the truth. Was it really over then, their awesome, all consuming love, truly and irrevocably broken, forever?

Sometimes, when Molly came out with one of her funny little comments, Grace would hold her tightly in her arms and long so much to share the moment with Tom. She was their child, their own little girl and he was missing so much already. Would it ever fade, that longing to share things with him, to be with him, or was it a weight that she would have to bear forever? And how long could she leave it before she let him see his daughter? The answer to that question was always the same. When she had finished writing down her story she *would* meet up with him, perhaps then she'd have things more straight in her head and be able to focus on… on what? In Grace's world there were just two places now, before… and after.

***

Grace's pen created the final word on a sunny afternoon in Heart Wood, on the day that she first noticed the strange little marble headstone.

***

She had approached the wood from a different direction, walking up the hill from the Allbright's rambling cottage, after leaving Molly to play with the two younger boys under the close scrutiny of their very capable mother.

"Get yourself off," Carol had insisted when she'd made her objections. "Have a bit of quality time, and don't forget…"

Grace had stopped then, looking back, returning the smile on Carol's round, cheerful face.

"Forget what?"

"You promised to let me read it."

She clutched her pad tightly at that and for a moment she hesitated; did she really want other people looking so deeply into her life? "I may have to edit it first," she said, trying to sound light hearted when her heart weighed so heavily that it threatened to engulf her.

"Never mind the edit," chortled Carol, as Grace headed off up the fell. "I want to read the uncut version."

***

Grace climbed hurriedly, stopping now and then to ease her aching muscles. It had taken a while to get her bearings from the unfamiliar angle, now she clambered over the crumbling grey stone wall, glancing at her watch as she headed for the clearing in the very centre of the wood. One pm. She had promised to be back by four so there was plenty of time. She paused for a moment, taking in her surroundings as if for the very first time. Dappled sunshine filtering through the network of branches that swayed gently above her head; the heady aroma of honeysuckle, from the huge bush that had entangled itself in a Rowan tree, filled her senses... And there was something else, something she had never noticed before. She walked towards it, pushing her way through the undergrowth, reaching down to touch the smooth cool surface of what appeared to be a miniature headstone. It was less than two feet high, but beautifully

Broken Heart Wood

made of a dark marble that must once have shone; now it was matted with moss and dirt. She rubbed it gently rubbed it to reveal a small patch of its former beauty.

It was set she, noted, at the very edge of the clearing, near to where she liked to come and sit on the flat, moss covered rock. So why had she never seen it before?

But of course… she looked around getting her bearings. Today she'd come into the wood from the other side, entering the clearing from a totally different direction; the stone was much more obvious from behind. And now that she knew it was there, even though from the other side ferns and bushes camouflaged it, she couldn't understand how she had never seen it before. Who had put it there though and why? Could it be a small grave, maybe for someone's beloved pet.

She scrutinised the stone, trying to read the read the words inscribed on the dark marble. Tomorrow, she decided, rubbing away the dirt, she would try and clean it properly… and then suddenly the words became clearer.

'GOODBYE MY LOVE'

She touched the letters with her forefinger, a familiar rush of emotion choking her throat. It made this place seem even more special to think that someone else had once stood here, suffering as she did, even if it *was* only for the loss of a pet dog perhaps.

Love came in so many different guises though. Someone must have truly loved whatever was buried in this peaceful isolated spot, to have gone to all the bother of having a headstone erected. But why was there no name?

Settling herself down on her favourite rock she picked up her pad, her mind slipping immediately back to the moment where she left off her story. For over an hour she sat quite still, her pen flying across the paper as she relayed the thoughts and memories that swirled inside her head.

Eventually she sighed, easing her cramped hand before dotting the final sentence. There, it was done, right up to the moment when her world came crashing down around her. Tears pressed like heavy, burning weights against the backs of her eyes. Had the person who placed the headstone there also felt total despair as they laid their loved one to rest, she wondered, glancing at it curiously. And were they all alone in their vigil?

Broken Heart Wood

Before she moved on Grace was determined to try and find out the truth, but for now... for now she just had to try and make some sense of her own life.

Picking up her pad again she flicked back through the pages, re-reading the final chapters, the secrets of the heart shaped wood and its marble headstone forgotten for now as her mind slid back in time.

***

We named the leggy three-year-old Quicksilver, after something we saw one rare day out together in Allonby. Trevor was at home, entertaining his new girlfriend, a sexy looking tanned blonde called Charlie Webb. Like most of his women she was half his age and so obviously just after what she could get; rides on his horses mainly. She fancied herself as a show jumper and I teased Tom that she was after his job. At first it had been just a joke, after their relationship had lasted for over a month though I was not quite so sure.

Fortunately, although a fair enough rider, Charlie didn't have Tom's exceptional talent, so I couldn't see her ever really taking his place. Who knows though, when the path of true love -or lust- is involved, and she was the very first girlfriend that Trevor had ever shown any real interest in. Once he had slept with his latest conquest his ardour usually waned quickly, Charlie however seemed to have managed to get under his skin. He'd even given her a couple of rides in novice jumping classes, much to Tom's annoyance.

The one good thing about Trevor's preoccupation with Charlie was that he put less pressure on his staff and actually agreed to Tom and I having the same day off for once.

We ran to catch the Allonby bus with our fingers entwined, sitting on the back seat giggling like two truanting school kids. An elderly woman with stern dark eyes shook her head at us as we raced down the aisle to jump off the bus outside the town hall. I smiled at her, feeling totally happy with the whole world and everything in it. The future stretched ahead of us full of promise and glory and for once we had a whole day to just spend together.

It was the shop on the corner of Marley Street that most took my fancy. It was named 'SURPRISE' and it was full of surprises. Everything from tricks and jokes to all kinds of unusual objects graced the shelves and we spent at least half an hour just rummaging through them.

Broken Heart Wood

"Look at this," cried Tom, holding out a slippery silver snake like item. It was really weird and difficult to keep hold of, almost as if it had a life of its own. He held it out towards me and it shot through his fingers, landing on the floor with a hollow thud, glistening in the sunshine that beamed through the large shop window.

"It's called Quicksilver," the small, kind eyed shopkeeper informed us. "Look..."

Reaching down to pick it up he ran it expertly through his hands so that it appeared to move like liquid, writhing like a living snake.

Tom glanced at the price tag on the box and nudged me before turning to look at him apologetically. "It's fantastic," he agreed. "But way beyond what I can afford."

"That," declared the smiling shopkeeper. "...Is because it's made of a brand new material... something very special."

It was half an hour later, as we sat in a tiny café sipping hot chocolate, that I had the idea.

"Guess what..." I began eagerly

Tom placed his forefinger into his drink, withdrew a large dollop of foam and deposited it on the end of my nose.

I giggled, removing it with my sleeve before going on.

"Listen, this is important," I insisted.

"Right...!" Tom held up both hands. "I'm all ears."

"We've been trying to think of a name for your horse, remember?"

He groaned. "How could I forget, we must have turned down a thousand already."

"Well..." My voice rose with excitement. "The weird silver thing in the shop was silver and different and very, very special wasn't it?"

Tom frowned. "And your point is?"

"Quicksilver," I cried, sure of my idea. "We could call the colt Quicksilver, you know, because it's silver and different and very special too."

"That," declared Tom, reaching across the table to plant a kiss on my nose. "Is what I love most about you, Grace Bryant... your exceptional imagination; Quicksilver it is."

And so our special horse was named Quicksilver, or Silver for short; although I have to admit that at first he didn't appear to live up to his very special name.

Tom seemed to have more and more horses to bring on for Trevor and less and less time to spend doing anything else, so a lot of the early work with Silver was left to me. I revelled in the opportunity, spending hours getting to know Tom's new horse and trying to improve both his balance and self-confidence. That may sound odd I suppose, but horses are really not so unlike people, they have weaknesses too, and insecurities, just like us; differently based perhaps but essentially the same. In fact I suppose in a way horses are not unlike children.

Quicksilver was a difficult youngster, spooky and nervous with legs too long for his body and a tendency to either try and test you out or just bolt off at the first sign of trouble. It took a whole lot of patience to try and win his trust but I believed that I was eventually beginning to get there.

Tom may have been forced to miss a lot of those very early days, but we discussed his horse's progress for hours, late at night usually when we were snuggled up in my caravan, content just to be in each other's arms. He always seemed to know instinctively how to deal with any horse's problems; I remember Trevor once telling him, when he had managed to calm down a particularly difficult young mare on a wild and blustery winter's day, that he was a naturally skilled horseman.

I'll never forget the pride in Tom's eyes that day. He made a joke of it afterwards of course but we both knew that Trevor had meant what he said. I could see how frustrated he was getting though, at never being able to take his charges further on in their careers.

"Thing is," he admitted one evening, holding me tightly in his arms. "I feel as if time is passing me by, you know, every time one of the horses starts to move up the grades it gets sold on and I've always been fine with that. Now though I feel like I want a keeper, something to aim for the top with."

"I've found my keeper," I murmured, nibbling his ear and a hot flood of passion transported us into a place where there was nothing in the world but the two of us.

"I haven't forgotten," I told him next morning.

"Forgotten what?"

Late as usual, he was standing on the bed struggling into his jeans. I gave him a push and he fell onto his knees.

"Forgotten what you said about time passing you by, you know, missing all your chances."

He went totally still for a moment, his eyes darkening. "There's nothing we can do about it so..."

"No!" I reached up to place my hand across his mouth. He took it, kissing my palm gently and I shuddered deep inside. "There is something we can do. As soon as Silver really gets going we can set up on our

own, you know, take in liveries and bring on other people's horses to fund your show jumping career."

He looked at me, startled. "You would do that... with me?"

I smiled but I had never felt more serious. "Tom Roberts," I said quietly. "I would do anything with you."

His eyes held mine, bright now with excitement; gold flecks flickered in their tawny depths as the possibilities sank in... the awesome, unbelievable possibility of forging our own future.

"I can manage the yard while you are competing," I told him. "And Quicksilver will bring you the success to get a proper sponsor."

A flicker of self-doubt clouded Tom's features at the enormity of the idea. "But do you really believe that we can do it?"

With no self-doubt I nodded firmly. "Yes" I insisted. "If we want it enough. You just need to have faith, in yourself... and in Silver."

Still the doubt was in his eyes. "But will he be good enough?"

The kettle started to boil, bubbling madly, its cut-out switch broken weeks ago. I moved quickly across the small space to switch it off, pouring the steaming liquid *into two mugs of coffee and splashing it all over the side in my haste.*

I handed him a mug and he sipped the scalding liquid, staring at me with a searching expression... depending on me. "I believe in Quicksilver," *I announced determinedly.* "And I believe in you. Silver is almost ready to start doing some novice classes, I'm sure of it. He is our future Tom, yours and mine."

"Our future," *he echoed, drawing me close.* "That's awesome."

"You'll have to persuade Trevor let you take him to some shows though," *I told him, my voice rising.* "He owes you that, surely, and you need to get the colt high enough up the grades to attract a sponsor. If he does really well then maybe, eventually, we could stand him at stud."

Suddenly Tom took both my arms, dancing me around in a circle.

"Grace Bryant," *he cried.* "I do believe we really are going places."

"Yes," *I agreed, giggling.* "To work, or we won't have a job to go too."

Broken Heart Wood

It was strange how things kind of kicked into place after that, as if it was all meant to be. As if someone was paving the way for us.

Two days later Trevor took Charlie for a rare day out, giving Tom the chance to spend some time with Silver. If he was honest –and I knew that he would never admit to it- up until now he had been a bit disappointed in his gift horse. When he arrived, despite the certain 'look' that both Tom and I had seen, the scrawny colt had proven to be so immature that he could hardly trot round in a circle, let alone manage to clear a fence. We had both agreed ages ago that he needed time to mature so it was a few weeks since Tom had even tried to ride him. Every time he and Trevor went off to a show though I had kept on working with the cheeky grey colt, ironing out his insecurities and finally managing to build up his confidence and balance. I was sure that Tom would be amazed by his progress now and I couldn't wait for his reaction.

When all the morning chores were done I brought Silver up from the meadow, brushed him off until his pale coat glistened and tacked him up, before walking him round into the main yard. Tom had just dismounted from a big bay four year old; he patted the horse on the neck and handed his reins over to Jen, letting out a long low whistle.

"Have you been working some kind of magic or is that a totally different horse?"

Pride brought a flush to my skin as I ran my hand across the silky smoothness of Silver's arched neck. "Just work, good food, and a lot of TLC," I told him.

"Well then let's see if his ride has improved as much as his looks," he suggested. "Have you been working on that as well?"

"Just a bit," I admitted, remembering all the hours I'd put in when he and Trevor were away."

Tom's face lit up. "And I thought that he'd just been turned away all summer. Trevor would be livid."

I think that day was the first time Tom really began to believe in our dream. Quicksilver had matured and grown into himself. He was boisterous and strong now, definitely not for the faint hearted, but his talent was obvious. With me he was a pussycat but he loved to test Tom's mettle, dumping him at any available opportunity. It took almost two months for the pair of them to really gel and the first show was a disaster, by spring though Silver's rosettes lined almost a whole wall of my caravan.

Broken Heart Wood

*

It was another twelve months before lady luck moved in, with an opportunity for us to try and realise our dream. We seized it with both hands.

*

I was hosing down the yard, swishing the pipe to and fro my mind a million miles away, when I heard Jen's voice. "Hey Grace," she called, appearing from the barn with a hay net over her shoulder. "Guess what?"

"What?" I asked curiously, turning off the hose pipe and looping it onto its hook.

"Well it's just an idea, but the cottage up the lane from us has come up for rent and I thought about you and Tom. It's a bit run down but surely anything would be better than that tatty old caravan of yours."

Excitement rippled through me. "Where is it?" I asked eagerly.

Jen smiled, pleased at my obvious interest. "It's only ten minutes from here, Ivy cottage. It's just a two up two down and it does need some work; I think it might have a yard with it too."

"A yard, what, you mean with buildings?"

I stopped in my tracks, possibilities whirling around inside my head.

She nodded eagerly. "I'm not really sure; it's just a bit further down the lane from cottage... So you're interested then?"

I gave her a quick hug, already looking around for Tom. "Too right we're interested, thanks for telling me, Jen..."

"I don't know what the rent is or anything," she called after me as I ran off across the yard.

We moved into Ivy cottage three weeks later but it took almost six months to get the yard sorted out. At first the owner decided that he didn't want to rent it out at all and when he did eventually agree to let us have it, the work it needed took all our resources.

***

On the day we finally moved Quicksilver into his new stable, Tom asked me to marry him.

"Well I suppose we'd better become a real team now then," he casually remarked, as the quirky silver colt snorted at his new surroundings.

His arm was draped around my shoulders, my head resting in the curve below his collarbone.

"...A real team?" I echoed, liking the sound of it.

"Well, if we really are to start our own enterprise," he went on, pressing his chin down onto the top of my head. "Then perhaps we should get married."

"Married...?" My mind reeled with shock. Had I heard him right?

"Look," he turned me to face him, staring deep into my eyes in the way that made my whole body tingle. "We are about to start a whole proper life together and I want it to be a total commitment. I love you Sarah Bryant, more than anything else in the world... Will you marry me?"

Suddenly I was in his arms, sobbing with emotion. "Yes," I cried. "Of course I'll marry you."

"Then let's start the rest of our life," he murmured against my throat, his hand moving to the buttons of my shirt.

"Tom," I groaned, unable to resist the sensation of his fingers against my naked skin. "Not here."

"...Why not?" His eyes burned into mine. "This place is ours and we can do whatever we like. The whole world is ours Grace and we are going to the very top... believe me."

And oh how I believed him.

CHAPTER TEN

Grace sighed, her mind reeling as she re-lived those early, happy days. They *had* begun to make their way to the top, she and Tom and Quicksilver. There were only six stables at the Ivy Cottage yard and Tom still needed to ride for Trevor if their venture was to survive, but very gradually they built up a reputation for producing young show jumpers. Their five livery boxes were permanently full with horses to break or bring on; Grace took over most of their care whilst Tom did the jump schooling. They even managed to buy their own horsebox, a bit battered and ancient but reliable enough to transport the youngsters to their first shows. The bigger competitions Tom still went too with Trevor, riding both Quicksilver and the Little Oaks better jumpers –the novices were now in the total care of Charlie who had managed to inveigle herself into a permanent position with Trevor.

It was a system that worked well for the first few years, she and Tom, working together in perfect harmony towards a joint goal; she used to feel so privileged, she remembered, to have such an uncomplicated relationship. They did have the occasional disagreement of course, usually over money or the lack of it, after all what couple doesn't? But how ever minor their tiffs might be they always ended up making love and then apologising to each other in the languid aftermath of total fulfilment.

Grace closed her eyes, remembering; the feel of his naked skin against hers, his musky aroma flooding her senses... And then, totally out of the blue, Molly came along to shake their world, shifting their priorities but never their dreams.

Grace picked up her pen again, her mind going back to that moment when she first realised their whole world was tilting.

***

'Why is it, that just when everything seems to be going great, something always seems to happen, as if someone up there can't bear to see things going smoothly? For me the event that coloured our world was double sided.

Broken Heart Wood

Quicksilver had just moved up a grade and we finally had a sponsor almost hooked. Denby horse feeds, a local company, were trying to negotiate a deal with Tom -very low key but at least it was a start. He was at a meeting with them on the day I took the test.

I held out the stick, watching the colour change with disbelief. Kids were nowhere on our scheme of things, never even mentioned, so when I first realised just how late my period was I didn't even dare to tell Tom. It was such an important, busy time for us and the last thing I wanted to do was worry him unduly. And now, I realised, with a flood of apprehension; I had to face up to the fact that I was pregnant.

'Pregnant.' I rolled the word around in my mouth, placing my hand on my belly. Why hadn't I noticed how plump I'd become? I could be weeks, or even months, for all I knew. Shock and disbelief pumped through my veins, leaving me weak and shaking. A baby... we were going to have a baby. But how would we cope?

It took me days to tell Tom, days to build up the courage to shatter his world. And when at last I did... I realised that, yet again, I had misjudged him.

Broken Heart Wood

He just looked at me when I told him, his changeable eyes darkening with passion, and then he reached out a hand and placed it gently on the mound of my belly. "It's a gift Grace," he said, pulling me close. I rested my cheek in the crook of his shoulder and let the tears slip slowly from beneath my heavy lids. "Anything that has been made by our love must be a gift. And we'll manage, don't worry."

And we did manage too. I worked right up until the day before I went into labour, not allowing our baby's imminent birth to change my life at all, and Mary Maddison, a serious, plain faced nineteen year old, arrived to help out with the heavy work. By the time my labour pains started she was capable enough to keep things ticking over for a while...'

***

Mary Maddison! Grace cringed as she re-read the name, a kind of sickness creeping into her limbs. She lifted her pen, wanting to erase it from her memories, to scribble it out of her life. But she couldn't could she. Mary Maddison, her one time employee and almost friend, was a part of the life she had to learn to live with now, had to try and understand.

Turning the page quickly she read on, making adjustments as she went and editing parts that she didn't want anyone else to read, soaking up the memories that brought a bittersweet pain into her heart.

***

'I didn't realise that our baby would bring such joy. After Molly slipped easily into the world one wintery morning though, our whole lives changed irrevocably... for now we were three.

Tom, Molly and me; a perfect unit: And we were then. We laughed and we loved and we watched Molly grow, revelling in her every tiny gesture, so fulfilled in each other, so proud of our little girl that it seemed almost too good to be true... was too good to be true. But life it seems cannot stand to see us happy for too long.

Quicksilver's career soared, our stables were full and, though money was still tight, I know that we both believed then that life could not get better.

Molly was almost two years old when Lady Luck decided to leave us.

I had formed a special bond with Quicksilver. Not in the same way as Tom -for whom he would do anything as far as performance went- but on a kind of personal level I suppose you'd call it. Every morning he whinnied to me as I crossed the yard and every morning he whirled around his box when I went to put the head collar on, refusing to be caught until I had given him a carrot. Then he would nuzzle me softly, blowing gently through his nostrils, totally trusting me... a trust that proved to be misplaced when I so totally let him down.

Silver was arrogant and naughty for Mary, playing her up like a naughty school boy. With Molly though, he was a saint. I used to laughingly tell Tom that I believed his horse to be part human in the way he worked us all. The main thing though was his inborn desire to jump, for his amazing performances had already put him and Tom on their way to the top.

"I feel as if I'm flying, Grace," Tom once told me when we were lying in each other's arms in the glowing aftermath of perfect love making.

"Then I am flying with you," I sighed as he pulled me towards him yet again.

*

It was autumn when our wings stopped working

*

Broken Heart Wood

One of my responsibilities was to keep Silver fit and sweet, by hacking him out along the country lanes. Mary wasn't really up to riding him, although she exercised most of the others, so when I went out on Silver she would stay at the yard and keep an eye on Molly, who was quite content to sit in her push chair for hours, happily watching us work, or sometimes wielding her own little yard brush with a kind of fierce determination that reminded me so much of Tom.

Autumn was full-blown, breathtakingly glorious. I mounted up with a sense of elation, waving to Molly as Silver sidestepped across the yard. "Won't be long sweetheart...." I called. "Mary will look after you."

Those words echo now inside my head as I remember... round and round and round: If only I had set off later, if only I had stayed at home: If only, if only, if only... Lady Luck had stayed a while longer to grace us with her presence.

The sun lit up the gold's and reds of the trees along the lane, Silver felt fresh and full of life, his steps bouncing and vibrant. I thought about Tom, he should be back soon from delivering one of our charges to its satisfied owner, rumbling into the yard in our well-used horsebox. The usual longing came over me, to be with him, just to catch his eyes with mine and know that he was there, understanding my every thought.

We were almost at the village when I saw the huge red feed wagon approach, looming above the hedgerow as it weaved its way like a monster along the narrow lane. I reined in, looking for a passing place. Quicksilver hated Lorries.

The stupid idiot driver had his hand on the horn, its deafening sound filling my head and driving Silver crazy. I ran my hand down his sweating neck, murmuring to him, trying to stay calm whilst panic rose like a tide inside me. "Steady boy.... It's fine..."

But it wasn't fine was it; there was nowhere to go. Surely he was going to stop.

His brakes squealed as the sound of the horn died away, a high-pitched shrieking sound. Silver bunched beneath me. I grabbed the reins, desperately trying to calm him... too late.

In the moment that I saw the lorry eventually grinding to a halt, only yards away from us, Quicksilver leaped into the air, beyond all reason, beyond my delicate strands of control, once again a flight animal *running for his life. The main road loomed ahead of us at the bottom of the hill. His metal shod hooves sparked and slithered along the tarmac of the lane. I yelled at him to stop, silently sobbing, wishing that he would fall rather than race out into the traffic on the busy road.*

Cars flashed by just ahead of us, colours, lights, sounds. I hauled helplessly on the reins, screaming at Silver to stop, watching the inevitable happen as if in slow motion. The force that hit us took away my breath. I felt the impact, saw my noble horse crumple, a silver mound splattered with crimson as my body was flung away from him, out into the road.

The screaming sound filled my whole world. Stars flashed inside my head... And then came the darkness.'

***

Grace flapped the pad shut, closing her eyes against the well of emotion that was opening inside her She had tried to write her story from a distance, jotting down the facts like a need, her every thought taken up by Tom and his treachery. Now though, re-reading what she had written, it felt as if the events of that tragic day happened just yesterday. And that was when their awesome love first became flawed, she realised.   The day their dreams died.

Broken Heart Wood

Her peaceful wooded haven with its tragic miniature headstone seemed suddenly stifling. Struggling to her feet on trembling legs, longing for the quiet comfort of Hillside Cottage and Molly's sweet, innocent smile, she pushed her way through the undergrowth, heading for the light beyond the trees. Somehow she had to find a way forward, had to try and understand why Tom's love had faded when hers still burned so brightly.

They were over; she knew that, for there was no way she could ever forgive what he had done… And yet she also knew, that despite it all, despite the pain, she would never stop loving him until the day she died.

CHAPTER ELEVEN

Lucky whined softly, still desperately insecure and disturbed now by the tension in his new master's eyes. Tom reached across into the passenger seat, gently scratching the fluffy white hair on the top of his head, reassuring him. "You'll love Molly," he promised, his heart thumping at the memory of her face.

God how he missed her… how he missed them both. Ever since Mick told him that he had seen Grace in Meredale he had been unable to think of anything else. She may not *want* to be found but it wasn't her decision to take. He needed to see her, needed to explain… but explain what? There was no explanation for treachery. He'd failed her and that was all there was to say.

He drove on autopilot, his mind going over and over the words he had tried to rehearse, his excuses. But what if she wasn't there? Meredale may only be a small market town but it was sprawled all along the bottom of the valley, near to the looming fells of the Pennines. She could be staying anywhere, or maybe only passing through.

For the hundredth time Tom cast his mind back to that conversation with Mick, the conversation that had rekindled a glimmer of hope.

The burly middle-aged driver had breezed in through the office door at the end of his shift, jangling his keys on his finger, a contained excitement in his dark eyes as he made his announcement. "Guess who I saw today?"

Tom's heart had turned over, his whole body tense with nerves. "Grace," he cried, instantly knowing. "You've seen Grace."

Mick nodded eagerly. "Yes... in Meredale, walking along the street with a red haired woman."

"And Molly...?"

Mick opened his palms apologetically. "Sorry mate. No sign of her."

Tom's mind had reeled with possibilities. "Then she must be staying with someone there. She wouldn't leave Molly with anyone she didn't trust..."

Desperation filled his eyes. "But who... who could it be?"

Mick frowned. "Look..." he said. "It's no business of mine but why don't you get yourself off to look for her before it drives you completely mad. I can manage things here."

A ghost of a smile flitted across Tom's drawn face. "You've noticed then?"

Mick grinned. "If you mean have I noticed that you look like shit and you can't concentrate then… yeah, you might say I have. You sent me to the totally wrong depot yesterday. They don't usually expect to get packs of an extra-special new line in fell bred meat, at a dry cleaner's."

"Or a very important dry cleaning delivery at a farm shop," groaned Tom.

"Ah," Mick laughed. "So you did the other delivery then, say no more…. So, are you going or what?"

The possibility of actually doing something, of going to try and find Grace and Molly, brought a shine back into Tom's eyes. "But do you really think you can manage here?"

Mick shrugged. "Well I can't do any worse than you are at the moment. Just get your priorities sorted out mate and don't worry about here. Go on, and I'll fill you in on exactly where I saw her before you set off. I would have stopped to talk to her but I was stuck in traffic."

Broken Heart Wood

It had taken Tom just ten minutes to throw some clothes into a bag and get out onto the road. Now he was heading out of Allonby, across the moors towards the North of England. Beside him Lucky sighed, wriggling down into a comfortable position on the passenger seat.

"You may as well get yourself settled in for the long haul," Tom told the little dog. "Because we're not stopping until we find them."

Apprehension clawed at his stomach. Obviously Grace didn't want to be found; what if she wouldn't let him try to explain, what if she wouldn't listen… and why was she in Meredale anyway? Distant memories filtered in as the miles rolled by. What had she told him about her childhood? She had spoken of the Pennine fells he was sure. Was Meredale the town where she was born? No… it came to him in a flash. It was a village near there, a village called Grey something… Greytown… Greydale…? Oh what the hell was it? He would know when he saw it, of that he was sure, but first he would just drive to Meredale and have a good look around.

Pressing his foot down harder on the throttle he leaned forwards over the wheel, as if to will the miles away, staring bleakly at the huge black clouds gathering overhead to perfectly reflect his mood. Thunder rumbled, rolling across the wild grey sky. Great drops of rain splashed onto his windscreen and he flicked on the wipers, listening to their rhythmic mind-numbing swish.

Suddenly it felt as if he was travelling to the ends of the earth. Oh how had his whole world gone so terribly wrong he wondered? How had he ended up losing his dreams, doing a job he didn't particularly like and letting down the only two people who really mattered in his life? Was he just weak, a weak snivelling bastard who couldn't cope with the tragedy that life had thrown at him... had thrown at them all come to think of it? Grace had coped though, she would never let him down; he knew that with no shadow of a doubt... So why had *he* grovelled in self-pity, for that's what it was. His only excuse for letting them down so badly was self-pity?

The miles slipped endlessly by. The rolling hills of the Yorkshire Dales, with its warm, mellow stone buildings, gave way to Westmorland's wild bleak fells. Grey stone walls lined the sides of quiet country roads. Grey stone built farms flashed by and quaint little villages, their charm totally lost on Tom who saw nothing but the bleak austerity of the mighty fells, echoing the emptiness inside him.

Broken Heart Wood

'*MEREDALE 20 miles.*' He glanced at the sign. It would be almost midnight by the time he got there; there was nothing he could do tonight so perhaps he should see if he could find somewhere to stay for the night.

The thunder that had been threatening all evening rumbled angrily and almost as if on cue, a flash of lightening cracked across the skyline, its sudden bright light falling on a small inn on the side of the road, '*The Fox and Hounds.*' Tom stood on the brakes, swerving off the road into the car park and cutting the engine, suddenly desperate to stretch his legs and find some food.

As he pushed open the inn door with Lucky sitting happily in the crook of his arm, the heavy buzz of conversation in the small room lulled.

He walked across to the bar, trying to get the attention of the brightly dressed barman. "Do you have any rooms available?"

The man leaned around the door behind him. "Alma… bloke here wants a room."

Tom curled his fingers into Lucky's curly white coat, breathing in the aromas of food and ale as the conversations around him struck off again. The whole place was warm and busy, buzzing with life and laughter and friendly camaraderie... Never had he felt so alone.

"It's too late to order hot food," said the bright-eyed pink-cheeked woman who suddenly appeared from behind the bar. "But I suppose I could make you a sandwich."

Tom forced a smile onto his face. "Thanks, and do you have a room?"

She looked him up and down pointedly, her eyes settling on Lucky. "Just a single and we don't mind dogs."

"Thank you, that's great and a sandwich will be fine. I'll have a pint of Guinness as well please."

The ham sandwich tasted like cardboard but the Guinness went down smoothly. Tom drank it hurriedly and took his room key from the barman. As he climbed the dark, narrow staircase at the back of the inn, he felt a heavy weariness kick in; sleep, that was what he needed, a chance to recharge his batteries ready for tomorrow.

Collapsing, fully clothed, onto the small single bed he closed his eyes in relief, trying to override the tension that filled his whole body by thinking of happier times...

Grace, singing as she carted water buckets across the yard. Grace, reaching down to place her arms around Silver's neck before kissing the big daft horse on the end of his velvety nose: Grace, holding Molly by the hand, looking at him with love in her eyes…

Suddenly jerked awake by something warm and wet against his cheek, for a moment he panicked… where was he? Disoriented and confused he sat up, trying to get his bearings in the darkness whilst Lucky scrambled up to lick his face again.

Everything slipped back into place and with a sigh of relief he gave the little dog a hug, before pulling off his clothes and climbing in between the cold sheets, tossing and turning until the pale light of early dawn brought him back to face reality again… a reality that left him unable to refrain from reliving his darkest moments… yet again.

***

He had been full of enthusiasm driving home on that fateful day, after dropping the four year old off at Ted Marchant's. Pleased with how his horse had progressed, Ted had happily transferred the three grand he owed them into their bank, and before he set off he had tried to ring Gwen, knowing that she would wondering how he'd got on. To his surprise she hadn't picked up.

Broken Heart Wood

When he rang her again on the way home and still she didn't respond, a flicker of unease made him pick up speed, needing to get back. It only eased as he approached the turn into Moss Lane. Five minutes and he'd be home.

When he saw the flashing lights he stood on the brakes, a sinking feeling in his stomach. Something really bad must have happened here. Some unfortunate person must have set out on an ordinary day and, by the amount of activity up ahead, it looked like they weren't going home any time soon.

From his high vantage point in the horsebox he could see over the vehicles in front of him; someone was unravelling a tarpaulin, dragging it towards... His tongue stuck to the roof of his mouth, a physical pain stabbed his chest and a sense of unreality set him apart from the gruesome scene on the main road up ahead.

Swerving the lorry into the side of the road he cut the engine, jumping down from the driver's seat on wooden legs. A silent scream rang around inside his head as he approached the glistening mound that lay so awkwardly on the bleak tarmac road. All around him were grim, closed faces and so much blood... dark, shining crimson, splattered all across the road... splattered all across the silver coat of his glorious stallion... Quicksilver. He fell to his knees, beyond reason; looking into the rapidly glazing eyes of his dear friend and ally as the world around them seemed to stop. He wanted to let the screaming out, to shout his anger to the whole cruel world but the huge emptiness inside him was like a vacuum, sucking him in. If Quicksilver was dead then he was dead too.

"Tom... I am so sorry but there was nothing else I could do... I had to stop his suffering."

It was the stark reality of the vet's familiar voice that had brought home the truth. His beloved horse was gone. This mass of bone and flesh and sinew on the road, that had nothing to do with the glorious spirited stallion he loved so much... really was Quicksilver. But where was Grace? Panic hit. She must have been riding him, he was still wearing... He heaved, retching into the grass beside the road. His tack, he was still wearing his tack. "Grace!" he yelled. His voice sounded as if it was a million miles away. "Grace..."

The heavy tarpaulin slid over the horse's motionless body, retaining his dignity. All except for the silver tail hairs that fanned out across the dark tarmac, beautiful still, even in death.

A pale, vaguely familiar face loomed into his line of vision; kind eyes, their expression wary. "Your wife's at the hospital, Tom. Come on, I'll drive you there. One of my men will see to your horsebox."

That journey lasted a lifetime, a lifetime of regrets: If only, if only, if only... Please God let Grace be all right. He ran through the hospital corridors, soaking in the smells and sounds, until he saw her... then he stopped.

She laid so still on the bed, like death its self, white and silent, her breath coming so faintly that he thought it had stopped. Tubes came from her nose. Her face was caked still with blood and a drip was suspended above the bed.

"Grace," he sobbed, clutching her limp hand. "Oh Grace."

He had sat for hours, motionless at her bedside, just staring at her face, willing her to live. Nurses moved quietly around them. A white-coated man spoke in lowered tones and then handed him the phone. Mary's voice had entered his head from another universe. "Don't worry... Molly's fine with me. I'll be here if you need me."

Broken Heart Wood

It had felt like days before a doctor finally arrived tell him how badly injured she was.

And it had felt like a lifetime before they could even begin to tentatively try and pick up the threads of their life again…

***

Alone in a strange bed, so far from all he held dear, the memories proved just too much to bear' Loneliness suffocated him and he turned his face into the pillow, fighting off tears…until a warm, friendly tongue licked his ear in comfort, bringing him back to now. A smile curled inside him, eradicating the tears as he turned to stroke the little white dog that had appeared so unexpectedly in his life and become a real friend.

"Don't take any notice of me boy," he said. "We will find them, you'll see, and they'll both love you as much as I do."

***

It had been so hard he remembered, setting off again with Lucky on the passenger seat, trying to face up to the stark reality. Quicksilver, the king pin of their whole enterprise, was gone, and as he hadn't been insured, that was it. No horse, no money, no business and a wife who might not make it. A future without Grace had been impossible to contemplate.

They had given him the best and worst scenarios. There was a slight possibility that she might come out of her coma and be mentally fine, but he needed to face up to the fact that there could be some damage to her brain. Worst case, she may never wake up at all.

It had felt then as if his whole life had collapsed around him. With Quicksilver, maybe even Grace, the love of his life, and all his dreams gone in one foul swoop, there had seemed little point in anything at all... except for Molly. Her neediness and naivety had stopped him from crumbling completely, helping him cling on to some kind of normality.

He should have been straight with Grace from the outset, as soon as she came home from the hospital, he knew that now. She had been so distant then though, so vulnerable and once their lives finally got back on track the time had never seemed quite right. Their lives never *had* really got properly back on track though, he realised, not to how they were before at least. Guilt had formed too big a wedge between them. Grace's guilt about Quicksilver and the collapse of all his dreams, and his own guilt over that stupid mistake... and the way he'd dealt with it after.

Broken Heart Wood

Thinking about it now he couldn't believe just how weak and naïve he'd been. He'd actually felt grateful to Mary Maddison for all her support, believing that she was there purely selflessly, for the three of them. Keeping it all together… as their friend. Now though he knew that she had just been there for herself, making the most of her opportunities… or was that being totally unfair? Perhaps she really had been in love with him and it was actually he who had used her to help get him through all the emotion and trauma. All he knew was that after the accident she'd seemed like a Godsend.

He had never really taken much notice of Mary before. As a groom on the yard she had always seemed pleasant enough, but characterless, nondescript almost, doing her job as best she could but putting no spark into it. With Grace close to death in the hospital however, and little Molly to care for, she'd blossomed, taking charge of the little girl, doing all the household chores, cooking cleaning and dealing with the owners and well-wishers who called in with gifts and sympathy.

As days and weeks had turned into months, Grace had still remained in a coma; looking back now Joe could see that he had come to rely on Mary too much but she'd seemed so pleased to help out.

Her suggestion, after the first week or so, that she could stay in Molly's room in case he was called to the hospital in the night, had seemed such a sensible idea. It had been too easy to just let her take over everything, giving him time to spend with Grace.

One by one all Ivy Cottage's owners had collected their horses, promising to bring them back as soon as the business was up and running again. The stables had stood cold and empty, reminding Tom on a daily basis of his loss… as if he needed reminding. The memory of the silver stallion's body crumpled in an undignified heap on the tarmac road had haunted his every moment, waking and sleeping… alongside Grace's still, pale face. He'd sat for hours at her bedside, just holding her hand or talking to her whilst she remained totally motionless, as still as death already.

***

Struggling with the memories, Tom sat up on the bed swinging his legs around to the side and dropping his head into his hands. Beside him Lucky whined, sensing his pain, but for once Tom didn't hear the little dog as his mind slid back to the moment when Grace first opened her eyes.

Seeing her eyes move behind her pale translucent lids, with a surge of elation he had taken her hand. When he felt her fingers quiver, hope had soared.

He'd murmured her name again and again, watching mesmerised as tears appeared on her translucent skin, rolling down her face onto the pillow to make small smudges on the pristine white cotton. "Wake up Grace, please wake up," he'd begged.

Her eyes had flickered, opening slowly bit by bit, staring glassily around the room. When they finally settled on his face he'd expected recognition, even joy… anything but the cold, empty confusion they had shown.

"Grace?" His voice was a whisper, a murmured endearment… a longing.

Snatching her hand from his she had cowering back against the pillows, cringing away from him in terror. Her voice sounded raspy and strange. "…Get away from me…"

"It's me Grace. It's Tom."

For an endless moment she had looked right into his eyes. There was no recognition though, in her empty, fear filled gaze. Grace, the love of his life, was going to live, but she was lost to him.

"Who are you," she'd cried, her voice high pitched and terrified... "Get away from me....

His heart was a heavy painful weight in his chest as he'd watched her struggle in confused and crazy panic. Two nurses had rushed in, the doors swinging behind them. "Just move back please Mr Roberts," they insisted, their voices calm but urgent. "We will see to her."

And he had done as he was bid whilst his whole world collapsed around him... yet again. He had been living for this moment, everything else put on hold, even his grief over Quicksilver. Now though it overpowered him. Everything was lost... Grace didn't know him, didn't know who he was. But how could that be?"

The kind eyed doctor had tried to explain, calmly and rationally. "We did warn you that there could possibly be some deeper damage but only time can really tell us how much. There will still be swelling around her brain you see; when that goes down it could be a very different picture. Go back in to see her and please try to stay calm. Then I would suggest you go home for a few hours rest. We will be giving her something to make her sleep for a while anyway so you may as well take the opportunity. Come back tomorrow and we'll reassess the situation."

Broken Heart Wood

Tom had stared at Grace's lovely, familiar face and looked into her eyes again, those eyes that had always understood every inflection in his... Now they were the eyes of a stranger and never, in his whole life, had he felt so alone; if she had died then at least she would have died loving him, but this... this was unbearable. "Grace, it's me," he begged. "You *must* know who I am... please."

He'd reached out to touch her hand, unable to resist, but she'd pulled it away again, still cringing from him with fear in her eyes. "No... no... Get away from me."

Emotions had overwhelmed him then, anger, helplessness and a deep sense of loss. He hadn't thought any further than the moment when she woke... and now.

One of the nurses placed a gentle hand on his shoulder. "It happens sometimes," she told him. "You go and get some rest and come back in the morning. Things will quite probably be very different then, you'll see. At least she is going to be all right."

"How, he'd cried. "How can that be alright?"

When he'd walked into Ivy cottage half an hour later, his mind still numb with shock and pain, Mary was there to meet him with a ready smile. "Come and get something to eat," she'd said quietly, taking his arm.

"Molly's in bed already, fast asleep and you look like you need to rest."

It was only now, after all this time, that he realised she hadn't even asked after Grace… hadn't cared.

He hadn't been able to touch the food she'd placed in front of him, but the large whisky she poured made his throat burn, bringing some life back into the empty vacuum inside him. When it hit the bottom of his empty stomach with a hefty kick, he had taken another gulp, and another and another; anything to dull the awesome sense of loss and emptiness.

He remembered feeling very strange, as if he was in another world where everything was inside out. In his dreams Grace had opened her eyes and clung to him, facing the loss of Quicksilver with him beside her to ward off the pain, united against what? …Circumstance… the world… life…? Yes, that was it, united against the shit that life had thrown at them… United he'd always known that they could face anything… All his dreams had been blown back in his face though when she'd finally opened her eyes. Grace… his Grace, staring at him with fear in her eyes, as if he was a monster.

"She doesn't know me Mary," he'd groaned, dropping his face down into his hands. "I've lost her. She doesn't know who I am and perhaps she never will."

Mary had just quietly sat down beside him on the sofa, leaning across him to fill up his glass again, lifting it to his lips as if to a child.

And he had taken it eagerly, tossing back the fiery liquid before handing it back for her to refill, again and again; anything to shut out the pain.

His memories after that were vague. He remembered the warmth and comfort of Mary's body as she'd pressed close against him, her arms holding him tight, caring; someone to cling to when his whole life was imploding. And when her soft lips touched his, for just a moment, before a vague sense of guilt and outrage penetrated the fog in his mind, momentarily, he had reacted to her kiss, anything to keep out his aloneness. She'd pulled away then, picking up his half full glass and encouraging him to finish it. "Bed time I think," she'd insisted, pulling him onto his feet.

Glad to have some help as everything whirled round and around him, he had clung onto her, grateful for her help as he clambered awkwardly up the stairs. After that though, however hard he'd tried to remember, everything else had remained a blank.

When he'd opened his eyes again the light had been so bright that it burned his eyes. Everything felt fuzzy... distant, and a mallet thumped so hard inside his head that he thought it was going to crack open. It was daylight. He was in his bed but where was Grace?

Vague memories had brought a flood of mind blowing pain. Grace's cold blank eyes... the terror in her face. He'd vaguely remembered swigging back the whisky but couldn't remember how he'd got into bed. Fumbling beneath the bed clothes, with a sense of shock when he'd felt his own nakedness, he had scrambled out of bed only to fall onto the floor, where his clothes lay in a tousled pile.

Vomit had risen in his throat as he'd rushed to the bathroom, retching again and again, emptying his stomach into the toilet bowl.

"Here, you need to drink this."

Somehow Mary had been standing beside him, a towel draped around her. "Here," she'd repeated. "...Drink this; it'll make you feel better."

He'd felt sick again then, sick with shame. "What the hell Mary," he'd asked. "What's going on?"

Broken Heart Wood

"She'd just giggled, allowing the towel to drop to the floor, preening her nakedness. "Stop pretending Tom… you were amazing last night. And I know you might be feeling a bit guilty right now we both know that it was inevitable… You can't help who you fall in love with."

Her words had resounded around inside his head. In love with… was she mad?

Grabbing her towel, with a wave of anger he'd thrust it at her. "Cover yourself up Mary… and get out."

He would never forget the look on her face as she'd pulled the towel around her. "I know how you're feeling Tom," she'd told him, smiling with a newfound confidence. "And I understand, so don't worry, I'll take temptation away from you for now but I think we both know it's just a matter of time. I'll go and make breakfast while you get dressed… Molly's in her high chair by the way. She's already had some cereal."

As soon as she left his bedroom he'd retched into the toilet again; the second time though it had nothing to do with his hangover and everything to do with the guilt that turned his stomach inside out.

Fully dressed and clean shaven, his head had felt a little clearer. Whatever had he been thinking he'd asked himself with a rush of shame? Grace probably needed him now more than ever, so how could he have been so weak and pathetic. He should never have drunk so much whisky and he should never have let Mary see him in such a state.

He'd felt awkward, walking into the kitchen, looking around for Molly, feeling ashamed for not checking on her last night.

"She's fine," Grace had told him. "I put her in her play pen so that we could talk."

"Talk about what." Anger had curled inside him. "I was weak and pathetic and I drank too much... end of conversation."

"Oh Tom..." She'd stepped towards him then, reaching out her hand. "We both know that it was so much more than that. You might be feeling bad right now, I get that, but it was always going to happen. I know it and you know it. We've been like a proper couple these last weeks, a family, and I've seen the way you look at me."

"Nothing happened," he'd told her, feeling sick; it was her insistence that had scared him.

"I know that you have to deny it because of Grace and I admit that the timing is bad, but we both know the truth… We've fallen in love and we are meant to be together."

"That's just rubbish, Mary," he'd insisted, his voice tight and hard. "Nothing happened and you know it. I stupidly got drunk and you are making all the rest up."

She'd just stared at him then, her tone calm and soft. "But you *must* know that I've been in love with you for ages. And you love me too; I know you do, whatever you say. Last night just proved it."

Pulling out her phone she'd scrolled frantically down it, thrusting it towards him in triumph. "Stop denying it Tom, look, I have pictures on my phone."

When he saw the images he'd had to hang onto a chair for support, vaguely remembering her lips pressing against his. He'd been crazy drunk and she'd taken a selfie. "You kissed me when I was too drunk to even notice and why the hell would you take a photo?"

She'd pushed her phone in his face then, crying out in triumph. "Well what about this one then? We spent the night together, Tom, so stop trying to pretend."

He'd felt sick to his stomach, reeling at the sight of them in bed together, obviously naked, at least from the waist up. His face was partially hidden, but she was smiling into the camera. "Now tell me that nothing happened," she said. "We are in love Tom and we are meant to be together… you, me and Molly."

A sense of desperation had taken him over at that but he'd managed not to totally lose it, knowing it would only make thigs worse. "I want you to get your things and leave, Mary," he'd told her firmly. "I'll pay you a month's wages but I want you gone before I get back from the hospital."

She had just stared at him in confusion, and then her face had crumpled. "But who will look after Molly?" She'd asked tearfully and he had felt like a total jerk. Yes, she was delusional, but she was also very young; maybe he was as much to blame for not seeing the signs; he should never have allowed her to move in, or allowed her to get so close to both him and Molly.

"I'm sorry Mary," he said. "But I really am going to ask you to leave. I'm taking Molly to the hospital with me now, so I need you to go and pack your things and I'll pay your next month's wages into your account today. Grace will be home soon and I don't want her worried by any of this nonsense."

Broken Heart Wood

To his relief she had just run upstairs, packed her bag and left, revving her car engine as hard as she could all the way up the lane.

When her first text message had arrived a few days later, declaring her love and saying that she'd wait for him, with a gut wrenching surge of guilt and fear he had blocked her number. The hand written messages had started to arrive just two days later and although he had burned each and every one of them unopened, the fear sat heavy in his gut.

He'd been determined to be honest with Grace, just as soon as she'd recovered enough to face it. It was the right thing to do, he'd known it from the start… and now he was having to face the consequences.

***

As Grace had struggled through the long slow fight to recovery he really had tried to honest with her; they'd never had secrets from each other and this one had torn him apart. The timing though had never seemed quite right and the heavy burden of guilt had dragged him down, making him keep a part of himself back, the closeness part that Grace had so desperately needed. And now it was all too late.

Broken Heart Wood

Pulling Grace's letter -the one that she'd left for him on the kitchen table before she left- from the from the pocket of his jeans, he read it for the hundredth time,

Tom

'Your dreams died with Quicksilver, we both know that, and I carried all the blame believing that it was all down to me when we couldn't get back to what we once were. Now though I know that it wasn't just my guilt that kept a distance between us for all this time, but your guilt too.

*I saw Mary Maddison today, Tom, she told me all about your love affair and she showed me the pictures so don't try and deny it. She was the real reason we couldn't get **us** back, wasn't she Tom, I know that now. All this time I've felt so bad, believing that everything wrong between us was because I lost both Silver and your dreams. I have carried so much pain and guilt with me when all the time you were guilty too... guilty of betraying us.*

There are no excuses for what you've done to us, Tom, so don't expect me to listen to any. What really hurts though is realising that that you only stayed with me because you thought you had to... and maybe

because of Molly. I truly believed in our love you know. What a fool I've been. Anyway, just so you know, am not running away, I just need some space so don't try to find me.   Grace

A ray of sunshine filtered through the small window that overlooked the wild bleak fells, its golden beam falling upon the hastily scrawled note. To Tom it seemed like a sign. The storm was over, the wind had calmed and a glorious patch of blue was bursting out from behind the confines of the drifting grey clouds, letting the sunshine through. It gave him hope. Ahead of the three of them stretched an unmapped future... for they were meant to be together, him, Grace and Molly, there was nothing more sure. He just had to somehow make it right and find a way to bring *their* sunshine back.

"Come on boy," he called to Lucky who was already at the door, waving his plumed tail. "Let's go find them."

CHAPTER TWELVE

"You have a nice sleep sweetheart," murmured Grace, stroking Molly's forehead as her eyelids began to droop. When the little girl's thumb slipped from the corner of her mouth she leaned down to touch her lips against her child's soft baby skin, reflecting on the last months. So much tragedy, so much emotion and, unforeseeably, an unforgivable act of treachery from the one person she thought that she could trust. "Oh Tom," she whispered, closing her eyes tightly against the images that swirled inside her head bringing with them an unfamiliar rush of hysteria.

Beside her Molly stirred, lost in dreams and Grace sat up steeling herself against the heartache. She had to be strong for Molly's sake, had to do what was best for her child for she was all that really mattered now. With a heavy sigh she walked quietly across to the door, pausing to glance back at Molly one last time before running down the narrow staircase into the hallway below.

Annie was in the kitchen. "I've brewed the coffee," she called. "Why don't you come and tell me all about your day while Millie's having her nap... What did you think of Meredale by the way?"

Grace sank onto the chair beside the Aga. "I only nipped in to the bank with Carol first thing this morning so to be honest I didn't really see that much of it. It looked nice though, quaint and kind of timeless."

Annie nodded. "It's a proper old fashioned market town. You don't see so many of them anymore. It's all high-rise buildings and concrete nowadays, more's the pity. Now tell me..." Her soft blue eyes sparkled. "Did you finish your story?"

For a moment Grace hesitated. "Yes... yes I did," she admitted. "I still have to re-read the last chapter though."

"So can I at least make a start on it then?"

Grace panicked. "No... I mean... well yes, of course, just not until it's completely done. You probably won't be able to read my scrawl anyway."

Disappointment flickered in Annie's face. "Okay, fair enough," she agreed, sensing Grace's reticence. "I'll wait. Don't worry though I'm sure I'll be able to figure out your writing. Now let's have this coffee before it goes cold."

Broken Heart Wood

Grace didn't get the chance to ask Annie if she knew anything about the miniature headstone in Heart Wood. She was about to broach the subject just as Molly woke up from her nap and as she brought her downstairs the Allbright clan descended on them for tea. As soon as they'd all eaten, making short shrift of Annie's huge cottage pie, the boys insisted that they play charades. Molly loved all the merriment, barking like a dog with Will and Timothy who were trying to describe the film 'Lassie,' and attempting to brandish an imaginary sword, like Luke, who valiantly and hopelessly tried to portray 'The Gladiator.' The whole game ended up with the boys in fits of giggles, Carol doing some kind of crazy dance and Annie wiped the tears of merriment from her eyes whilst Ben just shook his head in despair at his crazy family.

Witnessing the sheer happiness and obvious togetherness of the Allbright family made Grace feel so alone. She felt as if she was on the outside looking in, playing a game. A wave of sadness came over her as she suddenly saw the truth. All she was really doing here was hiding from reality, she realised. One day soon she would have to go back and face Tom, to listen to his lies and then get on with her life. She'd finished writing down her story now and that was the deal she made with herself, to finish it and move on. Yet still something held her back, a nagging, unresolved mystery that demanded her attention: The secret of Heart Wood.

After the Allbrights had finally left and Molly was tucked up in bed, Annie and Grace were relaxing in the sitting room. The old lady looked up from the crossword she was poring over. "A kind of endearment, four letters…" she said.

"Love," Grace answered automatically.

Annie put down her paper with a flourish. "There, that's it: I've done the whole thing."

Can I ask you something, Annie?" Grace asked.

"Yes." The old lady's eyes shone brightly from the wrinkled parchment of her face.

"Did you ever notice a small marble headstone in Heart Wood?"

Annie threw up her hands. "Oh my lord, I'd forgotten all about that. What did it say? No, don't tell me… 'Goodbye my love,' was that it?"

"Yes," cried Grace. "Yes. Do you know anything about it?"

"Your mother and I often pondered on that headstone when we were girls," she sighed, remembering. "We used to make up stories about it. I think we eventually decided that it must be the grave of someone's pet, a dog perhaps."

"Someone must know though surely."

Annie shrugged. "You could look in the library I suppose but it seems that the wood has always been shrouded in mystery. I don't think the person who had it planted there ever intended anyone to know why."

"There's such sadness to it," Grace said, "and a kind of peacefulness too. It *must* have been planted in memory of someone's lost love I'm sure of it; I wonder if that same person placed the headstone there though."

"Oh I don't know about that; the headstone could have been put there at any time. Your mother and I once had a crazy idea about digging down to see what was buried beneath it –if anything."

"And did you?"

Annie shook her head. "I think we decided that sometimes secrets are meant to be kept,"

A shiver rippled across Grace's skin. "And of course you might not have liked what you found."

"Come on," Annie determinedly changed the subject. "Let's leave the long gone secrets where they lie. I'm off to my bed. It's been a long day and I have guests coming in tomorrow."

Broken Heart Wood

"Then I'll help you," offered Grace. "Changing beds, vacuuming, anything you want."

Annie shook her white head. "You really don't have to you know, you already pay your way but... well... my old legs aren't what they used to be, so thank you."

"I'll be up at the crack of dawn," promised Grace. "It'll be good for me to have something proper to do."

Annie slowly heaved herself onto her feet, holding onto the chair arm for support. "Eight-o-clock will do," she insisted. "They won't be here until after lunch. And don't forget to..."

"I know," cut in Grace. "Don't forget to finish my story..."

After the old lady withdrew she waited a while, plucking up the courage to read her own words. And when she did it seemed to her that they had been written by someone else, as if she had committed her own thoughts down onto paper without being consciously involved... Re-reading them was a much more emotional experience.

****

"The darkness seemed to last for an eternity and yet it flashed by in an instant, leaving in its wake a vague blurry grey that cushioned my pain. People were around

me but I didn't know them, strangers staring at me, reaching out to me. Fear flooded over me; I was isolated in a strange, distant place with vague and awful sense of horror flooding my every vein, leaving me weeping silently inside. Something terrible had happened but I couldn't remember what it was... A smiling face bent over me. "Just a little prick to help you sleep."

A little prick that brought blessed oblivion.

When I opened my eyes again things were clearer... Tom, where was Tom? And then there he was beside me, looking at me through clouded eyes, blaming me for...? Memories flooded in, engulfing me. A silver mound, struggling on the road: The vivid rich crimson of lifeblood, ebbing away. Misery clamped tight inside my chest, taking away my breath. If only, filled my every conscious thought. If only I had stayed at home... If only I had set off sooner... The pain in Tom's face said it all. For the first time since we met he felt like a stranger.

With every passing hour my memories crept back, horrifically clarifying each painful moment. Tom was thoughtful and kind and yet he seemed distant and aloof. He brought Molly in to see me every day and being with her was my saving grace. She alone had no secret regrets, no awareness of the tragedy that hung over us, no all-consuming guilt.

"Is Mary helping you to look after her?" I asked, making conversation when once it had flowed so freely between us. "Or is she too busy with the horses?"

It seemed sensible to me for Mary to be helping with Molly, for although she was really employed to work on the yard I know that she loved to look after our little girl. In fact it was only when she was around Molly or the horses that she seemed able to let herself go. She was a strange quiet person, deep I suppose you would call her, keeping herself to herself so that you never really felt that you knew her. Sometimes I used to catch her looking at me with a strange brooding expression in her eyes. .

"Mary has gone and there are no horses left to look after," Tom didn't meet my eyes as he answered my question in a dull, wooden tone. "After... you know. Well it just seemed best if their owners took them away."

My heart clamped tight shut as my guilt expanded.

"And Mary...?"

"She had to leave suddenly... Some family crisis I think..."

I'd imagined coming home to the place I knew, the life I knew. The thought of it all being gone brought a rush of panic.

"But what can we do without the horses? They're our whole life."

Tom's face darkened. "Quicksilver was our whole life you mean...without him we have nothing... They are over Grace, all our dreams are finished."

I think that was the moment when everything clicked into place. The moment when I knew that nothing would ever be the same. Somehow though, for Molly's sake, we had to try and make a new life.

The day when I eventually came home was bittersweet, both happy and sad. I didn't dare even look in the direction of Silver's empty stable. It was good to be out of the hospital and so good to sleep in my own bed again -except that Tom insisted he stayed in the spare room. "You are still so vulnerable and sore," was his excuse. "You need space and quiet. I'm worried about rolling over in bed and accidentally hurting you."

He looked at me with those sad, empty eyes and something inside me died, for suddenly I knew... I knew what was wrong. Tom blamed me; however hard he tried he couldn't help himself from blaming me, for I was the

Broken Heart Wood

cause of the death of Quicksilver and the end of our dreams. He was right to lay the blame at my door too because it was all my fault, and how could I expect him to ever forgive me when I couldn't forgive myself?

I lived with that guilt for months, carrying it like a lead weight around my neck, dragging me down into an empty place where self-reproach stared me in the face at every turn... Stared at me with Toms' eyes, or so I thought then. Now of course I know the truth. It wasn't because he blamed **me** that my Tom had kept his distance; it was his own guilt that had driven the wedge between us, his own guilt that pushed us apart... and perhaps he had also resented me because he had to let her go.

I remember so well how my heart lifted on the day he ran into the house looking almost like his normal self again.

"Grace!" he'd cried, grabbing hold of my shoulders and spinning me round.

Molly held up her arms too and he lifted her off the ground, throwing her into the air and catching her again. She burst into a fit of giggles. "Again daddy, again."

Broken Heart Wood

Ignoring her plea he had rested her on his hip, reaching out his free arm to draw me close, just like the old days. His lean body felt warm against mine and I could hear his heart inside my head. For the first time in weeks I'd felt a glow of happiness.

"Everything is going to change," he told us in a high, excited tone. "We are back on the up again. We are in business Grace. We have a new future."

It may not have been quite the kind of business I might have expected, but to see Tom smile again I would have done anything. I snuggled against him, my heart pounding with an unfamiliar joy as he outlined the details of what was supposed to be our new beginning.

"A friend of mine, George Appleby, is going abroad and he needs to sell his business quickly. He says that we can have it at a rock bottom price. It's our chance Grace, our chance to move on... to get our life back on track again."

The business it seemed had the rather doubtful title 'Get it There' and George Appleby had built up a modest reputation for transporting very special items all around the UK, with one van and his wife to do the office work. With a resigned sigh I imagined myself sitting at a desk and answering the phone all day whilst Molly played beside me on the floor. It was a long way from the gentle wicker of hungry horses, their soft velvety noses snuffling against me as I breathed in the warm familiar stable smells in the cold sharp air of a winter's morning. Nostalgia swept over me and I took a breath, focussing on Tom's bright excited expression.

"You can do the paperwork and answer the phone and I'll do the deliveries," he cried. "We'll make a go of it won't we Grace?"

"Yes," I had agreed, suddenly infected by his enthusiasm. "We'll make a go of it."

We stayed up well into the early hours that night, making plans and trying to think of a better name than 'Get it There,' something that would stick in people's minds. A name we could be proud of

For what seemed to be the first time in months we laughed together, coming up with crazy suggestions, both of us totally high on possibilities.

"Quicksilver," I eventually suggested, my heart thumping. "We could call it 'Quicksilver Deliveries', in memory of... of everything we've lost."

Broken Heart Wood

At first Tom's face darkened but he saw the rightness of it. "It's a brilliant idea," he agreed, holding my eyes with his. I saw the bright sparkle of excitement in their tawny depths and knew that hope was back. "It will be like a tribute to him. "Quicksilver Deliveries' it is."

"Get It There with Quicksilver Deliveries," I suggested. "It will help with the name change.

That night we made love for the first time since the accident but it held none of our old passion. Tom treated me like a fragile piece of porcelain that might break at any moment, as if he was almost afraid to touch me. And afterwards, sleeping fitfully in his arms, I dreamed of the horror that had blighted our life; the vivid crimson of blood against the silvery whiteness of Silver's coat, the pain on Tom's face. Guilt was a flood that threatened to drown me. I was gasping for breath. I reached out for him, needing his closeness, but my hand had met cold empty sheets. Oh what had I done to him... to us, and could things ever really be the same between us again?

*

I thought he'd moved away from me that night because being close to me brought back too many regrets. Now though, thinking back, I can't help but wonder if, in reality, he was just longing for someone else. The thought hardened my heart, pushing away my guilt. It wasn't my fault.

*

And so our life took on a whole new face, a face that looked once again to the future, hiding the emotions that bubbled beneath the surface. Our business was an overnight success that kept us both busily apart. Tom went off on deliveries whilst I took over the office, answering the phone, sending out bills and trying to make more sales whilst caring for Molly who seemed ever more demanding.

Tom never stopped, he bought one more van and then another so we had two drivers to employ and I had to find someone to help me help in the office. I felt as if we were on a roller coaster that was going too fast for us to get off, and I longed so much for what was gone: The gentle companionship of horses, the rhythmic sound of hooves on tarmac, the sweep of my body brush across a silken coat and the heavy ache of tired muscles.

I dreamed all the time of how it used to be, whilst stoically turning my face to our new future. I had Tom and Molly, that was all that really mattered; and after all, I still believed that it was my fault everything we loved so much was gone.

Broken Heart Wood

It was on a Tuesday that the new life I was slowly becoming accustomed too turned on its head.

*

As I walked the short distance from Ivy cottage to the yard I remember smiling at the glorious sight of daffodils in the meadow beside the lane. They bowed their golden heads in the fresh spring breeze, dancing in a sea of green.

"Look at the pretty flowers," I cried, lifting Molly up to peer over the dry stonewall.

"Pwetty pink," she gurgled.

I squeezed her tight, kissing her chubby cheek. "They are yellow," I told her. "Say yel...low."

"Wewwo," she repeated with a grin.

I took a deep breath, absorbing the scents and sounds of spring: A new born lamb bleated for its mother, an early swallow swooped low across the grass and a rare rush of happiness suddenly flooded over me. Perhaps with all this new life surging up around us we could finally move on and forget the tragedy that had coloured our lives for so long. Perhaps we should have another child. The idea hit me like a thunderbolt and swelled inside me as the day wore on.

It was still circling around inside my head as I set off to town that afternoon, leaving Debbie, our part time help, to mind the office and keep an eye on Molly for me whilst I went to the bank.

I made my deposit in the austere interior of the old fashioned bank on Highgate and hurried back out onto the street, smiling to myself as the sunshine hit me again. Maybe a new baby would be the last piece to fit the puzzle, the final step to getting things back to how they used to be.

I saw her just as I was about to step out onto the street. I looked left and there she was, staring back at me, familiar and yet so unfamiliar.

"Mary!" I called with a rush of pleasure. "How are you?"

She walked slowly towards me. Short steps, indecisive, her pale cheeks shot with colour. "I've been better."

Her voice was low, angry almost.

"Why don't we go and get a coffee or something," I suggested. "And catch up. Tom told me that you had to leave suddenly because of some family crisis. I hope everything's okay now."

She looked at me oddly then and laughed; a short, harsh, angry laugh. "He didn't even have the balls to tell you the truth then?"

"The truth...?

An awful wave of fear rose up inside me as I saw the bitterness in her face. I wanted to turn and run, to get as far away from her 'truth' as I could before it was too late... It was already too late.

"What truth...?"

She took my arm, drawing me to the side of the street. I felt as if there were just the two of us in our own private world a million miles away from the honking cars and jostle of passers-by.

"You must have known... must have seen it."

I licked my dry lips, feeling their roughness beneath my tongue. "Seen what?"

"Seen how he was with me..."

"With you...?"

My voice was a stupid echo of hers, my heart a heavy aching weight that pounded inside my head.

"When you were away and we were on our own together we just couldn't fight it any more though, couldn't resist each other. Of course he felt bad with you being in hospital and everything..."

She looked at me with such a sad emptiness in her face that suddenly I knew... She was telling me the truth.

"He was in love with me," she said. "But you were so ill that... well he could hardly leave you then could he. And if I'd stayed on, you would have seen how it was with us as soon as you came home. He felt sorry for you Grace that's all, that's why he stayed after..." She wrapped her arms about herself, a dreamy smile on her face. "...Anyway, it's time you knew the truth. He should have told you himself."

Sorry... Tom was sorry for me. No! A wave of dizziness washed over me. I fumbled for support as the world around me tilted. "He doesn't.... He wouldn't..."

"Here, look." She pulled out her phone, scrolling down, pushing it in my face.

"Now do you believe me?"

Bile rose in my throat as I saw them together. I held onto a lamp post to stop myself from falling and my whole world stopped.

"We loved each other, Grace, we still do if I'm honest, and it was so much more than just sex. He knew he had to do the right thing by you though so..."

I was shaking inside, trembling all over as the delicate structure of my whole world came crashing down around me. She looked at me with a momentary flash of compassion. "I'm sorry Grace, you were good to me, but sometimes there are things that are just too big for us to resist. That's how it was with me and Tom.

Broken Heart Wood

He would have definitely come away with me if things had been different but he had to look after you. Anyway, I have someone new in my life now so you don't need to worry that I'll come back for him."

I clung to that thought after she walked away, still hanging onto the lamp post like an idiot, being stared at curiously by cautious passers-by. She had someone new, she didn't want my Tom anymore... but he wasn't my Tom was he. An image of them filled my head, locked together in ecstasy, his lips against hers as he caressed her naked flesh. Nausea gurgled up inside me and I retched into the bushes...

"You ok love?"

A kindly passer-by with a plump face and concerned eyes peered at me.

"Yes, thanks," I mumbled, attempting a smile. "It's just morning sickness." Now why did I say that? A shaft of pain cut through me as I remembered my thoughts of a lifetime ago, my dreams of having another baby.

The woman's expression lightened. "Congratulations," she exclaimed. "...Worth being sick for then. Can I give you a lift anywhere?"

I shook my head, unable to speak, hurrying off along the street: running away to hide from prying eyes, to lick my wounds and face the facts. Tom, my Tom, and Mary Maddison had an affair whilst I was in the hospital. Did he do it to punish me then? Was that his way of getting back at me for losing our dream, or had he really fallen in love with her and just stayed with me through duty... or pity?

Anger flooded over me as I clambered into my car and roared out of the main car park in the centre of the town. My tyres squealed on the tarmac. I liked that sound for it echoed the sound inside my head.

When I got back to the office Debbie was waiting to leave. She looked at me curiously but said nothing. I smiled goodbye with empty eyes and picked up Molly, pressing my face into her baby sweetness. She was the only real thing left in my life now; the rest was just a sham.

"I'll see you tomorrow?"

I nodded my reply and she hesitated. "Are you all right Grace?" Her dark hair swung as she turned and her eyes were a clear bright blue. Had he been with her too? Had he...? I shook my head. "I'm fine... Thanks Debbie."

"I'm only here until lunchtime tomorrow remember," she said, smiling. "And then I'm on holiday for two weeks."

"Oh... yes."

My voice sounded strange and distant, the voice of a stranger; I made myself smile back. "That'll be nice."

"Hope so," she said, rolling her eyes dramatically. "I'm going with Rob you see. It will be our first holiday together, make or break huh?"

"Make or break," I echoed, dying inside.

When she was gone I looked around the small office as if I had never seen it before, everything was familiar and yet so unfamiliar. Molly's bright little face smiled out at me from the computer in the corner and behind her I smiled too, the happy relaxed face of a woman who didn't know that her husband had cheated on her. But why had Tom put us both on the screen if it was Mary he really wanted?

On the desk just in front of the computer, beside piles of coloured files, the diary lay open. My writing was scrawled across the page, and Tom's, the two of us intertwined as always. But we weren't intertwined anymore were we.

Broken Heart Wood

I took a breath, my whole body trembling, holding my daughter tightly in my arms, clinging to her neediness. She was the only one who really mattered now I reminded myself; I had to be strong for her.

"Mummy cwying," Her tiny forefinger reached out to touch the tear that oozed from the corner of my eye.

I brushed it furiously away, swinging her onto my hip. "No darling, mummy isn't crying, come on we have to go now... on our holidays."

I knew that I should wait for Tom, to face him and listen to his lies, but he'd talk me round I knew it and I didn't want to be talked around. I wanted to try and get my head around what Mary had told me first, wanted to be on my own to think things through.

I left him a note on the kitchen table, just a few brief words but enough to let him know why I'd gone, and then I threw my hastily packed bags into the car, fastened Molly carefully into her car seat and slid in behind the wheel. An ache filled me, body and soul and my fingers trembled as they fumbled with the key. Was I running away? I hoped he wouldn't see it like that because I didn't feel as if I was running away. I needed space that's all, just a few days to think, a few days to let him suffer... Or perhaps he would he be glad that I'd gone? I saw his face in my mind's eye as it was this *morning, when he left in his silver van. I had watched it disappear around the corner, its Quicksilver emblem emblazoned on the side reminding us every day of what was gone.*

"No," I said out loud, remembering the look in his eyes as he kissed me goodbye, the feel of his lips on mine. For despite what had happened with Mary all those months ago, I knew that there was still something real between us. I would never put up with being second best though, never feel that I had to look behind me all my life and I didn't think I could ever forgive him for letting me believe that all the blame was mine. I turned the key and my car's normally temperamental engine roared immediately into life, without even a splutter of hesitation. Was that a sign, a sign that I was doing the right thing?

I gripped my fingers around the wheel and let out the clutch, seeing the last glimpse of Ivy cottage slipping from the corner of my eye.

"Daddy," cried Molly. "Daddy come too."

Tears forced themselves from behind my burning eyelids. "Daddy has to work sweetheart," I told her. "So it's just you and me."

*

Broken Heart Wood

Dragging my thoughts away from now I tried to cast my mind back to another, almost forgotten place, where once I had been happy: Way ahead of me, somewhere in the far distance, were the mighty fells I used to love a lifetime ago. Vague memories of a wide-open sky and steep stark slopes filled my mind's eye and suddenly I knew where to go. "We're going home," I announced determinedly, turning the steering wheel to head north off the roundabout.

"Home," repeated Molly solemnly.

***

Grace closed the writing pad with a thump. She had put so much of herself into telling her story that she wasn't sure she could let anyone else in just yet, and yet she had promised Annie. She would hand it over to her tonight she decided, she deserved to know the truth. Sighing long and hard she closed her eyes tightly. So was it time for her to go back now then, she asked herself. Was she strong enough to face Tom and hear his excuses?

Soon, she decided, but tomorrow she would go once again to Heart Wood and let its tranquillity soak over her, lending her strength. She lay back on her pillows, snuggling close to Molly's small form: Tomorrow and tomorrow and tomorrow, so many tomorrows to face… and so many yesterdays to regret. But they hadn't all been about regret had they. Her mind went back eagerly to happier times, to the days when Quicksilver had promised them glory, when every new day was a fresh challenge and a new delight. Could life ever be like that for her again, or were her happiest times all in the past?

Molly stirred, tucking her thumb into her mouth and Grace felt a smile rise up inside her. As long as she had Molly then she knew that there would always be happiness in her life.

CHAPTER THIRTEEN

"Come on boy," Tom called, striding from the murky interior of the Fox and Hounds to meet the bright new day with fresh determination. Today he was going to find Grace and Molly, no matter how hard he had to search for them.

It felt good, he decided, with an unfamiliar surge of euphoria, to be actually doing something positive at last, after going through the everyday motions of life with a heart like lead for what felt like a lifetime.

As if to reflect his positive mood, the sun pushed its way from behind a swirling grey cloud and he looked up to see a wide strip of clearest blue above the stark magnificence of the fells. "Come on boy," he called again. "…Lucky!"

The little white dog half-cocked his leg against a tree stump, almost but not quite yet an adult, and headed towards his new master, strutting across the smooth green lawn at the side of the pub with a new found confidence. Tom opened the van door and he leaped in, perching on the passenger seat as if it was his rightful place.

"Right then..." Tom jumped in beside him, slamming the driver's door with a bang. "Let's get this show on the road."

Twenty minutes later he hit the motorway, the wide faceless road that cut through the northern hills of the Pennines on its way to Scotland. It was a strange place to find such a fast road, and to see such amazing views all around him whilst having to concentrate so hard on his driving was totally weird, almost dangerous really he decided.

Way below him, in the valley, he could see a village. Grey stone houses and narrow streets. Was that where she was he wondered? Was that Meredale? But no, for Mick had definitely described a pretty, bustling market town, not just a tiny village.

The motorway swept around in a curve and he slowed his speed, suddenly uncomfortable with the sheer drop to the side of him that sloped sharply down to the bottom of the valley. Cars and lorry's overtook him, zooming through the timeless landscape on the starkly modern tarmac road. There was something slightly disorientating about the whole place he decided, slowing his speed whilst absorbing his surroundings. Now what number was the junction where he had to leave the motorway, thirty-eight, that was it? His mind slid back to Grace and the task in hand, his heart thumping hard inside his ribcage as he allowed himself a sliver of hope. He increased his speed, eager to get on, just as the sun suddenly burst through the swirling grey cloud temporarily blinding him.

His fingers clenched tightly around the wheel and he blinked hard, narrowing his eyes against its glare and pulling down the sun shield. He seemed now to be facing the vast fell side that loomed towards the endless sky. Shades of green and brown and grey splattered with tiny white dots filled his vision, stretching to infinity.

The dots were sheep he suddenly realised, taking his foot off the throttle, fell sheep way up on the stark hostile slopes, happily surviving in the only way they knew how. He felt suddenly humbled by the true face of nature, creatures that survived such austere conditions with no complaints. This was *their* life though he realised; the sheep knew no other existence than the isolated hardships of the lonely fells that were their home. He turned his eyes determinedly forwards, trying to concentrate of the road again. He however *did* have a choice and the stark severity of life without his two girls had gone on long enough, somehow he had to get them back and convince Grace that she was the only woman he had ever loved, no matter what it took.

Suddenly overcome by a surge of withheld memories, he swung his van into the slow lane, taking stock. How many long gone faces had looked upon this exact scene he wondered: The endless sky, the incredible sweep of the fells against its magical ice blue clarity: His puny life seemed totally inconsequential in comparison. A wave of loneliness swept over him. There was so much beauty in the world but it all meant nothing without Grace beside him...

He took a breath, trying to focus. Now was what counted, not what was gone. He had to think positive. Lucky whined as if in agreement and he smiled. "Sorry boy, I'm just behaving like a stupid sentimental fool," he said, turning his attention back to the road ahead.

It was then that he saw it; over to his right on the steep fell-side. Ten thousand shades of green; a close-knit mass of trees in the shape of a perfect heart, quivering restlessly in the breeze that rarely left these isolated slopes. It was a place as much in touch with God as anywhere he had ever been he realised; was that why someone had planted the heart shaped wood here then?

Had tragedy inspired it, or was it perhaps in the memory of great joy?

Something softened deep inside him as he took in what must surely be the living proof of someone's deep emotion. It made him feel a whole lot better, less lonely he supposed.

"Funny old world isn't it," he said out loud. Beside him Lucky wriggled with delight at the sound of his master's voice, caring for nothing but the here and now.

The little dog's whole world was complete with so little, realised Tom, reaching over to scratch behind his ears. There again, he supposed, that was what separated animals from humans, their acceptance of everything life threw at them. Never questioning, never blaming, and never bearing grudges.

"Well you'll never need to worry about anything again now that you're with me," he promised, turning his attention back to the road ahead.

The strange heart shaped wood was almost out of sight now, but, as he glanced back at it one last time, suddenly he saw something move, a tiny figure climbing the steep slope, a miniature dot of a person wearing a bright pink top. Something clamped painfully tight deep down inside him as he remembered the pink top Grace had worn last year, the one he'd bought for her at Midland County show.

Their whole lives had been before them then, their dreams still intact. Oh how he longed for those times to come back. They said that suffering made you stronger, character building they called it, all it had done to their lives though was to tear them apart.

Turning his mind away from the past and back to the job in hand, he tried to focus on the positive attitude that had brought him to this place. He'd come here to find Grace and Molly and he wasn't going to leave until he'd done just that.

At Junction 38 Mick had told him to take the Lambton road and then look out for the sign to Meredale. He exhaled with relief; at last he could see the roundabout just ahead.

Indicating, he spun the wheel left, rapidly reading the road signs. 'Scotch Corner, Lambton, Greyside…'

"Greyside," his heart lurched as he said the name out loud. There was something so familiar about it. Was it… could it be the village where Grace was born?

He repeated the word again and again inside his head as he headed for Lambton. No it just didn't feel right.

Broken Heart Wood

The Grey part was he was sure about that, but not the rest.

When another name jumped out at him from the greenery of the hedgerow that flashed by in a blur, he smiled inside. 'Meredale,' now that was a name that he did recognise. Turning sharp right he following the road that ran steeply down to the valley bottom, heading for the market town where Mick had spotted Grace just yesterday.

"Not long now boy," he told Lucky, reaching across to give him a scratch. "You'll soon be able to meet your new mistress and you are going to love her."

The little dog gazed adoringly at him with soft brown eyes, curling his pink tongue around his new master's fingers; all he cared about was the big kind man who had become his friend.

The road narrowed and Tom slowed his speed to negotiate a narrow bridge. Just up ahead now he could see the small town sprawled along the valley bottom on either side of the river. Grey stone houses, narrow streets and the tall steeple of a church. Meredale, was that where he would find them then, but where, and how? Doubts crept in as he faced up to the enormity of his task.

As he drove through the outskirts of the town he saw children dressed in green school uniforms, loitering on the pavement, chattering at bus stops, giggling together in small groups as they headed towards a large building. He noted the name, *MEREDALE HIGH SCHOOL*. It seemed a lifetime since he was at school, *was* a lifetime.

Weariness overcame him and with it the ever increasingly familiar rush of emotion. What if he never found them, what if he never saw them again? Character building! If this was character building then he didn't want a character. He glanced despairingly at his surroundings and fate suddenly lent him a sliver of luck.

Another, smaller sign, pointed up a narrow road beside the school. Overgrown as it was by bushes, he would never have noticed it if a small boy hadn't darted out into the road ahead, forcing him to have to stand on the brakes. 'Greythwaite, that was it, definitely; that was the village where Grace was born.

A vision of her face flashed into his mind, just as if it was yesterday, sitting half naked in his arms with dreamy eyes as they exchanged memories of their childhood. He remembered that moment so well. He had wanted to know everything about her, every last detail. 'I don't often think of the place where I was born,' she had told him. 'It was a small village, I know that, all I can really remember though is my mother crying on the day we left so it has always seemed a sad place to me. It was called Greythwaite, Greythwaite village in Westmorland.'

"Will you go back there one day?" he'd asked but in that moment she'd run her fingers through the hair at the nape of his neck and drawn his face down towards hers, so he never got an answer.

So was this where she had come too he wondered, had she come back home to find her roots when the life she knew now was crumbling around her?

Turning the van onto the narrow lane he headed up the hill again, his hands quivering on the wheel. There was only one way to find out. "Please be here Grace," he begged.

Beside him, on the passenger seat, Lucky squirmed. "You'll love her," he told the little white dog. "And Molly… everyone does…"

***

Annie settled back into her chair, picked up Grace's pad and began to read, her tired eyes finding new life as they flickered across the pages. There was so much of Sarah in her daughter that it made Annie's old heart hurt.

She had forgotten how her dear friend's luminous grey eyes used to shine with emotion, until she'd so unexpectedly found Grace. They both even had the same softly curling hair and elfin features.

It was so much more than that though, Annie realised as she read Grace's story, for it seemed that she also had her mother's loyalty and passion as well as her love of horses.

Long forgotten memories flooded over her, putting her back in touch with the past and all the emotions of the day when Sarah finally left forever, never to look upon the wild open fells of Westmorland again.

Annie put the pad down on her knee for a moment, reliving that long ago morning when Sarah came looking for her.

She was in the herb garden, here at Hillside, weeding her precious borders whilst little Ben played happily on the smooth green lawn, content with his own company, as always. She would never forget the expression on her friend's face that day.

"I've done a stupid thing Annie," Sarah expression was defiant but her eyes, dark with misery, defying her brave statement. "I'm... I'm pregnant. I've told Donald though and we're going to be married."

Broken Heart Wood

Annie closed her eyes, feeling once again the wave of misery that had washed over her all those years ago. Until that moment she had totally believed that Sarah, her wild, carefree best friend, was just having a fling with the sweet talking salesman who had arrived in Greythwaite village totally out of the blue. She'd been convinced that one day soon, when she was finally ready to settle down, Sarah would see Donald Bryant for what he really was and turn to her brother, Sam. That was what was supposed to happen. They were supposed to be sisters in law, bringing up their children together in one big happy family… now seemed that dream was burst.

Sarah had always been so against 'tying herself down' as she called it. When Annie proudly announced that she and Arthur were getting engaged Sarah had told her she was mad.

'But there's so much more to see and do in the world yet Annie,' she'd cried. '…So much fun to be had.'

Annie shook her white head, remembering that moment. Much good it had done Sarah, all that talk of having fun and living life to the full –not that she hadn't tried too, for she had certainly lived her short life to the full.

Broken Heart Wood

Riding had been her greatest passion. She was forever taking risks on horseback, always prepared to try and tame a rogue, or mount a half broken youngster at the stables in the village where she helped out. Annie smiled to herself as she remembered Sarah proudly showing off her bruises; even the very worst falls failed to make her lose her nerve.

'I will never let myself be tied down by a husband and children until I'm at least thirty,' she used to say.

Well she had managed to get herself 'tied down,' just a few years sooner than she'd wanted, and tied down to the wrong man.

Annie felt a sigh rise up deep inside as the heavy weight of regret settled over her. Oh why was it that people never seemed to appreciate what was right under their noses until it was too late? When Sarah had finally realised that she truly loved Sam as so much more than the friend he had always been, it was far too late.

"But you are supposed to marry Sam," she'd cried on that grey morning, here at Hillside, in the fragrance of the herb garden.

Sarah had just looked down at her hands and Annie would never forget the desolation in her eyes, or her reply. "I know... but it's too late now."

"You could get rid of it."

Even as she mentioned it Annie had known that it wasn't an option. Nowadays of course there would have been no social stigma for either Sarah or her child and she wouldn't have even thought that she'd have to marry Donald Bryant. They could have just lived together, or she could have brought her child up alone if she'd wanted to. Oh how times had changed. Was it for the better though... who knew?

She supposed that Donald really had loved Sarah in his own shallow way and for the first couple of years things seemed to work out. Grace was born on a bright spring morning bringing Sarah such joy. She hadn't expected the love and fulfilment motherhood brought.

Donald was away on the road a lot though in those early years and Sam took to calling in on her when her husband wasn't there, doing jobs around the house and helping with little Grace... The fateful day when Donald arrived home early and caught him kissing Sarah with far more passion than just a friend, was inevitable, simply a matter of time.

Of course he had insisted that they move away at once. Sam had begged Sarah to stay and so had Annie but she wouldn't do it. She freely admitted to them both that it was Sam she really loved but her loyalty lay with the man she'd married.

"It was my choice," she said sadly. "He loves me in his own way and he is Grace's father. Anyway, think how upset my parents would be if Sam and I just set up home together. No Annie…" She had wrapped her arms around her childhood friend on the morning she left, weeping on her shoulder. "This is goodbye."

"But you'll stay in touch?"

Annie had begged her to ring, to write, to stay in her life but Sarah had just smiled.

"When we get settled," she'd promised, and she had written, occasionally, but then the letters stopped and it wasn't until now, when she'd finally met Grace again, that Annie eventually knew why. Her dearest friend was dead and gone, just like her Edward, and Sam. Suddenly death didn't seem such an alien place.

With a sigh she cast her mind back to the pad in front of her. Reading Grace's story was like listening to Sarah all over again and she knew what her advice would be already. Follow your heart for life is short, forgive and forget and live for now before its too late.

***

Broken Heart Wood

Completely oblivious to the emotions she had aroused in either Annie or Tom, Grace was climbing up the fell once again, intent now upon finding out the secret of Heart Wood. It had become like a need inside her, something to take her mind off everything else perhaps. It made her feel better to have something to concentrate on, something that took her mind away from images of Tom with Mary Maddison.

She should ring him; she knew she should; for whatever he had done to her he still loved Molly to pieces and he would be missing her so much. Tonight, she promised herself, she would speak to him tonight.

She had intended to take Molly with her today, she had put on Annie for long enough, but when she'd called in at the Allbright's on her way to the fell, Carol had insisted on looking after the little girl.

"Please let her stay with me," she'd pleaded. "You'll never carry the little mite all the way up there and she's far too small to walk. Anyway, it will nice to have a girly afternoon for once, I spend my whole life with men… bless 'em."

Grace was uncertain. The Allbright's had been so good to her already, welcoming her into their family, the last thing was wanted to do was put on their good nature. "Well if you're sure," she began, weakening.

"Of course I'm sure," clucked Carol, ushering her towards the door. "You want to stay with your Aunty Carol don't you Molly?"

The little girl's response was to run to the bubbly red haired woman, arms outstretched. "Cawol got ice cweam," she gurgled.

"I've got a lot more than just ice cream," laughed Carol, swinging her up onto her hip.

"I won't be long," promised Grace.

Carol laughed, shaking her head. "Take as long as you need," she insisted. "I'm at home all day today… and when you come back we can have a coffee and a natter."

*

Grace climbed determinedly up the fell, trying to ignore the ache in her legs. Physical pain was far easier to bear than the heavy ache in her heart. She turned her face into the wind, gasping as it buffeted against her. Here, in this wild free landscape, she felt in touch with something so much bigger than her puny life. Was her mother watching over her she wondered, as she walked the path that *she* once trod? Was Silver there too, galloping through a field of dreams? She quickened her steps, labouring over the rough ground until her muscles ached so much that she was forced to take a break.

Collapsing on the coarse grass she looked back down the valley, drinking in the raw beauty of the bleak open hills, against the moody greys and blues of the ever-changing sky; and in strange comparison the busy, motorway, starkly modern, cutting through time. How could she have forgotten this place she wondered and why had her mother never really talked to her about her home after they left? Perhaps the memories were just too painful. Annie believed that Sarah had compromised on love. She closed her eyes for a moment, trying to see her mother's face and remembering only the sadness in her eyes.

They had never really been happy, her parents, she could see that now. When her father met vivacious, dark skinned Terri, after her mother's death, he had become a whole new person. Would her mother have been different if she had followed her heart and stayed here she wondered. Would she still be alive?

Her mind drifted automatically to Tom; so many if onlys. *If only* Quicksilver hadn't died. *If only* Tom hadn't done what he did: Life seemed to be built on if onlys. And what was he doing right now she wondered, her fingers reaching automatically for the soft familiarity of the vivid pink top she wore, the one that Tom had bought for her last year, at one of the summer horse shows? Was he missing her, did he care that she was gone? The familiar heavy ache made breathing difficult and she clasped her arms about herself as she headed on again, up the steep slope, needing the ageless serenity of Heart Wood to soothe her pain.

CHAPTER FOURTEEN

Grace pushed her way through the undergrowth, following the path that was becoming so familiar, the path that she had made. Did anyone else ever come here she wondered, knowing the answer at once, for it was obvious that no other human foot had trodden here for years.

Perhaps the last people to set foot in wood before her then were her mother and Annie; it was a sobering thought, like fate almost; and could they have been the very first to look upon that tiny grave with its marble headstone. But who planted the trees? Who marked out the shape of the heart and who built the crumbling dry stone wall that must have once stood sturdily solid, keeping out intruders? Somehow she had to know, it seemed so important to her that she found out the truth of Heart Wood before she moved on with her life. She would talk to Carol when she went back to pick up Molly she decided. Surely she must know something, or at least she might be able to tell her how to find out about it.

Sinking down onto her knees in front of the headstone, her forefinger outstretched, she carefully traced the letters on the front. '*GOODBYE MY LOVE.*' What beloved creature could it be she wondered, that lay here in this peaceful place?

Almost as if in answer to her question, from way above came a rustling sound. She shivered, looking up to see the treetops dancing in a sudden buffeting breeze.

"Who *are* you?" she murmured, smiling to see an inquisitive red squirrel peering down at her.

As if suddenly aware of her presence, a startled rabbit dashed from the undergrowth and suddenly the whole place woke up. Pigeons fluttered from the trees, a blackbird raised its voice in a sad sweet song and sunlight filtered through the branches, making golden, flickering patterns on the moss covered rock that formed the centre of the clearing.

Grace breathed in the wooded aromas of trees and moss and damp earth and a kind of peacefulness crept through her limbs, a healing kind of peacefulness that brought strength back into her heart. Whatever tomorrow brought she could face it with Molly beside her she realised, and tonight she would definitely ring Tom.

|***

Broken Heart Wood

Annie put down Grace's pad with a sigh, brushing the tears from her eyes with the back of her hand. She had written her story more like a novel than just the bare facts, allowing all her raw emotion spill out across the pages.

It seemed almost wrong for her to be reading it, as if she was prying into someone else's private affairs. Her heart went out to the two young people whose love had been put to the test by fate. Were their feelings for each other strong enough to survive though she wondered; could they eventually get past all the pain and blame and treachery? Tonight, she decided, she would talk to Grace and try and get her to meet up with Tom, or at least talk to him, after all there were always two sides to a story, although she hadn't got the to the end of this one yet.

When the hall clock struck twelve noon, chiming out into the silence, she jumped, glancing at her watch -the gold one that Edward bought for her not long before his poor old heart gave out. Her doctor's appointment in the village was at twelve thirty and she wasn't even ready yet.

Dragging her tired legs up the steep staircase, she hurriedly freshened up and put on a blue flowered blouse before going back down to grab the keys for her truck.

As she struggled up into the large silver four by four she found herself wondering why ever she kept such a daft vehicle. Edward had been gone for years, so maybe it was time she started driving something more suited to an old lady… as Ben was always suggesting. With a sigh she turned the key in the ignition and pulled out into the lane, peering over the steering wheel to negotiate the corner. It was a damned pain this old age business she decided; what she could really do with was a new body to house the parts of her that still felt young.

By the time she had driven into Greythwaite, squeezed the four by four into a parking place and walked to the surgery, Annie was almost half an hour late for her appointment.

"I'm afraid that Dr Fletcher's surgery has finished," his young, fair-haired secretary informed her as she hurried through the door.

When Annie's flushed face fell the girl smiled, waving her hand to usher the flustered looking old lady through a door to the side of her. "Well go on then, hurry up and go in. He's just packing up but he might see you I suppose."

Broken Heart Wood

Donald Fletcher was standing in front of his desk putting some papers into a black briefcase. He snapped it shut when he saw Annie come into the room, turning towards her with a broad smile.

"You almost missed me Annie," he told her, stroking his grey streaked beard. "I only do one surgery here a week you know and you must be almost out of those blood pressure pills I prescribed last time. You're taking things a bit easier now I hope."

Annie smiled. "You know me Alan; I always have something to do."

"Well it's time that you started to act your age and take more care of yourself," he admonished, pulling out a chair. "Here, sit yourself down and roll up your sleeve. Let's see if the medication is working.

Fifteen minutes later Annie stood up from her chair with relief and reached for her bag. Both her blood pressure and cholesterol levels it seemed were fine and she had a clean bill of health.

"I told you that I was a long way off dying yet," she declared with a broad smile as Alan Fletcher took her frail hand and shook it firmly.

"I'm sure you are Annie," he said. "But don't forget, you're not twenty one anymore."

"Oh no," agreed Annie. "I feel at least twenty five."

Broken Heart Wood

He shook his silver streaked head slowly from side to side, a twinkle in his grey eyes. "You are an inspiration, Annie Allbright," he said, returning her smile. "But promise me that you'll take care of yourself... and don't forget to take your blood pressure tablets."

Annie let her hand lie in his for a moment; they went back a long way, she and Alan Fletcher, for he had been her brother, Sam's, best friend since childhood.

"Sarah's daughter, Grace, is back," she announced on sudden impulse. "Here in the village, she's staying with me."

For a moment he was speechless, remembering all the heartache surrounding her hurried departure all those years ago. "...And Sarah is Sarah with her?" he asked, wishing with all his heart that Sam was still alive.

Annie looked down at her hands, lips trembling. "She's passed on." she told him, her voice barely more than a whisper. "She has been dead since Grace was six years old."

Alan looked at her with a heavy sadness in his eyes. "And poor old Sam never even knew," he responded.

"He never knew," echoed Annie on a sigh.

For just a moment he took hold of her shoulders, squeezing them tightly. "Live for today Annie," he

Broken Heart Wood

urged. "...For who knows what tomorrow will bring. And don't forget to take your medication."

"Don't worry," she promised. "I won't... Take care now."

After she'd left, Alan Fletcher still stood in the same place, remembering. All that heartache and she was already dead; all those nights when Sam must have lain awake longing for her to come back, not knowing that he was praying for the impossible. If only he had known. Perhaps he knew now though, perhaps they were finally together for always. He liked that thought, savouring it for a moment as he watched Annie's small, straight-backed figure, march purposefully off along the street. If Sam had been more like his older sister he thought, then he would quite probably have got his girl in the first place. There again, if that was the case then Sam wouldn't have been Sam would he.

Afraid of not finding a parking place in the centre of the village, Annie had parked her vehicle down Green St, behind the vets, and walked the short distance to the doctor's surgery. Now, walking back across the square, she could see that, as she'd thought, all the spaces were taken.

Broken Heart Wood

One vehicle in particularly took her eye. There was something oddly familiar about the silver van that was squeezed in between the post box and the village green. What was it she wondered, slowing her steps? The lettering on the side of the van jumped out at her. Of course, '*QUICKSILVER DELIVERIES*,' that was the name of Grace and Tom's business. Could he really be here looking for her, or was it just a crazy coincidence; maybe it was one of his drivers.

She approached the vehicle cautiously, If there was someone in it then she would have to speak to them... wouldn't she?

With a mixture of relief and disappointment she saw that the driver's seat was empty. She peered through the window... what was that? A small white fluffy dog stared out at her with bright friendly eyes. It jumped to its feet and stood up on its hind legs, scrabbling on the glass for attention and wagging its tail.

"Hello boy," cried Annie with delight, longing to stroke the dear little mite. Well at least now she knew that it must just be one of the drivers for surely Grace would have mentioned a dog if they had one. Driver or not, she decided, she was determined to speak to whoever it was and try to get Tom's address or telephone number. In her mind there were times when

Broken Heart Wood

you needed to get involved in other people's business for their own good, whether they liked it or not.

A few yards away from the van, just in front of The Woolpack Inn on the other side of the green, was a solid wooden bench. Annie walked towards it, looking down with nostalgia at the small brass plaque on the backrest.

In loving memory of Edward Allbright
A dearly missed friend.

Her heart tightened as she remembered Edward's two good friends, Ted Marley and Mark Jones They'd had the seat placed here soon after Edward's death, near to the place where the three of them had spent so many happy hours with a pint of local ale in front of them. Now Ted was gone too and poor old Mark couldn't manage the walk to the Woolpack anymore. She really must go and visit him, she decided, sinking down onto the bench to wait for the van driver to return.

She felt quite happy about approaching him now that she'd seen his dog she realised, thinking how strange it was how little things like that influenced people's opinions. Just because he was obviously a dog person she'd automatically presumed that he must be an okay kind of guy; and of course that was because she and Edward had always been dog people too. Their house used to be full of dogs before… She blinked hard, twisting her wedding ring round and around on her finger; so many dogs, from Edward's working collies to any poor sad homeless stray that either of them happened to come across. Where had they all gone she asked herself, trying to remember which dogs were left when Edward went?

There was Teddy of course, the three-legged mongrel, Edward's ancient Border collie, Jess, and how could she have forgotten the young sheep dog, Sky. Edward had thought so highly of Sky; the two of them won dozens of prizes in sheepdog trials. Her mind slipped back to sunny days spent on steep hillsides, watching the sharp black white and tan bitch skilfully herding sheep.

It was strange how only the sunny days seemed to stick in one's mind, she thought, for surely there must have been plenty of wet ones too. Were summers really brighter back then she wondered, or was it just her *own* selective memory that made it seem so?

After Edward went so suddenly it had seemed wrong to keep Sky as just a pet, so she'd given her to a local farmer, who Edward had always respected, to carry on doing the job she loved. She had kept the other two dogs of course, but after they'd both died of old age she hadn't been able to bear the thought of replacing them.

She'd really missed having a dog around though, she realised, so perhaps it was finally time for her to get another. She would keep a lookout for a rescue dog, one that needed a bit of love and care. Maybe the local vets would be able to help her.

What do you think Edward," she murmured, feeling very close to him. A deep melancholy settled over her as she imagined him, sitting here beside her, and yet with it came the smile that he had always brought into her life.

Edward had been larger than life, always with a joke and a smile on his lips; Bright by name and bright by nature. No problem was ever too big to be solved by Edward, be it his or someone else's.

"Think of a problem as a challenge and it no longer becomes a problem," had been his favourite saying.

Annie dwelled on that memory as she sat in the late spring sunshine, waiting for the dog loving van driver to return to his vehicle. That is what she must tell Grace, she decided. There are no problems in life, just challenges to be met head on and surely true love is a challenge well worth fighting for.

She was in such a dream in fact that she didn't even realise that the driver had actually come back, until the little white dog jumped up at her legs.

"Lucky," called a tall broad shouldered young man. "Come here."

"He's alright," she smiled, cupping the dog's cute little face between her palms and rubbing the backs of his ears.

The man walked towards her, smiling at the way the little dog was behaving. "He likes you," he told her. "…He's only young and I haven't had him long."

Annie looked up to meet the most extraordinary pair of eyes she had ever seen. They seemed to sparkle with a myriad of changing colours; that was the first thing she noticed, but it was far more than that. There was something about them, some intangible sense of honesty. Images from Grace's story filled her mind and suddenly she knew.

"You must be Tom Roberts," she said, holding out her hand. "I'm Annie, Annie Allbright."

***

As soon as Tom had parked his van in a small space next to the village green, he had walked determinedly

Broken Heart Wood

into the Woolpack and gone straight up to the bar, holding out a photograph.

"Have you seen this girl?" he'd asked hopefully.

The young chestnut haired barmaid was nursing a hangover from a party the night before and was not at her best. She glanced dismissively at the attractive smiling face in front of her and scowled. "She's never been in here."

"But have you seen her around?" Tom pleaded. "…Please try and think."

When she met his eyes a hot flush had prickled her cheeks. She hadn't even had time to do her make up properly this morning she realised; she must look a total mess. "No… I'm sorry," she responded, running her hand self-consciously through her unruly mass of hair.

Tom sighed and her heart went out to him. "I'll keep my eyes peeled though."

"Thanks," he murmured. "And I'll have a coffee please."

When Mia, the bar maid, took his coffee across to where he was sitting at a small corner table, she could see that he was miles away, staring down at the picture.

"Is she your girlfriend?" she asked, depositing the coffee mug on the cast iron table top.

"My wife," Tom told her. The tone of his voice was so sad that she'd felt like putting her arms around him and giving him a hug. More than a hug actually, she thought, desperate to tell her friend Kate about the handsome stranger with the sad eyes. He was like one of the hero's in the novels they loved to read.

"Where are you staying?" she casually asked. "So that I can tell you if I see her."

Tom scrambled in his pocket for a pen and scribbled down his mobile number, handing it to her. "Thanks, my name is Tom by the way, Tom Roberts. I haven't found anywhere to stay yet but this is my number. I'll probably be around for a day or so."

"We have rooms here," she offered brightly.

"I'll keep that in mind," smiled Tom dismissively, taking a sip of his coffee. As the first scalding mouthful hit his stomach suddenly he wished that he hadn't even ordered it. He needed to be outside searching for Grace not sitting here in this murky bar.

"I'll ring you if I see her," called the chestnut haired barmaid as he strode from the pub a few minutes later. Her offer fell on deaf ears.

With a quick glance around the small village green Tom headed for the van. He may as well take Lucky

Broken Heart Wood

with him on his search he decided. He would go to the little shop on the corner, and maybe even ask a few friendly looking passers-by if they had seen Grace. It would be good for the little dog to have a walk and his presence might kind of break the ice, make him seem more approachable.

The moody sky of earlier morning had given way to bright sunshine; it dazzled him as he turned toward the van and he blinked, narrowing his eyes and opening them again to see Lucky peering at him through the window. The little dog wasn't looking at him though he realised, he was wagging his tail at a slightly built, elderly lady, with white hair and a straight back. She was sitting on a wooden bench just across from the van, staring into space with a faraway look in her eyes.

When he opened the door Lucky leaped out and went racing across towards her, scrabbling on her knees with his front paws. "Lucky!" called Tom. "Lucky, come here…"

The old lady rubbed the backs of his ears. "He's alright," she insisted, smiling up at him.

Tom leaned down and scooped the little dog up into his arms. "He's only young," he told her. "I haven't had him long."

For a moment his eyes held hers. There was something about her, something familiar, or was it just the way that she was looking at him?

"You must be Tom Roberts," she said calmly, holding out her hand.

Tom froze, unable to take in what she was saying. "You *know* me?" he eventually managed.

She nodded. "I know *of* you."

He took her small hand; it was cool and frail. "…Through Grace," he breathed.

"Through Grace," she echoed.

"Where is she?"

"She is staying with me; at this moment in time though she's probably somewhere up the fell, or at my daughter-in-law's. Why don't you leave your van here? I'll give you a lift back to mine and you can wait there until she comes back. I'd better speak to her first though, prepare the ground so to speak. Come on, my vehicle is parked just round the corner."

"Well… if you're sure," Excitement, combined with apprehension, flooded Tom's veins as he followed her across the green towards her big silver vehicle. "But how did you know who I was?" he asked. "And is that great big pick up really yours

Broken Heart Wood

She smiled, pressing the unlock button on her keys. "It suits me," she said. "And the answer to your first question is, Quicksilver… your van, it is pretty distinctive. Come on then you'd better get in if we are to get home before Grace."

He climbed into the passenger seat with Lucky on his knee and she pressed the start button. "So how do you know about me… and about Quicksilver?" he asked, as the powerful engine roared into life. "…And how much do you know?"

Annie hesitated for a moment, remembering the story: Grace and Tom meeting at the fairground. Their young love developing and the tragic accident. "I know enough," she told him, carefully nosing the vehicle out into the road, "enough at least to know that you two need to talk."

"And Molly…?"

Tom's eyes lit up at the thought of his daughter and Annie's heart tightened. "She's fine," she said: "Bright and cute and adorable and totally fine."

"And what about… Grace…?"

Tom spoke her name in a lowered tone, hardly daring to ask, his fingers scratching the backs of Lucky's ears with a kind of fierce intensity.

"Grace is... Grace is fine too, but I think she's in limbo at the moment. I'll get her to see you and then you can talk."

"It's going to be a shock, her seeing me here like this when she thinks I'm miles away. Perhaps I should just wait at the pub and you can ask her if she wants to come and meet me there."

Annie imagined Grace's face when she told him that Tom was in the village. What if she just packed her bags and left? She was very fragile at the moment, insecure and lost. "I think you should come and meet her," she said. "I'll tell her that you're here and then leave you on your own to talk."

They drove in silence for a mile or so then Tom cleared his throat determinedly. "Did she tell you why we split up?"

For a moment Annie hesitated. She didn't want to be disloyal to Grace but she was drawn to this young man of hers and she wanted to be honest with him. "Not all of it. Not yet... I know enough though and I know that whatever it was that finally made Grace leave you must have started much sooner than that."

Tom nodded. "Everything started to go wrong... there was an accident and all our dreams went haywire."

Broken Heart Wood

Annie reached across, closing her small hand over his. "I know, she still loves you though, I'm sure of it. There's is always a way back you know, if love is still there, but it needs forgiveness too."

"I hope so, oh God I hope so," sighed Tom, "I'm not sure if she'll ever be able to forgive me though, or if I even deserve it. Oh Annie, I am so sorry for putting you in this crazy scenario. Look at me, a total stranger bearing his soul to you."

Annie just laughed. "But I don't feel as if you *are* a stranger to me so don't worry about it."

"Well I'm just glad that Grace found you," he said.

"It was a bizarre coincidence really," she told him. "Like fate…. I stopped on the motorway to help her with her car and realised that she was the daughter of my long lost and oldest friend."

She made a sweeping motion with one hand, glancing across at him before turning her attention back to her driving. "This place is her home. She may have pushed her memories of it to the back of her mind but roots go deep; it was always going to draw her back eventually, in mind if not in body."

Tom looked up towards the skyline, where the mighty fells towered majestically against a sky of clearest blue. "It's an awesome place," he said.

"A place that touches your soul," added Annie, glancing across at him. "Treat her gently won't you."

He nodded hopefully. "Of course I will… always. I just hope that she'll give me a chance at least."

Broken Heart Wood

CHAPTER FIFTEEN

Grace ran down the steep slope towards the back of Dove nest, the Allbright's grey stone built cottage, her breath coming in ragged gasps. Eager to speak to Carol she hurriedly pushed open the little wicket gate that led straight through from the fell, as it clicked shut behind her though she hesitated for a moment, overcome by the heady aroma of the flowers in Carol's beloved garden.

Ben had proudly told her, just a couple of days ago, that his wife loved her garden but however hard she worked it always ended up looking wild and free, just like her. According to Annie though it wasn't really so wild and free, for Carol spent many an hour on the flowerbeds, trying to achieve a totally natural, abandoned, cottage garden appearance.

And it worked, thought Grace, for wild flowers stood shoulder to shoulder with lupines and tiger lilies; blues and pinks and shades of yellow all vying with each other to take first place. The result was a glory of colours and scents that assailed the senses.

Broken Heart Wood

Grace took a breath and headed on across the smooth green lawn that seemed hardly able to hold its space against the abundance of blooms. One day, she decided, I am going to have a garden like this.

In her mind's eye then, for just a moment, she saw them, Tom and Molly playing happily together on their tiny lawn, just as they so often used to do. Tom would pretend to be a horse, bucketing Molly across the grass, or they would chase a bouncing ball together; they liked the red one best. She closed her eyes against the memories and a cold hand clasped her heart. Was that it then, was it to be just her and Molly now… forever. Tom must be missing his little girl much.

Closing her eyes against the thought and shivering deep inside despite the bright sunlight, she ran towards the open door of Dove nest cottage and into the cosy space of the Allbright's large kitchen.

Carol was on her hands and knees with a dustpan and brush, sweeping up what looked like a thousand tiny silver balls, rolling around on the rustic tiles whilst Molly sat at the kitchen table destroying an angel cake.

"Oh dear," cried Grace, brought suddenly back down to earth.

Broken Heart Wood

"Look mummy," announced Molly proudly, holding out the battered looking cake.

Grace took it carefully, "Oh Molly that is so clever," she told her beaming daughter.

"It was supposed to have silver balls on it," groaned Carol from under the table. "Until Molly here decided to tip them on the floor that is. I'm trying to retrieve some of the cleaner ones."

"I think you'd better just sweep them all up and put them in the bin," laughed Grace. "I'll buy you some more."

Carol clambered to her feet. "I'm not bothered about that, we just wanted the cake to look beautiful, didn't we Molly?"

"Bwootiful," crowed Molly, reaching out to grab the cake she gave Grace and taking a massive bite.

"We have some more," announced Carol. "Look!" She opened a tin to reveal a dozen fairy cakes, some were perfect and others held the proof of Molly's handiwork. "I bet you can't guess which ones your daughter decorated."

Grace laughed. "Well you've certainly been busy; I hope she hasn't been too much trouble."

"Molly… trouble… how could such a dear little mite ever be any trouble?" cried Carol, lifting the little girl up into her arms. "Come on, you put the kettle on while I clear up this mess and we'll have a cup of tea outside in the garden."

"Now that," agreed Grace. "Sounds like a good idea."

Twenty minutes later they were settled at the cedar wood table, on the patio area at the back of the cottage, with a pot of tea and a plate of the most edible looking of the fairy cakes in front of them, whilst Molly played happily with some of the boys old toys on the carefully tended grass.

Grace absorbed the beauty of the garden and was met once again by the heavy sadness that had flooded over her earlier, when she'd imagined Tom and Molly playing together on the grass.

"Did you have a nice walk?" asked Carol, sipping her tea.

Grace looked up to see concern on her usually lively face. "I love being in the wood," she said with a sight. "There's just something about it. And it takes my mind off everything else I suppose. When I'm there I hardly think about Tom... or anything."

"What are you going to do about Tom?"

Carol's question was so to the point that Grace found herself shrinking inside. "I…" she stuttered. "Well…I'm going to talk to him."

"When?"

She held Carol's gaze for a moment. "I'm hopeless aren't I?"

"Pretty hopeless, but you really do need to speak to him you know. You can't just carry on hiding."

"I thought I was healing," murmured Grace.

"Oh love…" Carol reached across and squeezed her shoulder. "You can't heal until you've faced up to the problem, dealt with it from the inside and not just covered it over."

Grace studied her fingernails. "You think I'm running away don't you.

"In a way I suppose, not that I blame you, I don't know how I would cope if I was in your shoes and it was Ben who… well, you know."

An image of Ben Allbright flashed into Grace's mind, solid and dependable. "I don't think that's likely do you?" she said.

Carol let out a heavy sigh. "And I don't suppose you thought it likely about Tom either."

For once her expression was serious and on impulse Grace took hold of her arm. "It was a bad time for both of us," she began. "I messed up and…"

"It's not your fault," cut in Carol. "I don't need to know the details to tell you that. Whatever the circumstances were he still broke your trust, the question is, do you still love each other and, bottom line, are you going to be able to forgive him?"

Grace took a breath. "I can't stop thinking about it, seeing him, you know… with her. She… she showed me pictures on her phone"

"Oh love… that's awful. And did you give Tom a chance to talk about it, to explain."

"What is there to explain?"

"Look," Carol sat up tall, an animated expression on her face. "You're besotted by Heart Wood, I realise that; I think it must be your way of dealing with everything and that's probably a good thing, but I'll make you a deal. If you promise to meet up with Tom, or at least talk to him, then I'll come with you to the library, help you scroll the Internet; do everything I can in fact to help you try and find out the story behind the wood, if that's what you want. What do you think?"

Grace blinked, trying to stem the tears that pressed against the back of her eyes. "Carol," she said quietly. "I think you're an angel."

"Well," Carol laughed, patting her generous stomach. "A bit of an unlikely looking angel to be sure, but thank you anyway. So you'll take me up on my deal… you'll speak to Tom tonight?"

"Tonight," agreed Grace with a smile. "I promise."

*

As she walked slowly along the lane, hand in hand with Molly, Grace realised that she felt better than she had done in days. She had a plan now, a way forward. She would speak to Tom, without getting over emotional, and then throw herself into her quest to find out more about the truth behind Heart Wood, whilst she decided what to do next. Could she forgive him? An image of his face flashed into her mind, those ever-changeable eyes, holding hers, his firm suntanned hands on Quicksilver's reins.

Emotion flooded over her in a suffocating tide. She would love Tom Roberts forever, there was no doubt in her mind about that, but not if she could no longer trust him. And did he really want her to forgive him, even if she could, or had he already moved on and it was just Molly he was missing…

How could he have let her down like that anyway, when she was in such a bad place… or perhaps it was his way of punishing her for destroying their lives?

"Come on Mummy."

Molly tugged at her hand and Grace took a gulp of air. There was more in this than just the two of them though; there was Molly's future to think about too.

"Sorry sweetheart."

Reaching down she scooped her daughter up into her arms, holding her close. "Let's go and see Annie."

"Ann..ee," announced Molly solemnly, her little face lighting up. "Wabbits," she cried. "See Wabbits."

"Rabbits it is," smiled Grace, hoisting her onto one hip and slinging her bag over the opposite shoulder. Whatever happened, she decided, Molly must always come first.

Grace entered the garden at Hillcrest from the back, taking the shortcut that led across the bottom of the fell, as Annie had known she would. As she opened the gate she hesitated, looking further down into the valley for a moment, towards Fellclose, the farm where she was born. She hadn't plucked up the courage yet, to go there, especially after Annie told her that it had been made into holiday cottages. Her memories were of her grandmother sitting with her knitting on the porch and of their sheepdog, Rusty, a red and white collie, running for the ball. It was a yellow ball, she remembered, and after they'd finished with it she always had to make sure that she handed it back to her gran, to be placed in a corner of the big kitchen drawer.

Everything had its place in her grandmother's house, perhaps that is why her mother had to leave; maybe if *she* had been a little more forgiving then Sarah would have felt that she could have stayed with Sam. There again, what about her father, Donald Bryant; what had he ever done to deserve being abandoned by his wife and child?

She tried to imagine his charming smile and expressive, sparkling eyes. He loved her in his own way, she was sure of that, but perhaps she'd been too much her mother's daughter for him to give her the kind of love he had for his new children. She would write to him, she decided, or ring him up. It wasn't fair to lay all the blame at his door. After all, he had never really done anything wrong, apart from marrying the wrong girl perhaps and how many luckless men did that.

Molly sat heavily on Grace's hip, thumb in mouth and eyes half closed. "Come on sweetheart," she murmured, placing her lips against the baby softness of the little girl's skin. "Let's go and see what Annie's doing."

*

It was the scent she noticed first, the heady aroma of spices and pine trees, deeply masculine and painfully familiar. Annie appeared from the front sitting room; she caught Grace's eye and glanced away, fingering the heavy woollen fabric of her tartan skirt. "Ah… Grace," she began. "You are back… I…"

"Tom's here isn't he?"

Annie's eyes were misty she noticed, feeling strangely detached; it was almost as if she was seeing the old lady's kind, worried face, through someone else's eyes.

"I saw his van," Annie told her. "…In the village. I'm so sorry… I should have asked you first."

"Where is he?"

Her voice too belonged to a stranger; her feet were glued to the floor

Annie motioned through the door behind her just as it opened and then there he was. Tom, her Tom, filling the hallway with his smile, comfortably familiar and yet still a million miles away.

"Daddy!" shrieked Molly.

He reached out his arms for his child and Grace's whole body went limp as her own self zoomed back into place. A shiver began deep down in the core of her, vibrating through her limbs and turning her legs into jelly.

"Here…"

She heard the concern in Annie's voice and wanted to reassure her, to tell her that it was all right for Tom to be here. It was just the shock that was all. Her tongue stuck firmly to the roof of her mouth though and her legs refused to move.

Tom held Molly close, staring at Grace with a hungry longing and for just a moment she stared back, drowning in his glorious eyes. Had they always been so beautiful she found herself wondering, with the same weird sense of detachment. It wasn't fair for a man to have eyes like that. A giggle began deep down in her throat; the room around her seemed to move, losing its form, and her hand went to her throat.

"I think you'd better sit down Grace." His voice filled her ears, deeply melodic and so, so familiar.

Annie took her arm and led her though into the sitting room. Her feet unglued themselves from the floor with reluctance. Was it really her, Grace Roberts, who was collapsing into Annie's floral patterned easy chair, or was this all just a dream?

"A nice cup of tea, that's what we need," announced Annie.

What was this strange belief that tea could cure all ills, Grace found herself wondering? And then they were alone, the three of them, Grace, Tom and Molly Roberts... a family. But they weren't a family any more were they. A pain settled deep inside her, a heavy lonely pain that dragged at her heart.

"How did you find us?"

Her voice was a broken whisper. She reached inside herself for some of the anger she'd felt earlier, wanting to shout at him, to yell, to scream. All she could find though was the aching emptiness.

"Mick saw you, in Meredale. I just came to search for you but then I saw the sign to Greythwaite and remembered the name. Annie saw my van there... She brought me here, to see you."

"And she told you everything I suppose?"

He lowered his eyes, his expression guarded. "We had a chat and... Oh God Grace I'm so sorry."

"Sorry," her lips curled on the word. "How can sorry even start to cover it...?" And then finally the anger was released, in a torrent of pain and humiliation and blame.

Broken Heart Wood

"For months I thought that everything was my fault, because of Silver. I lived with that guilt Tom and all the time you… all the time…?"

"Tea's here," announced Annie in a meaningful tone.

Grace snapped back to now. Molly's wide eyes staring at her in dismay as she clung to her father.

"Now why don't I take Molly to see Lucky whilst you two have a nice chat," said Annie. It was a command, not a question.

"Lucky?" echoed Grace, her white-hot anger draining away.

Tom smiled, placing Molly gently back down onto the floor. "Ah yes, of course. We have a dog, Grace, the cutest little white dog you ever saw. He's in the van. Molly will love him I know… and so will you."

Grace so much wanted to know all about the dog but she feigned indifference. They had always intended to get another dog after their old Border collie, Kyp, died, just before… before Quicksilver. So why had he got one now when she wasn't there to help choose it, and where had it come from? She caught her breath as a sharp pain stabbed deep. Had *she* helped him choose it?

Pushing aside the jumble of questions that begged to be answered, she ushered Molly towards Annie. "You go with Annie, sweetheart, to see the dog."

Now was not the time for questions. But what was it the time for then, recriminations... blame?

As the old lady and the little girl left the room hand in hand, uncomfortably aware of Tom's close proximity, Grace reached forward to take the teapot handle, trying to control the tremble in her fingers as she focussed her attention on the simple task of pouring tea. She clung onto her china cup like a lifeline as she sipped the scalding liquid.

Tom's uneasy cough reverberated in the heavy silence between them. "Grace," his voice was pleading, tight with emotion. "Say something, *please*."

She didn't dare meet his eyes. "What is there left to say? It's over, everything we had together is gone... thanks to you"

Reaching across he took hold of her hand; it sat limply within his but at least she didn't pull it away. "You know that's not true," he said, his voice breaking. "I don't know what Mary said to you but it's not what you think. Please Grace; let me tell you the truth."

"You were my best friend," she said simply, meeting his eyes for just a moment. "I thought I knew you so well, but I was wrong. It's all gone now Tom. Trust has gone and without that we have nothing."

"Daddy... daddy!"

Broken Heart Wood

Molly's high-pitched cry reached them before she did. Grace lifted her chin and sat up straight, forcing a smile onto her face as the door burst open.

"Sorry," Annie's apologetic voice followed the little girl in through the door. "She just ran off and my old legs aren't what they used to be."

"Come see dog daddy," cried Molly, tugging at Tom's hand.

"Go on," urged Grace. "Go with her. We'll talk later."

He stood up in one smooth motion, filling the room. "I think Lucky likes you already," he smiled, reaching down to pick her up, before looking back hopefully at Grace. "Is mummy coming too?"

A knife twisted in Grace's chest and she looked down at the floor. "Mummy will wait here with Annie," she said quietly."

After they had left the room seemed bleakly empty, Grace felt bleakly empty.

Annie was the first to speak. "Are you annoyed with me for bringing Tom here?"

Grace shook her head slowly. "No, of course not; it was inevitable I suppose that he would find me eventually and I know we need to talk. It was a shock that's all."

The old lady reached out her hand, gently stroking the hair back from Grace's brow in a comforting, motherly gesture. "Why don't I mind Molly for a bit," she suggested. "And maybe you two can go for a drive or something? Tom will need a lift to collect his van anyway."

"No!" Grace recoiled from the idea, afraid of her own reactions if they were in such close proximity. She had to keep herself detached.

"Well then arrange to meet up with him in a more public place. A pub perhaps, somewhere where you can talk things through properly... You need to do it for Molly's sake, if not for your own."

Grace nodded. "I know," she agreed. "You're right; I'll suggest it when he comes back."

****

Relief glowed in Tom's eyes when he realised that maybe there was still a thread of hope. "I'll pick you up," he offered eagerly when she suggested meeting up.

"No!" Grace's eyes met his and slid reluctantly away. For one giddy moment she felt seventeen again, back at the fair ground where they first met. Her heart thumped in the base of her throat. Excitement fluttered beneath her rib cage. This was crazy. Whatever was she thinking?

"No!" she repeated anger and hurt flooding back as the images on Mary's phone flooded her mind's eye. "…We have things to sort out, I know that, but I'll meet you there."

"Where…?"

His expression was lighter, more hopeful she noted but she knew that it was just for Molly?

"Just through the village, on the road to Meredale: There's a little country pub called The Highwayman. I'll meet you there later."

"Seven thirty?"

She nodded, already turning away. "If I can get Molly to bed by then… say goodbye to daddy darling."

The little girl ran towards him, arms outstretched. He scooped her up; swinging her round and planting a kiss on the smooth soft skin of her cheek, before placing her gently back down onto the ground. When she clung to his leg, refusing to let go, for just a moment his eyes found Grace's again.

Determinedly hardening her heart against him, she took a firm hold of Molly's small hand. "Come on sweetheart… you'll see Daddy again soon."

"Want daddy," Molly screamed as Tom walked out of the cottage and across the yard to where Annie was waiting. When the latch on the garden gate clicked shut behind him he could still hear her screaming his name.

On the short journey back to get his van, Annie said very little, but when they reached the village green she switched off the engine and climbed down from the pick up. Tom was expecting a lecture, so when she just reached up and give him a brief hug, he felt a rush of relief.

"It's between you and Grace," she told him. "So I won't interfere. If you really do still love her though, then please don't give up on her, she's just hurting right now and she needs some time... Oh, and if you hurt her any more than you already have, then you'll have me to answer to."

*

As Annie drove away Tom just sat in his van, the ache behind his eyes filling his whole head. Lucky scrambled all over him as if aware of his emotion and he held the little dog close. Oh what a fool he'd been, throwing everything away by being naïve and stupid; he who had always prided himself on being strong... And he couldn't blame it all on Mary; she obviously had serious issues but he had fed them by allowing her to integrate so closely into their lives.

Broken Heart Wood

That awful night, when Grace had woken up hating him and he'd got back in such a state, must have obviously been the trigger for her to try and make her crazy dreams real. He should have seen what was happening with her though, long before that... and he should never have let himself rely on such an impressionable young girl in the first place.

Pressing his forehead against the steering wheel, his mind went back to Grace, in that awful moment when she'd opened her eyes and looked at him for the first time in weeks, looked into his face and cried out in terror. It had felt a though his whole world had stopped, and so what had he done... gone home and got blind drunk. He would never forgive himself for that.

And the very next day, when he'd gone to the hospital with Molly, flooded with guilt and self-loathing; it was just how the doctor had said it might be... a very different story.

She'd opened her beautiful eyes, just like the night before, but this time they had held so much love that it had torn him apart; and the first thing she said, as tears rolled down her cheeks... was 'sorry.' It was him who should have been saying sorry.

He'd wanted to tell her, right there and then, about Mary, to put things straight. That would have been pure selfishness though, to relieve *his* guilt. Grace had needed love and reassurance and so much help. He would tell her when the time was right, he'd silently promised, when she was well again. Somehow though the right time had never come... and now it was all too late and she might never look at him with love in her eyes, ever again.

Sitting up he felt a sudden surge of strength. Feeling sorry for himself would get him nowhere, he knew that, he needed to talk to her, to make her understand... to prove his love and to prove himself.

"Never give up boy," he sad to Lucky, who was desperately trying to lick his face. "...That's the secret. Grace can't have just stopped loving me just like that; it's not possible. And somehow I just have to make her see that,"

***

For Grace, after Tom left, the rest of the day dragged. Moments of anticipation were interspersed by long, desolate periods of apprehension. She wanted to see Tom so much and yet, at the same time, she couldn't help wishing that he was still a hundred miles away. What was she going to say to him, the soul mate who had turned into a cheating stranger overnight?

"Be business-like and mature," suggested Annie. "Keep your distance, let him have his say and try not to get emotional."

Well that *sounded* all well and good, realised Grace, but since when could she be with Tom and not get emotional?

Molly splashed happily in a shallow bath whilst she showered and changed, debating for almost twenty minutes over what to wear; not that she had much choice, for the casual items she had thrown into a bag on the day she left were all she had, and they were mostly just jeans and tee shirts.

As she carefully applied lipstick and mascara and dusted a little blusher onto her sun-bronzed skin, a knock came on the door. It creaked gently open to reveal Annie, tentatively holding out a lovely, silky crimson top.

"I thought you might like to try this," she said, holding it out. "It was present I've never worn. Red isn't really my colour but I think it might suit you."

Touched by the old lady's generous gesture, Grace smiled. "Thank you, I'll try it on… not that I care about impressing Tom of course."

"Obviously not," agreed Annie, raising her eyebrows. "But it gives a girl confidence to know that she looks good."

"You always look good Annie," Grace told her, holding the top up against her. "What do you think?"

"I think that I was blessed to find you on the motorway that day: To think that our paths might never have crossed."

"It must have been fate," smiled Grace.

"And maybe it was fate that I also saw your Tom's van in the square today."

The breath caught in Grace's throat. "Do you like him, Annie?" she asked quietly?

"Yes…" Annie hesitated for a moment. "Yes, I do like him. Who wouldn't?"

By the time Grace was ready to leave it was obvious that there was no way Molly was ready for bed.

"Just leave her with me, she'll she fine," insisted Annie.

Grace shook her head doubtfully and when the little girl started to cry as she kissed her goodbye she reached for her cell phone. "I'll just have to ring Tom and cancel. I can speak to him tomorrow."

"No." Annie lifted Molly up onto her knee. "She'll be as right as rain as soon as you've gone, I'm sure of it, and I think your meeting with Tom is more than overdue don't you? We'll manage won't we poppet."

"Want daddy," wailed Molly.

Grace dropped down onto one knee beside her. "You can see daddy tomorrow darling. Be a good girl for Annie now."

"Me come wiv you," announced Molly determinedly.

When plump tears rolled down the little girl's cheeks, Annie just held her close. "Now why don't we get some crayons and paper to draw a nice picture for when your mummy gets back" she suggested.

As Grace stood fingering her phone, not wanting to leave, a chatter of happy voices floated in through the half open window and suddenly the kitchen door burst open to reveal a mass of Allbrights.

"We've walked here across the fell," announced Tim.

"That's obvious," laughed Annie. "Your face is a red as your hair."

"I think mine must be too," groaned Carol, holding out a large bunch of freshly cut blooms. "Now where can I find a vase and I'll arrange these for you."

"Grace is just about to go and meet Tom," remarked Annie, raising her eyebrows. Carol stopped in her tracks, looking round with a broad smile. "That was quick work. Go on then, off you go, you may as well get it over with."

Grace hung back. "It's Molly," she explained. "She's being a pain and I don't want to leave her with Annie if she's going to be hard work."

Carol made the chuffing sound that her whole family knew so well. No one questioned Carol Allbright when she had her determined head on. She shook her hands towards the door in a shooing motion. "Well we're here now so off you go."

Grace looked at Annie, who shrugged in response. "Better do as she says," cut in Tim with a broad grin. "Or else you'll cop it."

As the door of Fellclose clicked shut behind her, Grace felt as if she was stepping back into another world, a world where fear and pain stood side by side with a longing that left her weak. 'Be business-like and mature,' Annie had advised. 'Keep your distance and try not to get emotional.'

She took a deep breath, jangling her car keys on the end of her finger and lifting her chin. And that is exactly what she was going to do

Broken Heart Wood

CHAPTER SIXTEEN

Grace glanced up as the sign above her head creaked, swinging slightly on the balmy evening breeze. A dark figure wearing a wide brimmed hat clung to the neck of a rearing horse. A horse's head raised in fear... the past rose up to greet her as if it happened just yesterday. For a moment she hesitated, trying to control her shallow breathing, until suddenly Annie's words filled her mind, *'Just stay calm and business-like.'*

With a surge of confidence placed her hand against the door, pushing it open. It was over, she realised that, and the sooner she came to terms with it the better. All they needed to do right now was to sort out some details and plan for a future apart. With a determined stride she stepped into the gloomy interior of the low ceilinged, old-fashioned pub, just as the highwayman it was named for must have done all those years ago, she thought.

She saw Tom at once. A sliver of sunshine had managed to find its way in through the small window behind him, turning his dark blonde hair to gold. A hand tightened around her heart and she stopped in her tracks, shaking inside. Who was she kidding, she couldn't do this. And then he was beside her, ushering her over to the secluded corner table he had found, his hand under her elbow, burning her skin.

"…Drink?"

His eyes were soft, their colour hazy. His long tanned fingers rested lightly on the table-top beside hers.

"…Grace," he said.

She nodded, unable to look at him. "Yes…"

"A drink, what would you like to drink?"

A frown puckered her forehead. Were they now such strangers that he'd already forgotten what she liked to drink. Once he would have just ordered it without even needing to ask.

"I'll have a gin and tonic please."

Her voice sounded ridiculously loud, its northern twang grating. She drummed her fingers on the table as he walked across to the bar, desperately trying to remember her opening sentence. 'I am not coming back to Ivy cottage… ever, so we need to sort out what we are going to do about Molly,' that was it. She repeated the words silently to herself over and over. And then he would probably say. 'But you have to come back Grace, it was all just a terrible mistake,' and she would respond in a calm detached voice and not let herself be drawn into an emotional wrangle.

She took a deep breath, squaring her shoulders as he walked back towards her. The ice tinkled in her glass as he placed it in front of her. The tonic fizzed and sparkled just as his eyes did as they searched for and found hers. She looked away determinedly, picking up the glass and taking a large gulp. The bubbles made her splutter.

"Hey... steady on," smiled Tom, sipping his pint of Guinness. A froth of foam left a white moustache on his upper lip. She reached out automatically to brush it away, retracting her hand as if it had been scorched. He grabbed it before she could return it to the table-top.

"This is *us* Grace... you and me... remember?"

"No!" she cried, pulling her hand away. "There is no *us* anymore, you took care of that."

Her heart was pounding in her ears. This wasn't how it was supposed to be.

"It was a stupid mistake, Grace." His eyes, locked onto hers. "...And what she told you was a lie."

"A lie?" she repeated, remembering how Mary had pushed the phone in her face. "She showed me the pictures, Tom, so just stop lying."

Broken Heart Wood

"I was drunk," he groaned. "Too drunk to even know what was going on... she tricked me."

An inner strength came suddenly from nowhere, fuelled by anger. "She told me everything Tom. Told me how you fell in love when I was in the hospital... and how you only stayed with me through a sense of responsibility and pity?"

He lowered his head in such shame that she almost felt a prickle of sympathy. His voice was little more than a whisper. "No... it wasn't like that. That night, when you finally opened your eyes..." His whole body shuddered. "I thought I'd lost you Grace. I went home and stupidly got blind drunk. Mary was there, she was looking after Molly... I never realised how she felt about me though, if I had then I swear I'd.... I just thought she was being kind..."

"...Kind!" Grace struggled to contain her emotions, taking slow deep breaths. "You got drunk and obviously slept with someone else, Tom, when I was in the hospital. And just because *you* can't remember anything does not mean that nothing happened... So perhaps she is telling the truth and maybe you did have sex with her."

"No Grace," he pleaded. "You have to believe me. She took the pictures when I was unconscious because she *wanted* us to be a couple. It was all in her sick imagination."

There were tears in his eyes she noted, feeling strangely detached. "I thought we were special Tom," she said quietly. "And I really believed that we were forever. Maybe if you'd talked to me even… told me truth, then we might have had a chance, but now…"

"…Please listen to me, Grace, at least let me explain. Surely you owe me that."

Grace's voice was cold and calm, isolated from emotion." I owe you nothing, Tom. I took the whole blame for Quicksilver on my shoulders. For months after I came home I thought you were distant with me because you blamed me too… blamed me for losing our dream. I felt so very guilty for what happened that day and yet all the time…"

Desperately she tried to cling on to her composure. "…All the time it was you who was guilty. Can't you see Tom; this has nothing to do with what you actually did, it's about what you didn't do. And I really do believe that I could have forgiven you almost anything, if only you'd shared it with me and told me what you were going through… We've never had secrets before."

"I know that… and I wanted to tell you. I tried so many times to tell you but I could never find the right words. I love you Grace and I didn't want you to hurt any more than you'd already been hurt. You must realise though, that no matter what happens to us... you are the only woman I will ever love."

He took her two hands in his then and feeling drained of all emotion, for a moment she let them lie there. "At least give me a chance," he begged. "Let me tell you the whole truth now, right from the beginning. Or would you rather believe *her* crazy lies?"

Grace withdrew her hands, twisting them together as she studied the bubbles in her glass. "Okay then, tell me," she agreed. "But not here, we can go outside."

***

They sat at a table in a secluded corner of the pub's beer garden looking, to any casual observer, like a normal young couple enjoying a drink together when in fact they were anything but. An awkward silence fell between them as they self-consciously sipped their drinks. Tom looked into the distance, unable now to meet her eyes.

"Look Grace," he began. "I am not trying to make excuses because I know that there are no excuses. It was just..." His voice broke as the memories flooded in. "...After the accident, when you were in the hospital, I was just so afraid for you, so afraid that you weren't coming back. I really tried to keep it together, not just for us but for Molly too, she needed some stability.

I coped at first I really did, with all the horses going and everything. That was the worst; watching all our dreams crumble. The only thing that was really important though was that you were going to be okay; it was all I ever thought of and it was all that kept me going."

He lowered his eyes then, running a hand through his hair. It flopped back heavily across his brow and he pushed it impatiently aside. "Obviously Mary was still here then, working," he went on. "She helped out. She looked after Molly when I was at the hospital and she cooked and spoke to owners and answered the phone… There wasn't a hint of anything other than that I swear. I needed you so much, Grace, needed to know that you were going to be all right. They told me to expect the worst. They said that you were hanging on to life by a thread and if you did come out of the coma then I should be prepared for…"

For a moment he closed his eyes. "They told me that you might have some degree of brain damage, that you might be handicapped in some way or have personality changes. I sat with you; hour after hour I held your hand. I prayed Grace, I prayed and prayed and I waited for you to come back to me. I was so sure that you were going to be all right... so sure of us. It was the only thing that got me through it, that certainty... And then you opened your eyes and..."

He plunged his head into his hands, his words suddenly evaporating.

"And what Tom...?" Grace's voice was just a whisper.

He looked up at her, his eyes dark with pain. "You looked at me. After all the waiting, finally you opened your eyes and looked at me. You didn't know me though Grace... you didn't know who I was and you were afraid of me."

She almost reached out to touch him, feeling his pain, but she drew her hand back. "And then?"

He coughed loudly, clearing his throat. "I went back home. I don't know how I got there. I can't even remember driving. Molly was in bed and Mary was waiting for me. She'd made food but I couldn't eat it. I felt as if I was in some kind of weird limbo where my whole world had finally turned on its head. I just kept on seeing your eyes, a stranger's eyes staring out at me from your face. She poured me a whisky. It felt like an escape so I had another and another."

He reached out his hand to her but Grace ignored him, concentrating all her attention on the white knuckles of her tightly linked fingers. "Go on."

"She was sitting next to me on the sofa. She refilled my glass again and I remember feeling distant, woozy and strange. The warmth of her body pressed against mine. For a moment it felt good, having someone close… And then she kissed me."

A sharp pain ripped at Grace's guts. "And then…? Tell me the truth Tom."

Feeling sick, he dropped his head into his hands, unable to look at her.

"Please… she begged.

"For a moment," he admitted. "For just a single moment, I started to kiss her back… But then I realised what was happening, Grace. I pushed her away from me and I tried to stand up. My legs wouldn't hold me though and everything was going around in circles. The next thing that I vaguely remember was her laughing as she helped me up the stairs. After that everything is just a total blank… until the next morning."

Grace gripped firmly onto the sides of her seat. She wanted so much to just get up and go but she had to know. "Tell me the rest, Tom, she insisted, her voice like ice.

Tom looked at her, his eyes burning into hers, trying to convince her that he was telling her the truth. "The next thing I knew it was daylight. I was in bed, I was naked and my head was pounding so hard that I thought it might burst. I ran to the bathroom to be sick in the toilet and suddenly there she was, standing beside me wrapped in a towel. She handed me a drink. She said it was for my hangover, and then she started going on about how awesome last night had been and she showed me the pictures on her phone. I told her that she was delusional, that nothing had happened between us but she wouldn't stop, Grace. She just kept brandishing the photographs at me.

She told me that she'd given Molly her breakfast and put her down for a nap so that we could talk... then she dropped the towel down onto the floor and stood there, naked, I reached for it, pushed it at her and told her to cover herself up, but she just smiled at me. 'It was inevitable Tom,' she said, '...just a matter of time. We love each other and I know you feel guilty about it right now but you can't help who you fall in love with. We can be a real family now... you, me and Molly.'

Broken Heart Wood

*

A heavy silence fell between them as Grace fought to deal with what Tom had just told her. "So what did you do?" she eventually asked.

*

"She went downstairs. I washed and dressed... and then I went down to the kitchen and told her to get her things and leave right away. She kept on saying that we were in love and it was no good fighting it. I told her, again, that she was delusional and it was all in her head and I said that I'd pay her one month's wages if she left right away."

Grace's face was ashen "And did she... leave I mean?"

"Yes she did, but it didn't end there. She text me and when I blocked her number she kept sending me letters. I just burned them all without opening them. And then... amazingly, you came home and I let you down yet again... I should have told you the truth there and then, I realise that now, but you were just so weak and vulnerable."

Grace sat motionless, silent tears rolling slowly down her cheeks. "I think I've heard enough now Tom," she said quietly, standing up.

He reached out for her hand, gripping it tightly. "But what about us Grace… can you ever forgive me?"

Gently she disentangled her hand from his. "I need time to think. It's all just too much to take in."

"Do you still love me then, at all? Please give me that at least."

"It's not about loving you, Tom." Her voice was calm and firm. "It's about trust… and forgiveness. You tell me that you don't *really* know what happened between you and Mary that night and, let's face it, you probably never will. It's your word against hers and she has the pictures.

I do believe what you say about being blind drunk, but maybe, deep down, you don't really want to remember what actually happened. So unless I can truly forgive you, for everything, then the not really knowing will tear us apart. Loving is easy Tom, it's truly forgiving that's so hard."

"Grace," he called, as she turned to go. "…You said earlier that it wasn't what I did it was what I didn't do. And what I didn't do was to talk to you Grace, so please… hear me now, just for a few more minutes."

She hesitated, looking back at him.

Broken Heart Wood

"When you first came home from the hospital," he began. "You needed time just to heal. And I was there for you with that... wasn't I?"

When she nodded he carried on speaking quickly, as if to get it all out in case she walked away. "...And then, when you got well again, we just got on with trying to rebuild our lives didn't we. As if we were both afraid to really talk about what had happened."

Grace took a breath, wanting wanted to say 'and whose fault was that,' but she bit back the words. "...Tell me now then," she said. "Tell me how *you* felt, because all I felt was pain and fear and a terrible guilt for being the one who destroyed our dreams."

Tom closed his eyes for a second, his jaw tightly clenched. "When I saw Silver that day, lying dead on the tarmac... and then you, in the hospital, so pale and silent, like a ghost, it was as if I'd been plunged into a crazy nightmare.

Silver was gone, our dreams were gone and one by one the horses were all gone. If you had been with me then I would have dealt with it better, but you were lying at death's door... I needed you *so* much Grace. And then, when you finally opened your eyes, you thought I was a monster."

Grace stepped towards him and sank back down onto her chair. "I can't deal with this right now Tom," she said quietly. "I know how you suffered too, and I know we should have been able to talk about it, but can't you see? I blamed *myself* for Silver, for not setting off at a different time... for not doing thigs differently. And I have blamed myself all this time for our lack of communication, when really it was just you, harbouring your own guilt."

He reached out to her. "Please Grace... I have never stopped loving you and I never will, no matter what you decide to do. All I want is for the three of us to start over and be a proper family again with no more secrets... you me and Molly."

"Oh Tom..." She held his eyes in hers for just a moment. "I really am going to go now. I need to check on Molly... and I need some time to try and sort this mess out inside my head, No matter what happens though, I'm telling you now... I will never go back to Ivy Cottage."

Tom's eyes brightened, as if a light had suddenly been lit inside him. "So there is still a chance for us?"

"Honestly… I don't know. I need some space Tom, and there's still something unfinished here that I need to see through, so please don't pressurise me. And I'd like us to maybe try and learn how to be friends again first, like we used to be. You can come and see Molly at Annie's, take her out if you like… and then we'll just have to see."

***

Annie was watching out for Grace. As soon as she walked in the old lady got up and ushered her to a chair. "You look as if you need to sit down," she said. "Do you want to talk about it?

"Oh Annie…" Grace lowered her head into her hands, she'd felt so strong and calm when she'd been with Tom but now… "I do still love him," she admitted, "…I can't not love him; I don't know if I'll ever be able to trust him again though… or forgive him."

"You need to just give it time," Annie told her. "I know it's a bit cliché but time really is a good healer."

Grace nodded, looking up at her. "That's what I told him. I said that he could come and see Molly, maybe even take her out, but we need to just learn to be friends again first. We used to be such good friends you see, so close… of course that's only if it's okay with you for me to stay here a bit longer though."

Leaning down the old lady gave her a quick hug. "Oh Grace, you remind me so much of your mother. Of course it's okay. You can stay here for as long as you like and I know that you're pretty set on trying to solve the mystery of Heart Wood, so maybe you should make that your goal. Become friends with Tom but don't even think about anything more until after that. And it's not really about what he did or didn't do you know; we all sometimes make mistakes and stupid choices. What really matters is if you can find it in your heart to forgive him, warts and all. That's what really counts. Now, why don't you nip up and check on Molly. She was sleeping sweetly when I checked on her just before you got back. I'll make you a nice cup of tea and a bit of supper?"

"I can do it when I come down," Grace offered.

Annie shook her head. "Thanks, it's fine though I've got it all ready. I knew you'd be feeling fraught and there's nothing like a bit of comfort food to calm the nerves."

***

Just looking at Molly's contented face, flushed with sleep, brought everything into perspective for Grace. Molly was their future, hers and Tom's; they owed it to her to at least try and make some sense of all this. She might not yet be ready to make any firm commitments about their future, and she might never be ready, but she was prepared to try and remain open minded about it.

***

Grace hadn't thought she was hungry until Annie placed a plate of thick beef sandwiches in front of her. Half a dozen bites later however she pushed her plate aside, reaching for her tea. "I'm so sorry Annie," she said, "...when you've gone to all this trouble. My mouth just feels as if it's full of cotton wool."

Annie smiled. "Don't worry yourself, the sandwiches will keep. Now that you're settled though I need to tell you; I've finally finished reading your story."

"Grace could feel her heart thumping inside her chest. "And what did you think?"

"I think you're amazing" she said, reaching across to grip her hand. "... Oh Grace, why didn't you tell me about Quicksilver and that terrible accident? It's no wonder your lives have gone so wrong; no one can go through all that heartache and trauma without something suffering. I just wish you'd opened up to me sooner. You've had to go through all this on your own."

Broken Heart Wood

"It's was bad for both of us," said Grace honestly. "Being a top show jumper was Tom's dream, our dream, but we couldn't go on after… everything."

"But you're both still so young; you have lots of time ahead of you to work through all this."

Grace's response was immediate. "I'm not so sure. He was my soulmate you see, or at least I thought he was. Now I'm not sure if we can ever get that back. Anyway, I'm going to do as you suggested and focus on the secret of Heart Wood. When I've unravelled its mystery then I'll be ready to try and move on, one way or the other."

"But you will still do as you said; you know, try and at least retrieve your friendship with Tom?"

Grace nodded. "Yes, I really want to do that, for Molly, and for me too I guess… there'll be no pressure then."

***

Half an hour later, having said good night to Anne, Grace sat on the side of the bed where Molly was snuggled down beneath the floral duvet, her little face only just visible. As she leaned down to place a tender kiss on the little girl's smooth forehead, she felt an unexpected sense of peace.

Broken Heart Wood

She had finally met up with Tom. It had been painful, heart breakingly so, and yet in a way also somehow cathartic. For now though, at least everything was out in the open, which meant that, hopefully, she would be able to find a way forward again... in what direction though she wasn't yet sure.

Beyond her bedroom window the fell-side loomed, appearing silver in the moonlight. Against its bulk she could just make out the dark, mysterious heart shape of the wood; to her it wasn't mysterious though, to her it felt as if it held the key to her future. She knew that perhaps it was a crazy thing to think, maybe even a kind of obsession, but it had helped to take her mind away from her troubles and for that she was grateful.

Because of her preoccupation with its secrets she had a goal, some breathing space before she faced her future. An image of Tom's face flashed unbidden into her mind, his expression so serious and quietly determined when he rode his beloved horses. Had they given up on their dreams so easily because of the tragic loss of Quicksilver though, or because he wanted his dreams to be with someone else?

She didn't believe that, or at least she didn't want to, but it was such doubts that made it so hard for her to be able to forgive him.

Broken Heart Wood

CHAPTER SEVENTEEN

As Grace left civilization behind and headed up the rough steep slope, the sense of peace she'd felt the night before returned, replacing the nagging ache that had been lodged in her heart since Molly had run own the path to meet Tom that morning, eager to spend the weekend with her daddy and Lucky.

It had been kind of odd to watch them drive away together, giggling and laughing as they waved her goodbye. For a moment she had longed to go with them, back to the life she had lost… but it wasn't there anymore was it, that life. And she would never go back to Ivy cottage.

For a moment she stopped her furious climb, to ease her aching legs, looking back down the slope. Tiny houses, tiny figures, tiny lives, spread all along the bottom of the valley and a further up, below Heart Wood, standing solid like a part of the landscape, was a magnificent old house. Someone very grand must have once lived there she thought, living a very different kind of life from the rest of the community.

Taking a breath she carried on climbing, thinking what a crazy place this world of ours was with all its ups and downs. Every day was a game of chance. Sometimes it was difficult to understand how anyone ever dared to get up in the morning for fear of what might happen. Look at her for instance; she had set off on her ride that fateful afternoon, never guessing for a second that it was to be the last day of Silver's life and the end of her life as she knew it.

Her fingernails bit into the balls of her thumbs and she closed her eyes tightly, humming a tune, trying to think about what Molly might be doing now, anything to block out the sudden vision of the silver stallion's once proud body lying in a motionless mound on the tarmac.

Last night she had opened up her heart to Annie, finally unburdening herself of some of the pain that was hidden deep inside. When she'd tried to explain to her about her own guilt and how Tom had let her down however, the old lady had placed a sympathetic hand on hers, looking at her with a weight of sadness behind her eyes.

"People do things for many reasons," she said. "We are all vulnerable you know, however strong we may seem on the surface, and I know it really has nothing to do with me but, before you judge him too harshly, maybe try standing in his shoes, just to get a different perspective.

Grace had looked up at Annie then, suddenly knowing. "You've spoken to him haven't you... about everything?"

Annie smiled softly, nodding her white head. "Not everything at all, only enough to try and understand. He loves you Grace, he really does, but if you want a future together you need to find a way to forgive him and forget what has happened

Thoughts circled around in Grace's head as she forced her tired legs on up the steep slope. Her father had never really forgiven her mother, even though he had appeared too on the surface. She realised that now and she didn't want her relationship to end up bitter and blaming, like theirs.

As she headed towards the shivering greens of the trees up ahead, the wind suddenly buffeted against her, taking her breath. She sucked in air, filling her lungs with a gulp of its sharp clarity. *This* was true reality, she decided, this place where nothing ever changed for centuries, where the person who planted the wood once strode, all their experiences and emotions now lost in time.

They weren't really lost though she realised, for there was still Heart Wood and the tiny headstone, placed there perhaps as a testament to something special. And this very afternoon she and Carol were about to embark upon their quest to find out the truth by going to the library in Meredale.

It was almost lunchtime when Grace burst in through the kitchen door of Dove nest. Carol looked round with a smile, drying her hands on her green and white checked pinafore, her wild red hair a bright halo around her plump, pretty face. "So do you feel better now?" she asked.

Grace nodded. "Heart Wood always makes me feel better, it's weird."

Carol reached for the kettle, turning on the tap at the sink. "Well maybe there's some kind of spirit there that bonds with you."

Grace nodded again, moving her head slowly up and down as she pondered the thought. Carol may be only joking but she couldn't help thinking of the small marble headstone with its brief, moving message, '*Goodbye my love.*' She hadn't told her about that.

"Are you still coming to the library with me?" she asked eagerly.

"Yes, of course." Carol motioned towards the table. "I've left a cold lunch for Ben and Andy... I thought we could stop somewhere for ours on the way."

She pulled her phone from her pocket, putting it to her ear. "We're off now love," she said. "I'll see you later, lunch is on the table and the kettle's boiled."

Grace listened, envying her comfortable, secure relationship. "You are so lucky to have Ben and the boys."

Carol smiled, gathering up her flame coloured curls and scrabbling for a wild elusive strand. "He keeps my feet on the ground."

"And you've never had a... glitch?"

Carol's loud laughter erupted in a burst of mirth. "Glitch... Is that what you call it?"

She secured her hair with a diamante clip, looking at Grace more seriously. "Of course we've had a, 'glitch,' everyone does, it's natural. But neither of us has ever strayed, or even wanted to for that matter. There again, unlike you, I suppose nothing traumatic has ever really happened to us and we've always been too busy to be

Broken Heart Wood

bored. Come on, less of the maudlin thoughts; let's get to that library and see what we can find out about your precious wood. The internet didn't seem to have much to offer."

"It probably does if you key in the right words," Grace suggested.

"Just like life then," laughed Carol, pulling on her coat.

They stopped for lunch at a small pub near Meredale. "The name of these places never fails to amaze me," remarked Carol, locking the car before heading for the entrance of the ivy-strewn, mellow stone building. "…I mean, 'Dog and Fiddle' for heaven's sake. Whoever dreamed up that one?"

Grace shrugged, falling in to step beside her. "The names are supposed to have something to do with the surroundings of the place aren't they, or to remember some event. Maybe a fiddler with a dog used to come here."

"So what about the Drunken Duck then?" asked Carol, as they entered the warm cosy interior of the pub and walked across to the bar. "Honestly," she insisted. "There really is a pub called The Drunken Duck. It's in the Lake District."

"My father used to have that place," butted in the burly bar tender. "I was brought up there. It really was named after a drunken duck too, not that I ever saw it of course. Are you eating?" Before they could reply he handed them some menus. "Ducks off by the way," he told them with a totally straight face.

The two women were still giggling as they settled themselves down with a glass of white wine apiece.

"I feel positively decadent," announced Carol, "drinking wine at lunch time. And do you know…" She looked at Grace, a serious expression on her face for once. "I think that this is the very first time I have actually seen you enjoying yourself."

Grace flew to her own defence. "That's not true; I'm always smiling."

Carol took a sip of her wine, placing the glass deliberately down onto the oak topped table. "You're not though you know, not really. Oh yes you laugh at Molly's antics and smile along with everyone else, but this is the first time I've seen you without that pale haunted look."

Grace twisted her wedding ring around on her finger. "I do feel better, that's true. I suppose it's because I've spoken to Tom now. It was worrying me, keeping Molly from him… and I think I can see a way forward at

Broken Heart Wood

last..." She smiled then, the light back in her eyes. "I don't know where it's going of course but at least I can *see* the way."

To her surprise Carol did not join in with her attempt at light-hearted banter. "As long as you choose the *right* way Grace," she responded. "That's the trick. Now, what's on this menu?"

*

Despite the two women's determination to get to the truth of Heart Wood, the library was loath to divulge its information. After over an hour of going through books on local history neither of them had found out anything worthwhile.

"I keep finding a mention of it," sighed Grace. "But they never seem to say who actually planted it in the first place."

"I have a whole book here on the Pennine fells," added Carol. "It says that woods were often planted on the slopes above farms and villages to help prevent landslides."

"But why would they bother to make a perfect heart then?" objected Grace, suddenly horrified at the thought that there may not even *be* a mystery behind Heart Wood.

Broken Heart Wood

"We'll just have to go back on the Internet then," suggested Carol. "And key in some different words."

"If you don't mind me saying…"

A high reedy voice caught their attention and they turned simultaneously to see a tall grey haired man sitting at the next table. He wore small round spectacles on the end of his long nose and he sat very straight, his bushy grey eyebrows twitching as he spoke. "You need to speak to Martha Donnelly. She knows more about the history of this area than anyone, if she's still alive of course."

Grace gave him a grateful smile. "Well thank you Mr…?"

"Fletcher," he responded. "Charles Fletcher, retired school teacher."

"Thank you Mr Fletcher…"

"Charles, please."

"Thank you… Charles. And where might we find this Martha Donnelly?"

"Now there we might have a problem." He took of his chin between his thumb and forefinger, frowning thoughtfully. "She used to have a small apartment at Greythwaite Hall, in the only original part of the house that is left I believe. When he died, Major Dinsdale, the owner, left Martha the right to stay there for the rest of her days, or at least for as long as she required it. She'd worked for the family from the day she left school you see, never married or anything. Some say that she was in love with the Major. It caused a bit of a fuss when his son, Marcus, tried to sell the Hall off for apartments, but there was no way they could get her out. Anyway, to cut a long story short, she probably knows more than anyone else about the history around here, especially anything to do with the family."

"And has Heart Wood got something to do with the Dinsdale family?" Grace asked eagerly.

Charles Fletcher looked at her in surprise, his bushy eyebrows twitching again. Carol hid her mouth behind her hand, struggling to contain the giggle that was threatening to burst out at any moment. "I'm just nipping to the loo," she mumbled, dashing off.

"The Dinsdales owned most of everything around here until about sixty years ago, when the old Major died," went on Charles, ignoring her hasty exit. "I was twenty at the time so I remember it well. The family carried on for a while but young Marcus was a bit of a gambler; he gradually sold it off, piece by piece, until, all that was left was the apartment at the manor where Martha lives. He couldn't touch that however hard he tried. He's dead too now though, probably drank himself to death I shouldn't wonder."

"And you think that Martha may still be there?" prompted Grace eagerly.

"Well I haven't heard anything to the contrary but..."

"...But what?"

"Well... I mean, she must be very old now surely, so it's quite possible that she may have already died, or be in a care home of course."

Carol returned just then, her hilarity under control. "Sorry about that," she said, sliding back into her chair.

"Anyway young ladies," announced Charles, retrieving his trilby from the chair beside him and tweaking the peak. "I must be off, it was nice to meet you and I hope you find the answers you are looking for... but..."

"But what?" asked Grace for the second time, clenching her hands tightly together in anticipation?

"I was just going to say but don't get your hopes up too much," he finished with a smile. "And if she is still alive..."

"If she is still alive, what?" prompted Carol curiously when he hesitated for a moment.

His blue eyes twinkled, revealing a glimpse of faded charm.

Broken Heart Wood

"If she is still alive then, well would you please be so kind as to tell her…" He placed his hat firmly on his head. "Just tell her that young Charlie was asking after her; she'll know who you mean."

"Do you think he had a bit of a *thing* with this Martha Donnelly?" giggled Carol as she hurried along behind Grace, struggling to keep up."

"Well considering that he was probably twenty years younger than her," responded Grace. "I really don't think it's very likely, do you?"

Carol unlocked the car and slid into the driver's seat, her eyes alight with excitement. "Perhaps he was her toy boy."

"Trust you to think of that," said Grace. "Charles told us that the Major was in love with Martha so I hardly think that she'd have been interested in a young boy."

"Well they weren't as goody, goody as you think in those days you know," remarked Carol as the car engine roared to live. "Anyway, let's go to Greythwaite Hall and find out if she is still there."

"Now?" asked Grace, a flutter of excitement making her heart beat faster."

"Right this minute," responded Carol determinedly.

"Do you know where it is though?"

"Of course I do, you can't miss it. Surely you must have seen it when you went up to the wood."

"Of course..." Clarity dawned bringing a tingling rush of excitement as Grace remembered the beautiful old house on the fell-side beyond Heart Wood. "It's magnificent. But how do you get to it?"

"Ah..." Carol swung the car around a corner and into an even narrower lane. "That's the tricky bit. It has its own private entrance and to get to it you have to go right back down into the valley and along a narrow lane, although they may well have widened it now of course. I haven't actually been that way for ages; we used to go for Sunday afternoon drives along all the little lanes around here and stop for a picnic when we found a nice spot, we never seem to do that anymore though. I used to think that Greythwaite was the most beautiful house I'd ever seen, it was like stepping back in time just to look at it; I suppose they might have changed it altogether by now of course but I hope they haven't. Anyway, to be totally honest, do you *really* believe that there is any possibility, at all, of this Martha person still actually being alive... despite what Dr Jekyll said?"

"Don't call him Dr Jekyll," objected Grace, stifling a smile. "He was a lovely old man."

Broken Heart Wood

Carol nodded. "He *is* a lovely man to be honest, I've met him before. He just looks a bit odd that's all with those huge wobbly eyebrows; I can't think why he doesn't just trim them off."

As they drove along the valley bottom Grace looked up to see Heart Wood rippling in the sunshine. Her whole body tingled with an excitement she hadn't felt for months. Clenching her fists she closed her eyes for a second, desperately hoping that Martha Donnelly *was* still alive and fit enough to talk to them. It felt as if *their* whole future, hers, Tom's and Molly's, was dependent on her finding out the truth behind Heart Wood and the head stone that was hidden there; it felt like a mission.

"Look… Look!" shrieked Grace, jerked out of her reverie. "There it is."

The Hall loomed just ahead of them, set way up on the hillside looking down across the sweep of the valley.

Carol stopped the car and they both climbed out to get a better look.

"Why, it hasn't changed at all," cried Carol.

"It's breath-taking," sighed Grace. "The most magnificent house I have ever seen. You could search for years and never find a better setting."

"Well you'd never get planning permission if you did," declared Carol, bringing Grace back down to earth with a bump. "Come on, let's go and see if this ancient spinster of yours is still there... but don't hold your hopes out."

They bypassed the grand front entrance, driving cautiously around the side of the house into a courtyard that was set in block paving.

"Well if it *is* apartments now then they've been very carefully done to keep the original appearance," observed Grace, as they climbed out of the car. "I bet it didn't look much different in the Major's day. You could just imagine a coach and four pulling up here."

"...And a housekeeper in a long black dress and white pinafore coming out of that lovely old door," agreed Carol. "And do you know..." She walked eagerly across the courtyard; her heels tip tapping in the silence (Carol always liked to wear heels, Ben said that it was because she was so tiny but she insisted that they just made a legs look a better shape) "...The whole place appears to have been beautifully renovated but I do believe that this end bit is original."

Grace felt a tingle run down her spine. "Perhaps it is true then, about Martha Donnelly. Perhaps she does still live here."

Mary shook her head. "Well if she really is around one hundred years old then I wouldn't bank on it," said, raising her hand towards the faded wooden door. "…Anyway, only one way to find out."

She knocked firmly, rapping with her knuckles in an urgent rhythm.

"There's no one there," announced Grace, with a rush of disappointment tinged with relief. "Come on, we'll come back later."

Ignoring her, Carol knocked again even more loudly. "There's a light on inside," she insisted. "I can see it, and I'm sure I heard a sound."

"Perhaps they always leave a light on to deter thieves," suggested Grace as the door began to slowly creak open, just wide enough to reveal a tiny, snow white haired lady. She didn't reach much higher than the letterbox and her narrow, rounded shoulders were adorned with a plaid woollen shawl.

Grace stared transfixed, suddenly wondering if they'd stepped back in time as the door opened fully. Bright, penetrating eyes in a mask like face stared out at them, fleshless skin drawn across jutting cheekbones, cracking into a thousand tiny crinkles when she smiled. "Yes, can I help you?" Her voice was reedy and high-pitched.

Grace stepped determinedly forward, pushing past Carol's soft, generous curves. "Martha...?" she asked doubtfully.

The old lady nodded, inclining her head graciously. "Yes... I am Martha Donnelly, how can I help you?"

Taken by surprise, for a moment Grace was stuck for words. She hadn't really believed that after all these years the old lady would still be living here, at Greythwaite Hall.

Carol however, rose to the occasion, her warm bright smile lighting up the gloomy hallway. "Miss Donnelly," she said, holding out her hand. "So nice to meet you, would it be okay for us to have a little chat."

The little old lady pulled the shawl more tightly around her shoulders and ushered them into the hallway. "Are you the new carers?" she asked.

"Oh no, we aren't carers I'm afraid," Carol told her, shutting the door behind them. "We just wanted to ask you something, if that's okay."

"Charlie sent us," Grace blurted out. "He said to tell you that he was asking after you."

Martha smiled, her eyes softening. "Aye, he is a one that young Charlie. The Major will be after him if he doesn't watch it. Go and find someone your own age I'm always telling him…"

She glanced up at the two women who stood in her hallway, confusion clouding her face. "The Major is gone now though… Did you know that?"

Carol took her arm, drawing her gently toward the open door of a small sitting room. "Yes," she said. "Yes, we knew that. Now why don't I make us all a nice cup of tea and then we can talk."

Stepping into Martha's tiny sitting room, decided Grace, really was like stepping back in time. It held the faint scent of lavender combined with the musky aroma of ancient furniture, and something else, something spicy and exotic.

Martha fell heavily down into a well-worn, high backed leather chair. Dust rose in a cloud, hanging in the bright beam of sunshine that sneaked in between the ornate, half drawn curtains.

"He has gone, hasn't he?" Martha asked.

On impulse Grace leaned forward and took hold of her bony hand, concerned by its fragility. "Yes… yes the Major has gone I'm afraid. He left you this house though didn't he?"

"Until the end of my days," she said proudly. "He wanted to look after me you see. He always looked after me."

"I'm sure that he was a very good man, The Major," Grace agreed.

"Not like that Marcus."

The old lady sat up, agitated, glancing nervously towards the door. "He tried to get me out you know… he was a bad one that Marcus. The Major would turn in his grave."

"It's all right Martha… Marcus is dead now too, he can't bother you anymore."

"Dead," repeated Martha solemnly as Carol came back into the room with a laden tray.

"I've found some biscuits," she said brightly. "Now Martha, do you like your tea milky or strong?"

Carol's no nonsense presence brought clarity back. Martha drew herself up as tall as she could, smiling graciously. "So good of you," she said. "Are you from the village?"

Grace took over, pouring tea into thin china cups from an expensive looking teapot.

"We wanted to ask you about the family," Carol tentatively began. "Charlie said that you might know."

"I'm one hundred years old you know," Martha proudly announced. "Would you like to see my congratulations from the queen?"

"We'd love to," Grace said, already picking up the card from a small mahogany side table; Queen Elizabeth's face smiled back at her, set in a perfect pose. She found herself wondering if the signature really was that of the queen herself, or if they used a special stamp.

"I really do believe it's actually the queen's own signature," Carol said, as if reading her mind.

"It must be so marvellous to reach such a very great age," sighed Grace.

Martha shook her head slowly, her voice weak and quavering. "Not really… for everyone else is gone you see. The only people who come here now are the carers and they are usually in a rush. Why, I can't even manage to walk out into the garden anymore, let alone tend it."

Carol leaned forward, her heart, as always, on her sleeve. "But shouldn't they have given you a wheelchair if walking is so difficult for you? We could have *pushed* you out into the garden."

For a moment the old lady just stared at her. "That contraption," she announced. "I've never even been in it."

"Well perhaps it's time you did," suggested Carol, in the tone she reserved for her sons when they were being difficult.

"Surely it would be worth being in a wheelchair if it means you can go outside again," persuaded Grace.

Martha still looked doubtful. "And are you going to push me?"

Carol shrugged, smiling broadly. "Well, I've never pushed a wheelchair before, but I am good with a pram and I would love to take you out into the sunshine."

Martha snorted, taking a handkerchief from her pocket and snuffling into it.

"I tell you what," suggested Carol. "Let's have a bargain. We'll take you out into the garden and you can tell us what you know about Heart Wood."

Martha pushed the handkerchief back into her pocket. "I knew there was something," she chortled. "Heart Wood is it? Well come along then young ladies, the contraption is in the cupboard under the stairs."

Martha's cottage had its own small garden out the back; whoever cared for the perfectly manicured grounds of Greythwaite Hall apartments however, had obviously not extended their attentions to Martha's tiny square of unkempt grass and wildly overgrown borders.

Broken Heart Wood

"It's a disgrace," cried Carol, her cheeks flaming as red as her hair. "It would take no time at all to keep this bit tidy as well."

"I used to do it myself until my legs gave out last year," Martha sadly remarked. "I had flowers blooming all summer long... so many different colours. The Major used to love my garden; he said it was a little piece of heaven."

"And you'll have flowers blooming all summer again," Carol announced. "...Because I am going to call in every week and do it for you."

"She does love gardening," Grace added, wondering however Carol was going to find the time.

"There'll be a lot of pruning to do you know," Martha told her. "And I'll not have those modern slug pellet things put down."

Grace caught Carol's eye and raised her eyebrows, wondering if maybe her friend had let herself in for far more than she realised. In customary fashion though, Carol just shrugged. "Well I'm good at pruning," she said. "And I promise that I won't use slug pellets."

A comfortable silence fell between the three of them then, as they sat quietly together, gazing spellbound at the amazing view that stretched way out across the valley towards the awesome majesty of the distant hills.

Broken Heart Wood

Martha was the first to break it. She looked up at Grace, nodding, her eyes bright against the faded parchment of her skin. "So," she announced. "You want to know about Heart Wood. It doesn't have an entrance you know and there are those who say it is haunted."

She looked across at Grace, gauging her reaction, seeing the depth of sadness behind her smile. "I'm not too old to notice things you know," she said, reaching out to clasp her sleeve. "I can see the shadow in your eyes and if you are looking to find some comfort from the past, then I am the person to talk to."

"I..." Grace twisted her hands together on her knees. "I have been to Heart Wood a few times that's all... It is so beautiful there and I would just love to know more about it."

Martha nodded, her head bobbing up and down. "And you've found solace there... from your pain."

Grace caught her intense gaze with surprise. "But how did you...?" she began.

"It was obviously heartache that drew you there; some say that heartache planted it in the first place."

"...But whose heartache?" Grace blurted out, desperate to know.

"It was long before my time of course and no one *really* knows the truth of it," Martha replied slowly.

Broken Heart Wood

"Dorothea Dindsale owned the Hall then, and all the land around it. She is the one, they say, who planted the wood in memory of a man who broke her heart; that is why she never married. She died without disclosing her secrets though and everything went to her nephew, the Major's father."

"And is there nothing to say why she planted it," Grace pleaded, "…Nothing at all?"

Martha frowned "There is one thing, but no one has ever been able to make any sense of it. The Major once told me about it."

"…About what?"

The old lady raised her frail shoulders, fingering the heavy stuff of her shawl. "There's an old saying, I don't know where it came from or if there's any truth in it mind."

"What saying…?"

Grace ran her tongue across her dry lips, her heart pounding in her ears as she leaned forward to clasp the old lady's frail arm.

Martha looked at her for a moment and sighed. "Many people have tried to find out over the years, including me in the days when I was young and foolish. There is no truth in it, I am sure of that."

"Truth in what," Carol eagerly cut in?"

Martha linked her bony fingers together, holding them tightly in front of her chest. "It is said that the secret lies with the stone. So there you have it. I have been to Dorothea's grave and read the inscription on her stone but there is no clue... nothing."

"So is that what it means then... that the secret lies with Dorothea's *grave* stone?" Grace's mind was going round in circles. For the first time in what seemed like weeks Tom was not at the forefront of her thoughts.

"What else could it be," Martha responded. "She is buried at Greythwaite church, beneath a huge oak tree right at the back of the graveyard, you can go and see for yourself but you will be wasting your time."

Half an hour later, as they drove away from the imposing sight of Greythwaite Hall, Grace found herself looking back and imagining how it must have been for Dorothea all those years ago, living here alone with her servants, nursing a broken heart. Was there any truth in the story of the stone, she wondered, and was it really this Dorothea Dinsdale who had the wood planted in the shape of a perfect heart. What tragedy though could have affected her so much that she spent a whole lifetime alone, or was it just an old wife's tale spread by gossip?

Broken Heart Wood

"Let's go and see," suggested Carol, her bright blue eyes twinkling with excitement.

Grace snapped from her reverie, her whole body tingling. "What… now?"

Carol shrugged. ""Why not? Annie won't mind having the kids for a bit longer I'm sure. Anyway, she'll be as keen as us to find out about Dorothea's stone. I can't believe that we've lived around here for all these years and never heard that story."

Grace glanced back towards the imposing elegance of Greythwaite Hall, remembering the lonely old lady who had reached her 100th birthday all alone. "I suppose all those who knew of it are long dead now and poor old Martha doesn't get the chance to talk to many people anymore."

"Well I'm going to make a point of calling in to see her every week from now on."

"And you're going to do her garden remember," Grace reminded her, smiling.

"Oh yes!" Carol rolled her eyes. "Me and my big mouth: Anyway, at least this whole business has taken your mind off your problems for a while."

Remembering Molly's glowing face earlier, as she skipped happily along beside Tom, her tiny hand held tightly in his, Grace's heart tightened. The little girl had been so pleased to be with her dad and very excited about seeing Lucky; his cute face had been pressed up against the van window as he watched them approach. When they'd waved goodbye before driving off, loneliness had cut deep, now she found herself wondering if maybe she was destined to be like Dorothea, alone for the rest of her life... No, that was ridiculous she told herself, for she still had Molly to love... and Tom? The weight of longing dragged her down, pushing all thoughts of Heart Wood and the secret of the stone to the back of her mind for a moment. Would she ever be able to find it within herself to be able to forgive and forget though?

"Here it is," announced Carol, breaking Grace's train of thought. She nosed her car carefully in through the narrow entrance to the church car park, before cutting the engine and clambered eagerly from the driver's seat. "Come on then, let's go and see if we can make any sense of Dorothea Dinsdale's head stone."

She marched purposefully across the graveyard towards an ancient oak tree in the furthest corner, whilst Grace followed more cautiously. "Come on," she called eagerly. "This it, Dorothea's final resting place."

Broken Heart Wood

Grace froze as a weird feeling flooded over her, taking her breath. Could the person who had planted Heart Wood really be lying here, dead and rotting beneath the earth, all that heartache and emotion just a distant, forgotten memory? It wasn't just a forgotten memory though, she was sure of it. When she first went to the wood that day and stood in the clearing, she'd known instinctively that the whole place was founded on heartache. And then, when she'd come across the small stone that must have been hidden beneath the undergrowth for a lifetime, she had felt the aura that surrounded it. The very essence of the emotion that had created it in a perfect heart was still there, she was sure of it, lingering in wait… but in wait for what?

The answer to that she didn't yet know but one thing was for sure… no matter what the inscription on her stone said, this place, here, where Dorothea's final remains lay was not where they would find her secret…

Broken Heart Wood

CHAPTER EIGHTEEN

Tom stood back to look at his handiwork. It seemed like a lifetime he realised, since his whole body had ached with the effort of good solid hard work. The sun was sinking down behind the awesome hills, lending a burning glow to the vast sweep of the countryside, where small clusters of trees made dark shapes against the golden glory of the sky. It was a magical place he thought, staring around in wonder, and never had he been more sure than this that he was doing the right thing.

Turning back, he carefully inspected the fence he'd been mending, just as evening shadows crept furtively in across the meadow. 'We'll keep it a secret from mummy,' he'd told Molly when he brought her up here at the weekend. "…For a surprise."

"Supwise," she'd echoed, her small face contorting earnestly and then she had smiled, as only Molly could...

Tom's heart twisted inside him as he thought of his daughter. Grace had to forgive him, surely, she just had too, and then they could become a proper family again.

He would spend the rest of his life making it up to her if only she would give him the chance, and this... this would be the start.

Standing stock still in the half-light, he watched the sun slowly slip down over the horizon, remembering how it used to be. That totally comfortable understanding they'd shared, the complete togetherness that had never wilted beneath the weight of familiarity as is so often the case... The togetherness that had left them on the day Grace took Quicksilver out for his final ride.

Tom determinedly closed his eyes against the painful memories. Somehow he had to get that back, had to find a way to revive those happy days when he and Grace worked and strived and laughed together, side-by side, reaching for the same goals.   And even if they never did manage to rekindle that partnership despite all his efforts, one thing was for sure; it wouldn't be for lack of trying.

Flinging his bag over his shoulder with a warm sense of achievement, he heaved it into the van. Would Grace ever actually get to see the result of all this effort, he couldn't help wondering. Or was he just wasting his time?

Broken Heart Wood

By the time Tom finally drew up outside Ivy cottage his eyes were grating with tiredness. The engine shuddered into silence, magnifying the loneliness of the night and calling to Lucky he stumbled wearily from the van, totally forgetting to even lock it.

The nerve shattering jangle of the phone burst into his brain as he opened the front door. Cursing loudly he felt for the light switch, his every joint aching. It was almost midnight, whoever wanted to speak to him at this hour?

"I've an urgent delivery… it must get there by tomorrow lunchtime…."

A man's voice, high pitched, desperate. Tom resisted the temptation to just slam down the phone and scrabbled for the diary, listening with half an ear to his tirade and questioning why ever he had got into this crazy business in the first place.

"Yes… No problem. If I set off at 5am I can be there for lunchtime…Give me the address again…"

He heard his own voice in his ears as if it was a stranger's, putting down the receiver with a heavy clang and suddenly feeling as if he'd finally woken up. Where had the last twelve months gone and how had he let all their dreams slip away so easily, giving up everything just to become a glorified deliveryman? It was as if, with the tragic death of Quicksilver and all its aftermath, he and Grace had both lost their way. His one stupid, meaningless, weak mistake had ruined three lives and destroyed the closeness they could still have shared... even *after* Quicksilver. But guilt and blame had proven to be bedfellows far too tough for his and Grace's suddenly fragile relationship to withstand.

When a cold nose pushed against his hand, putting aside his maudlin thoughts, he reached down to scoop up the little white dog. "You, Lucky," he announced. "Are the one good thing to happen around here in over a year."

The dog's warm tongue found his chin and despite himself Tom smiled, placing him gently back down onto the floor. "And now we'd better get to bed, it'll be time to get up before you know it. We'll see Molly again at the weekend though... you'll like that won't you."

Lucky's response was to run around in mad circles chasing his tail. "We'll be a family again one day boy," he promised. "You'll see; the four of us... a proper family."

Falling into bed, Tom slept restlessly, his mind overflowing with crazy dreams, until the alarm clock beside his bed burst into life at four fifteen. Opening his eyes with a groan he rolled over to bury his head under the pillow, Lucky was having none of it though. The little dog snuffled against him, nibbling his ear.

"Okay... okay, give a guy a break," pleaded Tom, clambering awkwardly out of bed and pulling on his jeans whilst still rubbing the sleep from his eyes. "We don't need to set off until five."

He frowned into the bathroom mirror, running his hand across the harsh dark stubble on his chin before splashing cold water onto his face and hurriedly cleaning his teeth.

Who *was* the crazy guy with such an urgent delivery anyway he wondered, as he fed Lucky and buttered a piece of toast. He was still holding it, uneaten, in his hand, as he let the front door slam shut behind him and headed down the path.

He had been back so late the night before that he hadn't bothered to park his van at the yard. It was a relief now to see it gleaming through the darkness just outside the garden gate, saving him having to walk further down the lane. Lucky leaped eagerly into the passenger seat and Tom slid in beside him, turning the key in the ignition. It was going to be a long haul he realised, right across country to the West coast. If he shaped himself though he might have time to stop off on the way back and get on with his project. Maybe he was just wasting his time with it, but there again, who knew what the future might hold. Perhaps it wasn't too late to turn back the clock after all; at least it gave him something to focus on.

"Nothing ventured nothing gained," he said out loud to Lucky, nosing the van along the lane and out onto the highway. As he picked up speed the pale light of the moon shimmered on the tree tops. The little white dog just wagged his tail, his pink tongue slipping from the side of his mouth as he gazed happily out of the window. Anything his new master did was okay by him.

"At least I've got you for company, Lucky," said Tom, fumbling in his pocket for his phone so that he could leave a message to tell Mick where he'd gone. "I suppose I could say that you were my saving grace… Saving Grace! That's it boy. That's what I'm trying to do isn't it, save Grace… Damn…!"

He had picked up the phone he remembered, as he went to get his jacket… and then put it down again beside the sink when he went to grab a bag of crisps from the cupboard. His heart sank; he was miles from home with no phone and he hadn't even left a message to say where he was going.

"Too late to turn back now boy," he groaned, turning his attention back to the road ahead. "They'll just have to manage on their own."

As dawn broke over the horizon, a pale mist cast an eerie glow across the farmland all around him. Tom felt strangely detached from everything familiar, as if he had suddenly been transported into another world. "Perhaps we've died and gone to heaven boy," he said, determinedly turning up the radio to bring back a sense of normality and channelling his thoughts onto his, as yet, unfinished project. He couldn't wait to show Grace what he was doing, if he ever got the chance that is. But he would never use it as a bargaining tool. If she was ever going to forgive him then she had to do it for the right reasons... and only then would he reveal his hopes and plans and see if she wanted to share them.

***

As Tom took the long lonely road towards the North East, Grace was sitting with Molly cradled on her knee. She pressed her lips against the little girl's burning forehead, glancing anxiously across at Annie. "She's had this fever for almost twenty four hours now; perhaps I should get the doctor to come out?"

Annie placed a carefully folded sheet on top of her ironing pile and walked across to rest her palm on the child's forehead. "You know what children are like," she said, her tone reassuring. "They can have a raging fever in the morning and be playing happily by the afternoon. Leave it until after lunch and then see how she is."

"You're right of course," agreed Grace. "Carol said that this flu virus is all around at school and it just has to burn itself out. I just feel so helpless though…"

She held Molly close, annoyed at the injustice of it. "She won't be able to see Tom this weekend either, unless she makes a rapid recovery."

"Have you told him that she's ill?" asked Annie.

Grace glanced away, her lips set into a grim line. "I rang him early this morning, just before six. I'd been up with her for hours and it seemed like the right thing to do…"

"And…?"

"He didn't answer the house phone so I guess he must have been out all night; and he isn't answering his mobile either. Just when I'd almost allow myself to start believing in him… again he lets me down… again… and." Anger and disappointment flooded over her. "It's a total waste of time Annie, he's probably been out with some woman all night of course… or he's still seeing *her* and everything he said to me was just a lie."

Annie sighed, placing a sympathetic hand on Grace's shoulder. "You don't really believe that, I know you don't."

"Don't I, Oh Annie...I don't really know *what* I believe anymore?"

"Well you do still believe in the secret of Heart Wood don't you? At least that has helped to take your mind off your troubles."

"I don't think that I'm even sure about that anymore," admitted Grace sadly. "I knew we'd find nothing at Dorothea's grave though. We read the inscription again and again; 'Here lies Dorothea Dinsdale...' and the dates of course. Anyway, too many other people have already looked there with no success so obviously *we* were never going to find anything. Perhaps there isn't even a secret at all and we are all reading far too much into it. After all, Martha's saying, '*the secret lies with the stone*,' might simply just mean that the secret of Heart Wood is lost forever, buried with Dorothea."

"And do *you* believe that?"

Grace looked up, holding Annie's bright gaze for a moment. "No..." she said slowly. "No... at least I hope not. But I don't believe that it has anything to do with Dorothea's grave stone either."

Annie nodded. "You think it's the other stone don't you, the hidden one... Did you tell Carol about it?"

For a moment Grace hesitated. "No... I didn't and, to be totally honest, I feel really bad about that... I just don't want anyone and everyone going up there though, you know, rooting around. If there *is* a secret then I'm beginning to think that it has been kept for far too long now to ever make it public knowledge."

"Your mother and I never told anyone about the stone either," admitted Annie. "Because it was so obviously *supposed* to be hidden I suppose, there in the undergrowth. We were just girls when we first saw it of course and it seemed like our romantic secret. You'll go back and look at it again though surely?"

Grace nodded determinedly. "As soon as Molly is feeling a bit better hopefully ... if you'll look after her of course?"

"You know I love having her," said Annie, smiling. "And I'd love to come with you to the wood to be honest, but my old legs aren't up to that steep climb anymore."

"I almost asked Carol to come with me," admitted Grace. "I felt so guilty about keeping the Heart Wood headstone a secret from her. I know how enthralled she would be by it."

"Look," Annie sat down beside Grace, placing a hand on her shoulder. "You know what Carol's like. She is a dear, kind, fun loving person, but she can't keep a secret to save herself and she wouldn't even see any reason too if she knew the truth... So best spare her the dilemma... eh?"

Molly moaned restlessly in her sleep and Grace pressed her lips against the little girl's cheek. "Why, I think she feels cooler already," she cried with a sigh of relief. "So perhaps you were right about not calling the doctor out... and I think you're probably right about Carol too; I think the world of her and I feel really bad about keeping secrets from her... but maybe the secret of Heart Wood needs to be kept."

Annie nodded, looking at Molly. "She'll be running around by tea time, you mark my words. Now, why don't you try Tom again, there's sure to be a good reason why he isn't answering his phone and he'll want to know if Molly's ill."

"Me want Bockle," announced Molly, opening her eyes with a smile.

"I'll get it," offered Annie. "You see, I told you she'd soon fling it off."

Broken Heart Wood

Later that afternoon, convinced by Annie, Grace took a reluctant leave of Molly, who was happily cuddled up on the sofa sucking her thumb and watching Peppa Pig on the TV.

She hesitated at the door, still worried by the little girl's flushed complexion. "Perhaps I should leave it until tomorrow?" she suggested.

Annie would have none of it. "That's not a feverish flush you can see, she's just a bit warm," she insisted, smiling. "Or is it maybe that you think I am not fit to look after her?"

"Of course you're fit to look after her," cried Grace. "More than fit... Well maybe I'll just go straight there and back then, if you really don't mind... I know I won't find anything of course... I never have before."

"Ah..." announced Annie. "But you weren't really looking before were you."

A mist had settled over the hills, merging with the sky and leaving a silvery sparkling film across the countryside. Even the fell sheep that nibbled the coarse grassland were rimed with a halo of tiny droplets.

Grace turned her face up towards the sky, feeling totally isolated. Somehow it felt good, to be all alone in this mystical silence, as if she had entered a private place where pain and treachery could not enter. Where *was* Tom though, she found herself wondering, and why hadn't he answered his phone. Perhaps he'd had an accident, perhaps he was he hurt? The thought left her trembling. She punched his number into her phone yet again... no reply. With shaking fingers she dialled the business line.

"Quicksilver deliveries..."

Mick's familiar voice filled her head.

"Hi... I.... It's Grace..."

"Grace!" He exclaimed. "Wherever are you... are you okay? Is Tom there?"

For a moment she hesitated, overcome by the memories the driver's voice brought rushing in. "I'm all alone on a hillside in the mist," she eventually responded. "And I'm fine but... do you know where Tom is?"

"Now there is a difficult question," grumbled Mick. "He was supposed to be doing a run into York today but he's gone AWOL and left no message. I was hoping that you might help me track him down."

"He isn't answering his phone."

"Well that's because he left it at the cottage. I found it this morning when I went to look for him. He hadn't locked up either so he must have left in a hurry."

Broken Heart Wood

"And you don't know where he is?"

"I wish I did... and I wish that you'd come home and help him sort his head out."

"Thanks." Grace's voice came out in a hoarse whisper. "Tell him to call me if you hear from him."

The phone flicked into silence and she looked ahead again, searching for the familiar sheep track that led right past the wood. It disappeared before her into the opaque silence and she walked along it tentatively, her mind going off on a tangent. What if she became lost in this weird world forever... What if there *was* no way back...What if... what if... what if...? Tom had used to tease her about her crazy imagination. 'You should write a novel,' he used to say. '...Something really weird and wacky.'

Suddenly the determined independence that had carried her so far totally deserted her. The hot swell of tears pressed against the backs of her eyes and loneliness descended in a smothering blanket. She started to run in a shambling clumsy pace, slithering and stumbling up the narrow track towards the dark clump of shadowy trees ahead. Here lay the answer, she was sure of it.

Within the familiar confines of Heart Wood there lurked a very different world, free of mist and shadow.

Grace clambered over the grey stone wall, putting all her fears, doubts and energy into reaching the tiny head stone.

At first, with a rush of panic, she couldn't find it. There was the clearing where she liked to sit on the flat, moss covered flat rock; surely the stone should be just over there, near the large holly bush. She pushed through the trees, remembering the first time she'd stumbled upon it and suddenly there it was, hidden by bracken and one wild, wandering blackberry bush. Eagerly she pushed the vegetation aside, ignoring the sharp prickles against her skin.

'GOODBYE MY LOVE'.

Carefully she traced the letters, searching the smooth stone for a clue, another tiny word, anything.

Could it have been Dorothea who put it here? But surely she couldn't have carried it up the steep slope of the fell and dug it into the ground all by herself. Perhaps she'd got one of the gardeners to do it of course, and sworn him to secrecy; that made sense. At least now though she knew that it was Dorothea who designed and planned Heart Wood in the first place. But why... why had she wanted it here? Even Martha didn't know that though so how was *she* ever to find out?

She placed her hand on the ground in front of the small marble stone as if feeling the earth would reveal what was buried beneath. *'The secret lies with the stone.'* Was there some truth in the saying or was it just an old wives tale carried on through time?

"Tell me Dorothea," she begged. "Give me a clue."

Her cry was met by an empty silence, followed by the rhythmic dripping of water as the mist on the fell-side turned to rain. Slowly she stood up, running her hand through her damp curls. Perhaps the saying really *did* mean that Dorothea's secret lay with her in the grave and perhaps it *was* just someone's beloved pet that rested here in this peaceful haven from the world.

Her mind slipped, as always, back to Tom, a familiar wave of pain cutting into her like a knife as she stumbled out of the woodland and onto the wild open slopes beyond it.

Did nothing ever last? She had always believed that their love was strong enough to face anything, and it had; it had survived the tragedy of Quicksilver and the loss of all their dreams. It wasn't really even Tom's stupid mistake with Mary Maddison that had finally torn them apart... it was the fact that he'd let her bear all that guilt for so long.

Broken Heart Wood

Increasing her pace she started to run down the hill, desperate to see Molly, desperate to put her arms around the one being she could love unconditionally.

CHAPTER NINETEEN

Grace burst in through Annie's living room door, her mind whirling with concern for Molly; only to find her daughter sitting in exactly the same position as when she'd left, happily snuggled up next to the diminutive old lady. The little girl looked up, removing her thumb from her mouth for a moment to give her mother an angelic smile. "Peppa pig," she announced with delight before turning her attention back to the screen.

"We haven't actually moved since you left," said Annie. "And Molly has been fine, so let us hope that that's the end of it. Did you find what you were looking for?"

Grace sank down onto the sofa beside them, running her fingers gently across the smooth plumpness of Molly's cheek, her heart tightening with a rush of love. "What do you think?" she sighed. "I'm beginning to believe that there really is nothing to look *for*... or if there is then we'll never find it."

Annie smiled, slowly shaking her white head. "Ah well, at least it's giving you something to think about."

Broken Heart Wood

"That's why you're pushing me isn't it," cried Grace. "So that I won't sit and brood."

"Ring Tom," urged Annie. "Talk to him… Give him a chance to explain properly."

"He's already tried and there's nothing to explain anyway."

Grace's tone was flat, masking the rapid beat of her heart.

"Nothing ever goes right all the time and no one is perfect you know," Annie told her "Everyone deserves a second chance don't they?"

Grace stood, uneasily. "You don't give up do you, Annie," she said sadly. "Anyway, why don't you two stay here and I'll go and make us a cup of tea."

"There's some freshly baked lemon cake in the flowered tin," Annie called after her. Grace couldn't help but smile, she had eaten more home-made cake since arriving at Hillside Cottage than in the rest of her entire life. "I'll be fat by the time I leave here," she called back.

"Well you could do with gaining a few pounds." Annie chortled. "Oh, and by the way, Carol called in earlier."

Grace reappeared around the door. "She can't have stayed for long then."

"No, not long… she was on her way to do Martha's garden and she wondered if you wanted to go with her. She'll probably drop by on the way back."

Grace was peeling potatoes for the evening meal when Carol eventually appeared.

"Well I've done my first stint," she announced, flopping down onto a chair. "And I'll tell you what, that woman is a tartar. No wonder she's never been married."

Grace put down her potato peeler and looked round with a smile. "And here I was thinking that it was because she'd always been in love with the Major who was already married to someone else."

"Well there is that too," admitted Carol. "She talked about him actually."

Grace walked across to sit down next to her, a bright prickle of interest in her eyes. "And…?"

"Seemingly he arrived to take over Greythwaite Hall after Dorothea died. Martha was in service there and she was obviously smitten by the Major from the first, you can tell by the way she talks about him. Of course, not only was he years older than her and from a totally different class, he was married too, so there was no way they were ever going to get it together –not officially at least."

"Poor Martha," sighed Grace. "But did she ever actually get to meet Dorothea?"

"The old lady was ill when she first arrived at the Hall but she did see her once or twice I think. She died when she was sixty six so I've been working out that she must have planted your precious wood when she was about twenty, in the late eighteen hundreds.

"But how can you know that?" asked Grace eagerly.

"Well within a year or two I suppose, but, if you think about it, surely in those days she must have been in her late teens or early twenties if it was in memory of a love affair."

"But we don't know that she had it planted there because of a broken heart," argued Grace, "and anyway you can fall in love at any age surely? Or perhaps it had nothing to do with a love affair at all… maybe it was put there to commemorate the death of her husband or something."

"Pay attention Grace," barked Carol, laughing. "Dorothea never married, remember, that's how the Major came to inherit the Hall."

"You two sound like Sherlock Holmes and Dr Watson," said Annie with an amused smile. "Are you staying for a bit then Carol, shall I put the kettle on?"

Broken Heart Wood

"No," Carol jumped up, glancing at the clock. "I'm late already. The boys will be waiting at the bus stop."

"Are you going to say goodbye to Auntie Carol, Molly," Grace asked.

The little girl scrambled up from the floor, where she was busily piling up coloured wooden bricks, holding out chubby arms."

"Next time you want to go exploring in that wood of yours then bring her to spend some time with me," insisted Carol, picking her up and swinging her round before placing a hefty kiss on her cheek… "See you sweetheart."

Molly waved her hand madly and Annie smiled across at Grace. "You would never believe that she was so ill earlier."

"No," responded Grace slowly. "It seems that maybe she will be able to go to her dad's this weekend after all."

An image of his face flashed into her mind and something inside her fluttered. Oh why couldn't she just hate him? Reaching for her iPhone she headed out the door behind Carol. "I'll just try Tom again," she muttered.

As before, the phone rang a few times and then switched on to answer phone. Grace listened to the beep, trying to think of something to say, but the words stuck in her throat. She felt empty inside, totally barren, as if all feeling was being drained away from her. "Damn you Tom Roberts," she said out loud.

****

For Tom it had been a long and lonely day, financially rewarding, as he kept reminding himself, but somehow finances seemed less important now than they had ever been. Its only reprieve had been the three hours he'd spent on his project on the way back; now that did help to fill the yawning chasm that gaped inside him.

Loneliness loomed again as he walked into Ivy Cottage, glancing around the familiar and yet strangely unfamiliar space. It seemed empty now, soulless, as if with Grace and Molly leaving all life had gone from the place he had once thought of as home. The front door slammed shut behind him and he immediately went to find his phone, flicking it open. Poor Mick would be going mad.

'*Ten missed calls…*'

"What do you think boy?" he said out loud to Lucky, who was sitting on his haunches waiting impatiently to be fed. The little dog jumped up at his leg as he scrolled down the numbers, drawn at once to Grace's message.

Broken Heart Wood

'*Damn you Tom.*'

Her voice was a hoarse whisper in his ears. Her words brought a quick sharp pain into his heart. He tapped his finger down impatiently onto the reply button.

"Tom!" She sounded breathless, surprised almost.

"I love you," he said. Where had that come from he wondered bleakly and what happened to the sensible, take it one step at a time, approach?

"So you think that you can just disappear for an entire day and those three words will make everything all right I suppose? Well its way too late for *I love you* to work, Tom."

"Look…" His mind was whirling, trying to think of the right thing to say. He settled for the truth. "I have been driving all day and I left my phone at home that's all… Anyway…"

He felt a smile begin. If she was angry then it must mean that she still cared. "I didn't think you'd even notice that I was gone."

"When our daughter is ill I, obviously stupidly, thought you might like to know."

The smile faded instantly. "Molly! What do you mean… ill? What's wrong with her? …Shall I come over?"

"Don't bother, she's better now."

For a moment there was a silence between them, awkward and painful.

"I meant what I said," he murmured. "Those three forbidden words... and I am sorry that I didn't take my phone today."

Her voice softened. "I'll see you at the weekend then... saturday morning, about ten?"

"Grace..."

"Yes."

"Molly is okay though isn't she?"

"She's fine... now. She had a fever but you know how children are."

"Do you think perhaps? ...I mean... Could we talk... when you are ready of course?"

"What more is there to say?"

Grace's voice was so hard and cold. Tom felt as though something was clawing at his chest. "Surely what we had must mean something still...?"

"Oh Tom... can't you see?"

Grace's voice broke, her breath coming in shallow gasps. "What we had is gone. So much has happened to us over the last twelve months, this last thing was just the final straw and ... Look, I'll think about it okay, if you really do still want to talk I'll think about it."

A flicker of hope penetrated Tom's despair. "That will have to do for now," he told her. "But I'll never give up on us you know."

Grace snapped her phone case shut, closing her eyes against the agony that filled her lungs; *us*... one word that meant so much. But how could there ever be an, *us,* again when trust was gone?

"Are you all right dear?"

Annie's kind, troubled eyes, shone through Grace's confusion; she blinked, trying to smile. "Tom has been driving all day and he left his phone at home. I told him about Molly."

The old lady nodded. "It really is time to think forwards you know Grace. You're welcome to stay here for as long as you like of course, I love having the two of you, but you need to decide where you are going with your life now."

"I'm never going back to Ivy cottage, no matter what happens."

"Talk to Tom," urged Annie. "...Now that you've had time to think things through. Time is a great healer... and I know that I've already told you that."

"And trust is the hardest thing to regain," responded Grace sadly. "I would rather be on my own than spend every minute wondering, watching his every move. I don't know if I can ever forget you see and that would be like a canker in any relationship."

Annie sighed, shaking her white head slowly. "Life is too short to make wrong decisions."

Grace caught her gaze, holding it for a moment. "Then why do we all just keep on doing exactly that?"

"Because we're human," suggested Annie, taking her arm. "Come on… there's a good drama just starting, let's lose ourselves in someone else's problems for a bit."

"Now that," agreed Grace. "…Is an excellent plan."

Despite her determination to enjoy the TV programme, Grace found her mind wandering, to Tom, to Heart Wood, to Dorothea Dinsdale and her secret. An idea crept into her thoughts, slowly materialising, at first indistinct and then gradually more viable. She needed to go to the wood again though to follow it through but tomorrow Carol had insisted that she, Annie and Molly went out for lunch and then they were taking Annie to see Martha at Greythwaite Hall.

Grace was looking forward to meeting the old lady again and Annie was really excited about it, anyway she couldn't let poor Carol down; she felt guilty enough already for not telling her about the Heart Wood head stone.

"Well," remarked Annie as the credits began to roll. "Whoever would have believed that it was him all the time?"

Grace looked at her vacantly and Annie laughed. "You didn't really take in any of it did you?"

"My mind just kept wandering," admitted Grace. "Anyway, I think I'll get off to bed. Is there anything I can do for you before I go up?"

"Ring your husband and tell him that you still love him."

Grace shook her head. "You never give up do you Annie."

"Not until I see you happy again."

"But I am happy, I love being here at Hillside. It's like home."

"Well you didn't look very happy just a minute ago."

Four hours later, as midnight came and went, Grace still lay sleepless next to Molly, tossing and turning with crazy ideas milling around inside her head. The memories she'd tried so hard to stifle burst out from their self-enforced barriers. Tom's eyes the first time she saw him that day on the fairground, their hopes, their dreams... and Quicksilver; the warm silkiness of his gleaming silver coat, the feel of him beneath her as he stretched into gallop and his oh so familiar smell. The whole glory of the noble horse that was to be their future, a glory that went so badly wrong on that fateful day

Beyond the bedroom window was a blanket of darkness, thick cloud masking the moon. Grace crept from her bed and went to peer outside into the gloom, wrapping her arms about herself. Up there was the answer to Dorothea's secret, she was so sure of it now. All she needed was a few hours to go and look just one more time.

There wouldn't be time tomorrow though and on Saturday morning Tom would be here, wanting to talk: Would she talk to him, would they go somewhere for a coffee and a civilized chat? She didn't even know the answer to that herself. Dare she go was perhaps a more pertinent question, for if her life with Tom Roberts really was over then a dose of nostalgia was the last thing she needed. Truth was she longed to talk to him, to tell him everything just like she used to do. And there lay the heart of the problem she realised; she'd lost her best friend.

Suddenly she felt like ringing him right now and just telling him everything that was going on inside her head. But it had all been just a lie hadn't it, the caring, so what was the point, for when the going got too tough he'd her down. No, it was just she and Molly now and that was what she had to concentrate on. She slipped back into bed, snuggling up next to the little girl's small sleeping form… and Heart Wood of course.

Images floated through her mind as waves of sleep overcame her. Dorothea in white, running through the wood, the Major, chasing after her and flowers, everywhere there were flowers. Carol's bright face, smiling sadly from a halo of red hair, "You should have told me Grace… should have told me… should have told me…"

**

"Cup of tea dear…?"

Annie's hand was on her shoulder. She blinked, groaning. "It can't be morning already."

"It's past morning," laughed Annie. "And Molly is already dressed and fed."

"Oh no…!" Grace sat up. "What kind of mother must you think I am?"

"A mother who has been under a lot of strain and needed to catch up on her sleep; anyway, Molly didn't make a sound when she woke. We crept downstairs so that we didn't disturb you."

Grace rubbed her eyes as clarity flooded in. "But I should have helped you do breakfasts for the guests…"

"Don't worry. I haven't booked anyone in for B&B this week, or at least just two couples in self-catering, so there are no breakfasts to do."

"I'll be down in five minutes then," promised Grace.

When she arrived downstairs, still bleary eyed, Carol was already in the kitchen. "Don't panic," she explained, noting the surprised expression on Grace's face. "I know you're not ready yet. I've just dropped the boys off at school though and as I was passing by here anyway, I thought I'd call in and see what time you wanted picking up.

"Half ten?" suggested Annie. "It's market day today; we could stop off and have a look round… Have you got time for a coffee?"

Carol was already heading for the door. "Better not, I have to leave some lunch for Ben and Andy and I've a load of washing to put in. I'll see you later."

Broken Heart Wood

Despite her misgivings about the whole trip, Grace found herself enjoying the day out with Carol and Annie. Shopping had never played much of a part in her life; when they still had the horses every spare moment was spent with them and afterwards... afterwards she realised she and Tom had both just lived on autopilot, going through life in a kind of daze. A wander around the busy market in Meredale with two shopaholics like Annie and Carol, was a whole new experience, despite the fact that Molly kept on trying to grab everything she could see that was coloured pink. In the end Annie bought her a large pink fluffy dog; the little girl immediately named it Lucky.

After a wonderful lunch at a tearoom in a garden centre just outside the town, Grace was happy to sit and relax in the back of Carol's big family run-around, reflecting on the last twelve months whilst Molly dozed beside her. It was strange how things worked out, she realised, how good could sometimes come out of bad. If things hadn't gone so badly wrong in her life then she would probably have never even met these two women she'd already become so fond of.

After the tragedy that had plummeted both of them into a spiral of total darkness for what seemed like an eternity, Tom had plunged into their new business with a feverish determination and she had followed in his wake, trusting him... how wrong she had been.

Turning her attention back to the awesome scenery beyond the car window, she opened it to breathe in the heady scents of early summer, closing her eyes against the fresh breeze that took away her breath. Where was he driving too today she wondered, imagining his long tanned fingers curled firmly around the steering wheel of his Quicksilver van. For a fleeting moment another image flashed into her mind, of those same hands, skilfully controlling the real Quicksilver; she blinked hard, trying to fight off thr hard painful lump that swelled inside her.

"Wake up Grace," called Carol from the driver's seat. "We're almost at the Hall."

Grace's mind flashed back to now. "Sorry, I was miles away."

"No guessing where," smiled Carol.

"Look," cried Annie, taking their attention. "There it is...why, it hasn't changed a bit."

"That's what I said when we came here last time," agreed Carol.

Grace just stared, spellbound. Today the house seemed even more beautiful than the last time she saw it.

"We are going to see a very old lady," she told Molly, who had woken up with all the excitement. "And you must be a very good quiet girl."

The little girl clamped her lips tightly together, screwing up her nose.

"Preferably without the funny face," Grace told her, smiling.

Martha was delighted to receive her visitors, especially Molly –although she seemed to think that Carol was there just to do her bidding.

"I think she sees me in a whole new light since I offered to do her garden," she whispered to Grace, leaning down to pour out her tea.

"Yes," giggled Grace. "As a servant I think… or a gardener"

Carol shrugged. "Oh well, if it makes the old girl happy…"

Annie was intrigued by Martha's stories of times long gone. The two younger women had to prise her away after almost two hours, with promises to bring her back next week when Carol came to do the garden.

"I can't believe that her memories are so clear," she cried delightedly as they headed homeward.

"I think she *lives* in the past to be honest," remarked Carol. "Anyway, *we* need to think of the future. Did you manage to find out any more about Dorothea?"

Annie shook her head. "Not really, only what you told us. She's more interested in the memories of her precious major and what might have been."

"Do you think we all do that?" asked Grace. "Dwell too much on what might have been I mean."

"Well I don't," announced Carol determinedly. "There's no point in it is there. No, we just have to get on with what is happening in our lives here and now... and deal with it."

"That," responded Grace. "Is a very astute point of view... and as from now it is what I intend to do."

Suddenly she couldn't wait to see Tom tomorrow. It was time to talk she realised, to move on with her life in whatever direction... but not just yet. At the weekend, when Molly was away, she would go to Heart Wood, for somehow she knew that this time she *would* find some answers. Only then would she talk to Tom... when she finally knew in what direction she wanted her life to go.

Annie glanced back at her from the passenger seat, catching the expression in her eyes.

"That is one of the most sensible things I've heard you say since you came to Greythwaite," she said, reaching out a hand to Molly who grabbed for her rings with a gurgle of delight.

Grace let out a satisfied sigh. "Today I *feel* more sensible."

CHAPTER TWENTY

Grace woke at dawn, a prickle of excitement completely obliterating any ideas of further sleep. She slipped quietly from her bed so as not to disturb Molly, moving silently over to the window to watch the sunrise creep across the fell, marvelling in the glory of colours that brought the earth to life.

Every living being relied on the sun, she thought, taking its regular rise and fall totally for granted, but what if one morning it didn't appear and the whole world remained in darkness, what then? She knew what Carol would say of course, smiling to herself as her friend's loud, positive tones, flooded her imagination. *'You just have to get on with whatever happens in your life and deal with it,'* which seemed to be her immediate response to any situation, no matter how serious. Grace took heart from Carol's positive approach to life and the way she took everything in her stride.

Thinking about it now she felt a sense of peace. So, as of today, she was determined to just get on with her life and deal with it; she hadn't done a very good job so far, and she knew that wasn't fair on Molly... or Tom.

Turning away from the window with a fresh sense of purpose, her eyes settled on her daughter's sleeping face, so innocent, so trusting. Anyway, she thought, why should she care what was fair for Tom? The truth hit like a sledgehammer. Because she still loved him, whether she wanted to or not. He was a part of her whole being... or used to be.

Turning her attention back to the glory of the dawn, she let out a heartfelt sigh. Maybe, if she was a better person, she would just be able to forgive and forget and move on.

Shaking her head at the idea, she remembering what she had said to Annie. *'Trust is the most important thing; the lack of it would be like a canker in any relationship.'* That was so true. So surely it must be better to just to step back and savour the *memories* of a good relationship, rather than let blame and distrust destroy them altogether and turn your love into hate.

Today felt like a turning point in her life, the day when she was finally able to take some decisions... and it started right now. Excitement fluttered inside her, mingling with the ever-present heavy misery and easing the ache that was wearing her down.

She slipped from her pyjamas, allowing them to settle in a silky heap around her feet as she reached for a fluffy white bath towel. The prickle of excitement still bubbled inside her as she stepped beneath the shower and impulsively she turned down the temperature, drawing in her breath as the cold water hit her skin, bringing with it a sharp vibrant tingle. She was alive and her whole future stretched out before of her; that was enough for now. Whether or not it included Tom was yet to be decided.

By seven thirty Grace had tidied the kitchen, emptied the dishwasher and prepared breakfast.

"I don't know what I'm going to do when you're gone," cried Annie with delight, when, after rapping her knuckles against the old oak bedroom door, Grace appeared around it carrying a loaded tray. "...Never have I been so spoiled since Edward died."

"Well I'll never be totally gone now will I," Grace reassured her, settling the tray down on the old lady's knees. "... Because I'll be coming to see you all the time no matter where I end up. And I could never miss my regular dose of the Allbright bunch; they are like a happy fix."

Broken Heart Wood

"Well they were certainly funny last night?" Annie exclaimed, chuckling like a teenager. "The way the boys played with little Molly…"

Grace smiled at the memory. "She adores them all and they are so good with her. To be honest though it's Carol who really makes me smile, she must drive poor Ben mad at times."

Annie took a sip of her tea, her mind in a faraway place. "When I look at him I just see my Edward," she sighed. "He had that same long suffering personality. A truly *good* person… there aren't many of them around you know. Anyway, what time is Tom coming to collect Molly and are you going to have a talk with him today?"

"You never give up do you?" groaned Grace. "He's coming at around ten this morning and I have decided that I'll meet up with him on Sunday, when he brings Molly back… if that's all right with you of course?"

"You know it is," said Annie. "And I suppose that as soon as he and Molly have left this morning you'll be off up to the wood?"

Grace nodded determinedly "Just try and stop me."

Tom arrived early, eagerly anticipating seeing Molly and Grace. He parked his silver van in the lane outside Annie's cottage and let Lucky out for five minutes, pacing up and down as the little dog raced around in excitement, sniffing and scrabbling in the hedgerow where a rabbit had recently hopped by.

For some reason he felt uneasy today. Everything had seemed to be going a bit better with Grace and yet now there was something that he couldn't quite put his finger on. A change in her attitude he supposed it was, a newfound strength. He could sense it in the tone of her voice on the phone.

"Come on boy," he called as Annie's front door opened and then Molly was running down the path towards him, her chubby legs travelling too fast for her body.

"Hey, steady on," he cried, hurrying to meet her.

Lucky got there first. He bounded happily towards the little girl just as she lost control of her legs, breaking her fall. Together they rolled across the ground towards Tom who scooped his daughter up into his arms, planting a kiss on the soft smooth warmth of her cheek.

"Hey Molls, it's okay… don't cry… Lucky saved you didn't he."

When the little dog whined with excitement, scrabbling at Tom's leg, he crouched down to let Molly to stroke the fluffy white hair on the top of his head.

Broken Heart Wood

Lucky whined softly, licking her tear-streaked face, his tail wagging madly.

"Say thank you to him," urged Tom.

Molly hesitated, torn between laughter and tears, reaching out one plump finger. When Lucky licked it happily she burst into a fit of giggles. "Wucky," she chortled.

To Grace, watching unnoticed from the cottage doorway, it was a scene of such togetherness that she felt suddenly isolated, lost in a lonely place. Until Tom looked up, catching her eye. Then, for one fleeting moment, she was back at the fair ground again, seeing him as if for the very first time. Her heart lurched, beating erratically and she turned abruptly away. That was in the past; it was the future that mattered now.

He caught up with her in three big strides, his fingers firm around her elbow.

"You said we could talk today," he said hopefully, hitching Molly higher on his hip.

Grace shrugged off his hand, unable now to meet his eyes. "I said we *migh*t, she reminded him.

"Please Grace, give me a break. Just a few minutes will do."

Annie's clear vibrant voice broke the tension. "I will look after Molly when you bring her back and you two can talk then," she announced determinedly. "Maybe even go for a drive…"

Suddenly Grace smiled. "Ok," she agreed. "…If you insist."

"I do insist," she said.

"And so do I," added Tom.

Suddenly, despite herself, Grace realised that she was actually looking forward to it. She waved goodbye to the pair of them with a warm flood of emotion; was it hope she wondered, was hope back in her heart?

Although eager to go up to the wood, Grace insisted on first helping Annie to change the beds in the self-catering apartments adjacent to the cottage.

"You get yourself off," the old lady insisted but Grace was adamant.

"How can I go off doing my own thing when you are heaving duvet's about?"

Annie tut-tutted whilst hiding a smile, sometimes it felt as if Grace was her own flesh and blood. Poor dear Sarah would have been so proud of her daughter, for despite all her problems the girl's heart was definitely in the right place.

Broken Heart Wood

At eleven am, just as Grace was finally about to leave, there was a babble of sound, high-pitched laughter and running feet. Ben's huge figure appeared in the kitchen closely followed by Will, Tim and eventually Carol. She rolled her eyes, going immediately across to put the kettle on. "Boys… who'd have them," she cried, turning to look at Grace. "Give me a little girl any time; where is she anyway."

"Oh they have their moments too," laughed Grace. "And she's gone to spend some time with her dad."

Carol rolled her eyes. "Things are moving on then?"

"They're meeting up for a chat on Sunday," Annie told her, raising her eyebrows

"And about time too," declared Carol.

"We're off to town mother," explained Ben, cutting in on the conversation. "It's Carol's birthday next week and I'm going to buy her a new outfit."

"Now there's a first," smiled Carol, glancing affectionately across at her husband. "…Ben dragging himself away from his precious cars to spend some quality time with me."

"We were hoping that the boys could stay here," he went on, ignoring her.

"Why of course they can," agreed Annie. "You'll have a coffee first though…?"

"Just a quick one then," Carol agreed. "Or it'll be time to come back before we've even got there."

"Ah," Ben grinned. "I see you've intercepted my plan."

Carol stood as tall as she could, her bright red head still just reaching his chest, but before she could explode he picked up her dumpy figure as easily as if she were a child and swung her round.

"Put me down," she shrieked, loving it.

Grace's heart turned over …God how she missed Tom.

*

She thought about that episode as she climbed the steep slope half an hour later. They were such an unlikely couple, the huge, quiet man and the diminutive explosive red head, but they had something very special. That was what Tom and she had together, until he destroyed it, or was it just circumstance that had changed their lives? If something awful happened to the Allbrights would they just crumple, or would they stand stalwart in the storm like the trees in the poem that Annie loved so much?

Ahead of her Heart Wood shivered in the breeze and she hastened her steps, hitching the bag she carried further up onto her shoulder and ignoring the dull ache in her calf muscles.

Anticipation sent a shiver rippling down her spine as she clambered eagerly over the crumbling stone wall and stepped into the wood, immediately feeling its familiar tranquillity settling over her. It seemed so silent at first, totally and restfully bereft of noise, and then she began to pick out the tiny sounds, a mouse scuttling through the undergrowth, the snap of a twig, a blackbird singing in the tree up ahead.

Moving on, beneath the canopy of trees, she looked for the route she usually took, entranced for a moment by the sight of a red squirrel scampering through the branches above her head. A hand seemed to tighten around her heart; was today really the day when she would finally get to the truth of Heart Wood and lay Dorothea's secret to rest?

Lifting the bag from her shoulder she looked inside. Dare she really do what she had planned? Was she totally mad and perhaps in for a terrible shock? Stepping forward determinedly she pushed her way through the dense woodland towards the clearing, one thing was for sure, she was going to follow it through now, no matter what.

Broken Heart Wood

As usual it took a while to find the headstone. Dorothea had disguised it well, or perhaps when she'd had it placed there the wood was open and new and it was nature that had formed its hiding place. Grace sank down onto her knees beside it, tracing the letters carefully. *'GOODBYE MY LOVE.'*

Apprehension gurgled inside her. Should she really be doing this?

Despite her reservations she opened the bag, withdrawing the small shovel she'd borrowed from Annie's garden shed. Now... where to start? Panic flooded over her as she began to dig. This was insane, what if she uncovered the bones of an animal... or worse? Carefully she worked away at the stony ground, her heart beating so hard that it echoed inside her head. When she hit something solid she drew back, dropping the shovel. Her breath came in ragged gasps as an awesome silence descended and it felt as if the whole world had suddenly stopped... Sacrilege, this was sacrilege.

The word screamed inside her head, spiralling round and round. A shiver rippled through her whole body leaving an icy emptiness in its place. Was it a tiny coffin she'd hit? What if Dorothea had lost a baby, what if it's small secret body rested here?

Broken Heart Wood

Unsure of what to do she moved back, slumped on her knees in the undergrowth. "What now?" she whispered into the emptiness. "What now?"

A strangely familiar voice filled her ears, emanating from the air around her as naturally as breathing. "Dorothea?" she whispered softly.

The silence descended again, heavy and still. She had heard a voice though… hadn't she? The words it spoke were indistinct, it's feeling clear. She had to go on now. Whatever happened she had to see this through.

With careful fingers she prised away the earth, revealing something smooth and hard, dreading to feel the shape of a tiny coffin. It was square thank God, or almost square with gently rounded corners and not much more than eight inches across. Frantically she scrabbled in the ground, her confidence soaring, longing now to reveal the contents of the box that she cautiously withdrew from its hiding place.

Carefully clutching the earth caked box, she moved out from the darkness of the undergrowth, carefully placing it down on the flat, moss covered rock. The sun's rays filtered through the trees above her, making dappled, golden patterns across its soft green surface and for a moment she hesitated, overpowered by the awesome realisation that perhaps she really did finally hold the truth of Dorothea's long kept secret. The small box sat in front of her on the rock, a solid, real object. Dropping down onto her knees she began to wipe away the soil with trembling fingers, gradually revealing its once gloriously patterned exterior. Now the different shades of wood were just vague shapes, merged together and blackened by time.

Grace knew at once what it was, remembering seeing a similar item on Annie's welsh dresser just a week or so ago. It had been slightly hexagonal in shape and inlaid with mother of pearl but she was sure that it was the same type of object.

'It's a tea caddy,' the old lady had explained. 'Left over from the days when tea was rare and valuable and needed to be locked away from the servants. They would even take the used leaves if they could, so they say, for tea was such a luxury in those days.'

Made to last from a hard wood such as mahogany, and lined in pewter, a tea caddy was the perfect object to protect its contents, even against the damp earth that had encased this one for so long. Holding it carefully in her hands, her heart beating erratically, Grace tried to open it. There was no key though in the tiny lock so perhaps its secrets would remain intact after all; perhaps they were meant to be forever locked away against prying eyes.

Moving nearer the centre of the clearing, to take better advantage of the light, she tried to prise open the box with the edge of her small shovel. It gave remarkably easily, as though thankful to be found, revealing its contents to the world for probably the first time in well over one hundred years. For a moment Grace just stared in amazement. She had imagined tiny bones, or something even more sinister, but here, still carefully folded, were what seemed to be letters, or documents of some kind… And on the top, smiling up at her was a young man in uniform. Her heart twisted inside her chest for even now, after all these years, she could see the emotion in the eyes of the handsome soldier. Was he once Dorothea's lover? Perhaps he died at war and Heart Wood was his shrine.

Carefully she removed the rest of the items. There was small bundle of what had to be love letters, folded neatly and tied up with a faded silken ribbon. She held them reverently in her hand. Was it fair to reveal their secrets, to read the words that were never intended for a stranger's scrutiny? Guiltily she undid the bow, carefully unfolding them one by one, unable to resist, devouring the contents that were so carefully and beautifully written in a strong and sloping hand.

'My dearest darling D

I was so loath to leave you – especially after last night- now I know that you are truly mine... forever. Don't worry my love, the time will soon pass and then I will stay there with you forever and we will never spend a night apart again...

Sweet dreams my love

Ever yours

Jonathan x

***

Dearest D

Are you thinking of me still? Do I dwell in your heart as you do in mine...? Hold out your hand at midnight and I shall hold out mine, together we will reach across the miles and feel our fingers touch.........
We will be together again soon, despite these horrors...
I promise.

Ever yours   Jonathon

***

Grace read each beautifully written letter one by one, skipping guiltily through Jonathan's protestations of love and imagining a young Dorothea, feasting on his every word. Her heart swelled inside her as she felt the young man's growing unhappiness, had Dorothea felt it too, had she sensed the misery in his unspoken voice?

For a moment she paused, placing the letters carefully back down in a small, neatly folded pile. These words of love had been written for Dorothea's eyes only, it felt so wrong to intrude, and yet she knew that she had to read on, had to know why they never married. Did he die there in that alien, unhappy place; did he never come home again to these fells? Would the last three letters tell her? One by one she picked them up, devouring their contents.

My darling D

There is not much time for writing now. We are about to depart for foreign shores as yet unknown to us. Pray for me my love and I shall dream of you...

All my love forever J

***

Oh my darling Dorothea

This is a dreadful place, the only thing that keeps me going are thoughts of you. Light a candle in your window for me my love, to guide me home and I shall see you light it in my dreams.

J.

***

Dorothea my love

It may be some time before I can write again. I am not allowed to tell you why for my mission is of a secret nature. Please try not to worry for there is nothing in either heaven or earth that will stop me from coming home to you: Keep the light in your window burning to guide me home...

J

***

A heavy weight settled in Grace's heart as she read what appeared to be Jonathan's final letter; so had he died then, been killed in action maybe? Carefully she retied the ribbon, placing the letters back into their resting place before picking up the photograph again. The young man smiled out at her from across the years. The handsome soldier whose future it seemed had turned sour.

With a heavy sigh she turned her attention back to the rest of the documents that were loose in the bottom of the box. They also proved to be letters but written on a different paper in a much more spidery hand; her heart lit up as she realised that they too were written by Jonathan, so perhaps he hadn't died after all.

Dear darling Dorothea

At last, after all this time, they are finally allowing me to come home to you my love. I feel as if you are the only real thing left in this ugly world of ours for so many dreadful things have happened, here, in this godforsaken place: Things that I will only be able to forget when I look once again upon your dear sweet smile and walk hand in hand with you across the awesome majesty of the fells. Please say that you are waiting still after all this time, reassure me that you have not imagined me dead and fallen for another. There are things I need to tell you, to keep the record straight, to be totally honest and true, but first I need to see you face to face, to feel your soft sweet body in my arms once more. I shall be home within the month, please be there for me and keep my light burning, for without you I really will be truly lost

All my love...forever. *Jonathan*

***

Broken Heart Wood

Grace carefully read the letter through again. So if Jonathan *did* come home then why…? She picked up the very last loose letter in the box with a feeling of pending doom, her hollow sobs resounding through the silence of the trees as she read his desperate admission of an awful guilt and felt his pain.

***

My Dearest, Darling Dorothea

Have you spoken with your cousin Charles yet? He left for home before me and I fear that he plans to dishonour my name. I pray that I am not already too late? I know that he cares for you and so will try to tell the worst of me, but I want you to hear the total truth of it from my own lips. I had intended to wait and tell you face to face, to see your eyes sparkle at the sight of me for at least just one more time. Now I shall have to relate my sad mistake in a letter, so that you know the real truth of it from my own hand, for I would never lie to you, even to save myself.

I cannot expect you to ever begin to understand the atrocities of war. I have seen things that I would never wish on any other human being… monstrous things beyond all human decency. There are no excuses; I know that my darling, but sometimes, when a man is at his lowest ebb, he makes mistakes, irretrievable mistakes.

Throughout it all though please believe me when I say that you were my one guiding light, my only goal and my reason for living.

One's mind can become tarnished when all hell rises around you. The short of it is my love...the real truth... I have a child, or will have by now. The result of a stupid half-crazed indiscretion for which I have no excuse except to say that in the midst of death I wanted to feel alive, just one last time. Or perhaps there was no child at all; perhaps it was just a desperate native girl's way to get money from me. No matter her reasons, the wrong is all mine.

How can I ask you to forgive such treachery, except to say that I was lost for a while and could see no way forward except to die... and I so desperately did not want to die.

I am pleading for your forgiveness Dorothea, for I have always loved you more than life itself and if you turn me from your door, if you have extinguished my light, then I shall prove that to you. For without your guiding light... I have nothing.

Please do not give up on us my love... yours forever, no matter what happens.

Jonathan

***

Oblivious to the hot tears that flooded down her face, Grace reached for the faded sepia newspaper cutting that lay in the very bottom of the box. Somehow she knew what it would say.

SOLDIER FOUND DEAD

The body of a solder, recently returned from foreign parts where he was serving with the Queens 9th regiment, was recently discovered on the Howgill fells in Westmorland. The man, twenty five year old Jonathan Darley, died by a bullet from his own gun; no foul play was suspected.

So Jonathan had finally proven that he really did love Dorothea more than life itself.

For what seemed hours Grace just sat with his last desperate letter in her hand. How would she have felt if she had been Dorothea Dinsdale, waiting impatiently for her love to come home only to find out that he'd been unfaithful… more than just unfaithful, if that was true? And yet she realised that no matter how many times she

Broken Heart Wood

ran it through in her mind her sympathies still lay with Jonathan.

Surely though, if Dorothea had gone to all the trouble of planting the heart shaped wood and even made this shrine to him, then she must have regretted turning him away from her door. But why hadn't she left something herself, some explanation perhaps, or apology. Carefully Grace went through every letter again, searching for something more, finally picking up the photograph of the poor doomed soldier who had taken his own life, here, in this lonely place. The breath froze in her throat as she turned it over to reveal what surely must be Dorothea's hand….

Jonathan, my love

I have sat for so many precious hours, here in this place where your lifeblood ebbed away; soon though I fear that I will no longer be able to climb the steep fell slope, so perhaps then this really is goodbye my love, until we meet again. Are you here with me now perhaps, reading these words that have taken so long to write… Oh how I hope so.

I saw you from my window that night when Mary turned you from the door. The slope of your shoulders, the desperation of you, and I regretted extinguishing your candle. I remembered our love and realised its truth, no matter what you did in that terrible place, for who am I to judge. I was too late though my love. I saw you raise the gun. I called to you... I saw you lying there...

I never married, Jonathan, for there has never been anyone but you, and, ironically, my cousin Charles did not even make it home so you could have told me your secret face to face after all... for I really do believe that you would have done so.

So goodbye my love -or at least to this, your place on earth, for surely where a man's heart beats last must be his true resting place. And I pray that we shall meet again in heaven. Wait for me there my darling... I won't be long.

D

The afternoon shadows were lengthening by the time Grace finally closed the wooden box on Dorothea Dinsdale's secrets. Then she carefully placed it back into the ground, re-covering it with earth and patting it down before disguising the hiding place with leaves and branches. The words, written with such pain and passion,

Broken Heart Wood

were never meant for public knowledge; they belonged there, in the earth where Jonathan Darley, Dorothea's soldier, breathed his last breath.

Would she tell Annie? As Grace set off back down the steep hillside with a heavy heart it occurred to her that perhaps the old lady already knew.

CHAPTER TWENTY-ONE

Grace walked slowly back down the fell, acutely aware of her surroundings. The bleak tranquillity of the lonely slope where Jonathan Darley died; the awesome majesty of the hills against the vast, endless sky... An image of him lying there, breathing his last desperate breath only minutes too late, filled her mind's eye. How twisted is fate when as if on a whim it can just change what should have been. Or was it always too late; was Jonathan Darley's fate always to die so tragically?

If he had lived, if Dorothea had forgiven him sooner, then there would have been no Major Dinsdale at Greythwaite Hall for Martha to fall in love with... so many repercussions, who knew where they might have led.

And what about her own fate then, what was Grace Robert's fate to be? Had the powers that be decreed that she forgive her Tom, or was she meant to move on, just she and Molly together forging a new life? Who decided where your life went anyway, God, or man?

Broken Heart Wood

She paused for a moment, watching the tiny people way, way below; tiny people with tiny lives… But they weren't tiny were they for no one's life is tiny, except perhaps to another. And in that moment she made her decision, with a sudden certain clarity she saw her fate before her, her life as she wanted it to be.

With a final glance back towards the wood where heartache lingered, grabbing her bag she began to run, awkwardly bounding over the tussocks of grass, feeling totally liberated by the discovery she had made. Now she could move on with her life again for tomorrow was to be the start of a whole new future.

The warm comfort of Annie's kitchen beckoned; would she tell the old lady what she'd found? Perhaps she really did already know, perhaps she had uncovered Dorothea's secret years ago. And what of Tom… tomorrow she would talk to him for now at last she knew what she had to say.

Annie was out in the garden busily weeding, when Grace came through the small gateway from the fell. For a moment she paused; the old lady looked so frail and tiny, stooped over the ground. A warm rush of affection brought a lump to her throat, life was so short she realised, so fickle; you had to grab it with both hands and live it before it was too late.

"Hello," she said.

Annie looked round, startled, the vibrancy in her face denying the march of time.

"Well?" she smiled, standing awkwardly.

"You knew the truth didn't you?"

The old lady sighed, wiping her brow with an earth caked hand. "Some secrets are better just left to lie," she said. "Come on, I'll put the kettle on."

***

The fluttering excitement that had kept Grace from sleep that night was still there the next morning as she showered and dressed. What did you wear for a special occasion she wondered, discarding the meagre items in her wardrobe one by one before picking each one up again? She settled for jeans and a bright pink tee shirt, dabbed on some lipstick and bounded down the stairs to find Annie already in the kitchen.

"Do you feel better this morning?" she asked, as Grace walked into the warm sunny room.

"I felt alright yesterday," she responded with a smile. "Although I would have been better if you had let me tell you about Heart Wood… or Broken Heart Wood as I now prefer to call it."

Broken Heart Wood

Annie turned her attention determinedly back to the eggs she was mixing. "There is nothing to tell." she insisted, without meeting Grace's gaze. "...Anyway, in my book secrets are meant for keeping and if you did stumble across some answers... well then I hope they helped you. But just remember..."

"Remember what?" asked Grace curiously.

"...To be able to forgive is a gift, don't leave it too late."

"As Dorothea did," finished Grace in awe. "And now I know that you really have seen it."

Annie shrugged, looking away. "Come on," she said, changing the subject. "Put on the kettle for me and I'll make you scrambled eggs. A good breakfast sets you up for the day you know."

Realising that that was to be the old lady's final word on the matter, Grace did as she was bid. Annie really had once found the small box that contained the truth of Heart Wood though, she was sure of it now. Well she too would respect Dorothea's wish to keep her secret and leave the sad story there in the spot where her one true love had breathed his final breath.

"Scrambled eggs would be great," she announced feeling better deep inside than she had since what seemed like forever. The future stretched before her, positive and true... whether or not Tom was in it remained to be seen.

His silver van came into view at exactly three o clock. From her position at the window Grace watched it pull up in the lane at the front of the cottage, its Quicksilver sign standing out in the sunshine, a constant reminder to what should have been. She rushed outside to see Molly, walking eagerly up the path.

Tom grinned as he opened the driver's door and something funny happened just above the inverted V of her rib cage. She bit her bottom lip, trying to slow down her breathing.

"Does this greeting mean that maybe I'm allowed to stay for a bit?" he asked hopefully, reaching across to unbuckle Molly from her car seat.

"Annie said to ask if you wanted to come in for a coffee..."

He unfolded himself from the van with Molly held firmly in his arms. "Just Annie or are you asking me too?"

The little girl reached out her arms to her mother and Grace took her eagerly, burrowing her face in the sweet softness of her hair. "It was Annie," she insisted, suddenly unable to meet his gaze. "But I *have* decided that perhaps it is time we talked."

"Come on you three," called Annie from the open doorway. "The kettle is on."

To Grace, as they walked down the pathway together, it seemed as if the aroma of summer flowers that grew in abundance in Annie's borders, had somehow become stronger, making her head swim. Had Tom noticed it too she wondered? For a moment a cold hand seemed to clasp tightly around her heart as she sneaked a glance in his direction; was she really doing the right thing, was the path that *she* had finally decided upon the one that she was really supposed to take? Dorothea got it so wrong what if she had too?

Annie's kitchen was bright with afternoon sunshine, her brass pans sparkling on the shelf above the stove. "Now you two," she asked brightly. "…Tea, coffee or a cold drink?"

Tom cleared his throat. "Coffee for me please, Annie."

"I'll make it," offered Grace, placing Molly down onto Tom's knee and jumping up to grab the kettle."

"Oh for heaven's sakes," laughed Annie, breaking the tension. "Never mind the drink. Why don't you just go for a drive right now and have a chat. I'll see to Molly."

"That's hardly fair though is it," objected Grace.

"Look…" The old lady took the little girl's chubby hand, holding it closely, steering her in the direction of the hallway. "Do you want to go for a drive with mummy and daddy, Molly?" she asked. "Or would you rather just stay and watch Peppa pig with me, and when the boys come later on then they'll take you to see the rabbits."

Molly beamed up at her. "Peppa pig," she shrieked with glee, jumping up and down. "My want Peppa pig."

"Are you sure?" Grace glanced doubtfully across at Tom. After all her good resolutions suddenly she wanted to put off their moment of truth.

"I insist." Annie shooed them towards the door. "Leave Lucky here as well, he'll be fine with us…. And you don't need to rush back. Ben is dropping the boys off with me shortly and then he's coming back later on with Carol. They're bringing a Chinese for us all too so I don't even need to cook."

Panic fluttered in Grace's stomach. "So we don't have a choice then?"

Tom took a firm hold of her arm, ushering her towards the door. "Thank you Annie," he said, smiling.

Broken Heart Wood

As the Quicksilver van headed up the steep incline out of Greythwaite village, an awkward silence fell between its two occupants.

What to say, wondered Grace. How to tell him... and when? How could this man who had once seemed like an extension of her own self have suddenly become a stranger?

She took no notice of where they were actually going, totally oblivious for once to the raw beauty of the scenery that passed them by. All she knew was the tension that spanned the short distance between them and the words that kept going round and around inside her head. Small talk seemed unnecessary; there was already too much to say and yet silence sat heavily between them as the miles rolled by. Did he know where he was taking her Grace wondered, had he planned this route, or was he just driving for driving's sake? She glanced across at him but he just stared straight ahead, jaw set, totally concentrating all his attention... on what? Why wasn't he at least trying to make conversation?

When he eventually pulled over into the side of the lane and cut the engine, Grace's attention was taken by the awesome view from the window. Climbing out of the vehicle as if in unison, she and Tom stood side-by-side, almost touching and yet still a million miles apart as they looked down into the valley beyond the wild slopes of the fell. Way, way below them now, right at the very bottom, was civilisation. A tiny village, matchstick people, the distant sound of excited children released from school, whilst up here…

Grace turned her face towards the sky, vast… endless… infinite: So many words sprang into her head and none of them the ones she had so carefully rehearsed on the way here. "It's awesome," she breathed. When Tom's fingers curled gently around hers she let them stay there, no longer seeing the view.

Her heartbeat was deafening, pounding in her ears and her whole body pulsated with the relentless rhythm of life… of love. All her good intentions faded, evaporating before the rush of emotion that left her trembling helplessly.

"Well," he murmured. "You wanted to talk?"

Helplessly her fingers returned the pressure of his. She tilted up her face to look into his eyes and then somehow she was in his arms, where she was supposed to be… His warmth, his scent, the life of him… the memories that intoxicated her every naked sense flowed over her.

Broken Heart Wood

For what seemed like an eternity he just held her, waiting for her to make the first move, a word, a sign… anything. A hollow emptiness opened up inside him when she drew away from him, moving across to sit down on the bench that had been placed there to get the best view of the valley. His arms dropped limply to his sides and slowly he sank down beside her, not quite touching, longing to take her in his arms again; an ache swelled in his heart as he watched the expression on her lovely face. Was this the moment when she was to tear his world apart? Was their moment of closeness just a goodbye?

"I love you Tom," she began, without looking up. "And I think I always will, but up until now I didn't believe that I could move on beyond…"

For a moment she glanced across at him, looking away again at once, but not before he'd noticed the shimmer of tears. He half reached out a hand to her then dropped it back, the dull ache in his heart spreading throughout his entire body.

"It was so much more that pushed us apart, more than just your one stupid mistake," she said quietly. "It was blame and guilt and regret… and you let me take that blame for so long. My guilt and regret for ruining our future may have dragged us down, Tom, but, as it turns out, it was actually your treachery that ruined our love and destroyed my trust in you."

Tom leaned earnestly towards her. "And now... how do you feel now?"

She ignored his question, staring down again at her tightly clenched fingers. "I've spent a lot of time thinking about what went wrong, Tom, and I've come to realise that there were four main factors in our relationship, you, me, hope and dreams... and when hope and dreams..."

She took a breath, closing her eyes. "When hope and dreams left us with Quicksilver... that was when you and me first began to crumble. What you did..." Looking up, suddenly defiant, she faced the full agony in his glorious eyes. "The thing that finally broke us in two was just the result of all that. I'm not making excuses for you; you hurt me so much, took away the one thing that I still truly believed in, apart from Molly. And since the day I found out... the day when I saw her in the street, when she showed me the pictures on her phone, I haven't been able to see a way back to what we once had. My trust in you went that day you see, Tom, and without trust then it seemed to me that everything was finally lost forever, every precious moment. But then..."

"Then what Grace?"

Broken Heart Wood

Reaching across she took his hand in hers, gently stroking the contours of his fingers. He hardly dared to move as hope sneaked back.

"Something happened," she said, in a calm determined tone. "…Something that helped me to see things more clearly... We all make mistakes, I know that. Life is never perfect for anyone and none of us are perfect either. The kind of love we had though was special… too special to just throw away, even when things went so badly wrong. It's easy though, when your heart is broken, to take the wrong path and possibly ruin the rest of your life… I know that now."

Tom closed his fingers tightly around hers. "And which path are you taking Grace?" he murmured, his voice breaking on the words.

Grace sat rigid beside him, determined to say her piece.

"I love you Tom and that's all that really counts. I know that now. I'm not going to dissect it all over again, I've already done that a thousand times and I don't even want to discuss it anymore. As far as I'm concerned it's the future that matters now, our future, yours Molly's and mine."

Turning her face up to look at him, she boldly held his eyes in hers. "Hope is back, Tom, if you want it. I'm ready to move on at last, with or without you. If it's to be with you though you need to know right now that I can never go back to Ivy cottage again, into the life we had before…"

A total silence fell between them, deafening in its intensity. Tom was the first to break it with his sweet familiar smile. "So three of us are back on track again then," he said. "You, me and hope; we just have dreams to find again."

Grace sighed, a final heartfelt sigh. "I think our dreams went for good along with Quicksilver so I guess we'll just have to settle for you, me, hope… and Molly of course."

"And that," cried Tom, jumping up and pulling her to her feet, "is where you just might be wrong…Come on."

For a fleeting moment he held her close against him in a quick hard squeeze, and then he was dragging her back to the van by one hand. "Perhaps I can supply the last piece in our puzzle."

Grace had gone over this moment in her mind so many times, since she discovered Dorothea's secret and began to realise what really mattered in life. And every time, in that moment, Tom had held her in his arms, begging her forgiveness and declaring his love. So what was going on? Where was he taking her?

He drove fast, too fast for the narrow lane, his eyes fixed determinedly on the road ahead and his jaw clenched tight.

Grace held firmly onto the sides of her seat, wanting to tell him to slow down, to ask him where they were going... Her heart thudded hard inside her as images flashed by, her lips remained tight shut. Perhaps their fate was to die here on this lonely road... but then what about Molly?

"Slow down Tom," she eventually managed, her voice just a croak.

He flashed a grin in her direction. "I can't wait though Grace, I just can't wait."

He pulled up eventually at a cluster of run down looking buildings, stamping on the brakes and flinging open the van door almost before the wheels had stopped turning.

"Here," he announced, appearing at the passenger side and holding out a purple scarf.

"Here what?" asked Grace nervously.

He opened the door and took her hand, drawing her gently up to face him.

"Trust me Grace," he murmured. "Please."

With trembling fingers he fastened the scarf around her eyes and placed his arm about her shoulders. "I have been waiting for this moment for so long and I thought that it was never going to happen. I wanted you to forgive me first you see, before I told you. I wanted you to want me for the right reasons... and now you have... haven't you?"

She reached round to find his face, touching his cheek. "Forever, if you'll have me."

His lips touched hers, warm and soft and tingling. "For eternity," he promised.

He led her forward across the lane. The creak of a gate opening filled her ears and she stumbled as her feet met rough grass. His arm supported her, drawing her close.

At last they stopped. "Well... are you ready?" he asked, reaching up to unfasten the scarf.

"...Ready for what?"

"For our dreams," he told her, his voice bright with excitement. "...And for the rest of our lives... together."

When he removed the scarf with a flourish for a moment all she could see was sunshine, glorious golden late-afternoon sunshine lighting up a jumble of dilapidated buildings. And then she noticed that someone had been at work there; the fences had been repaired and there were new doors on the crumbling stone stables...

"I can soon fix the walls," Tom told her, pleading his cause into her confusion. "And there are thirty acres out back. Just think of it Grace, thirty whole acres..."

"But Tom..." She stepped back, unsure. "What are you talking about, who owns this place and is it really you who has done the work on it?"

He stepped up behind her, wrapping his arms firmly around her waist and placing his chin on the top of her head as they both surveyed the scene before them.

"Annie," he announced, to her surprise. "Annie owns it... In fact, to be fair, it was she who first put the idea in my head. The old guy who has rented it from her for years has finally gone into a home; it fell vacant and... well... it just seemed like fate. There's a cottage too, it needs some work but ... Oh please say yes Grace."

He turned her to face him, needing to look into her eyes, to gauge her reaction. "It's not even to show jump or compete again, at least not really, this is just for us, for our dream. We can take liveries, or buy and sell, I've even spoken to some of our old owners and I have at least three who'll send us horses to break and school if we want... We can be a family again Grace, with a whole new future... working together. We could even have another baby... And there's one more thing." Reaching up to where an old sheet was suspended over what looked like a sign, he dragged it down with a flourish.

What Grace saw beneath it brought her barely contained well of emotion bursting from its confines in a torrent of tears. They ran down her face and into her mouth, splashing over Tom as he reached out his arms to her, holding her so close that she could barely breathe.

"Say yes Grace," he pleaded. "Please say yes."

The oval sign swung gently in the afternoon breeze; a silver horse, staring out towards the horizon... and above it... beautiful lettering in a perfect arch.

QUICKSILVER STABLES
Proprietors G and T Roberts

Slowly she turned to look at him, her eyes burning into his; glowing with an emotion she had never expected to feel again.

"Yes Tom... Yes," she murmured.

As he slowly lowered his lips to meet hers a warm glow swelled inside her. Hope and dreams were finally

Broken Heart Wood

back in their lives again, fused together with love into all the tomorrows that stretched towards infinity.

***

<u>HOME</u>

Tomorrow is another day and yesterday has gone

Today is just a flash in time…

Forever leads me home

By T J Darling

Printed in Great Britain
by Amazon